All around Bree the air tingled

"Alexander!" she called. "Are you here? Are you truly here?"

Standing at the edge of the cliff, Bree held her breath. But she heard only the waves breaking against the rocks.

Still, surely he was there. "Alexander, you must hear me! Just give me a sign."

Her words were cast back at her as though not even the gods believed in the power of faith. Blast. Coming to Marauder's Point had been an exercise in illusion, in trying to make real the stuff of dreams.

"Alexander!" she shouted again, defiant now. "I was a fool to believe in you! I'm not in love with you! So get out of my dreams!"

Suddenly thunder rolled. A slash of lightning split the sky.

And Bree watched in horror as the waves below—the very sea that had swallowed Alexander Devane a century and a half before—seemed to rear up in fury...

Dear Reader,

What can be more romantic and more mysterious than a gorgeous man traveling through time to meet up with you...a man destined to share your life? We're especially proud to present TIMELESS LOVE, a unique program in Harlequin Intrigue that showcases these much-loved time-travel stories.

So join Eve Gladstone as she brings you the mysterious nineteenth-century sailing captain who haunts Bree Kealy's dreams...until Bree meets Alexander Devane in the flesh—a man more powerful than any mere mortal.

We hope you enjoy *Time and Tide*...and all the special books coming to you in TIMELESS LOVE.

We welcome your comments on this unique program.

Sincerely,

Debra Matteucci
Senior Editor and Editorial Coordinator
Harlequin Books
300 East 42nd Street, Sixth Floor
New York, NY 10017

Time and Tide

Eve Gladstone

Harlequin Books

TORONTO • NEW YORK • LONDON
AMSTERDAM • PARIS • SYDNEY • HAMBURG
STOCKHOLM • ATHENS • TOKYO • MILAN
MADRID • WARSAW • BUDAPEST • AUCKLAND

ISBN 0-373-22295-5

TIME AND TIDE

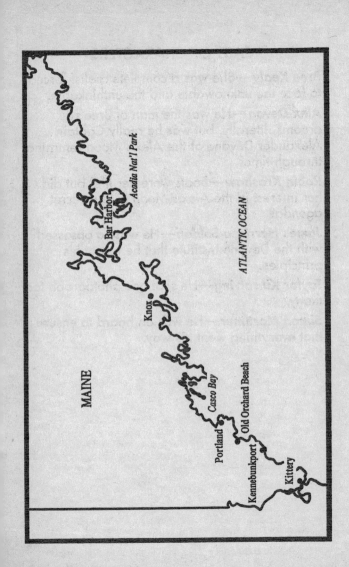

CAST OF CHARACTERS

Bree Kealy—She was a complete realist forced to face the unknowable and the unthinkable.

Alex Devon—He was the man of Bree's dreams, literally, but was he really Captain Alexander Devane of the *Alexis Moon* returning through time?

Robin Krashaw—Boats were her life, but did her interest in the *Alexis Moon* hide a secret agenda?

James Harrison Seldon—He was so obsessed with the Devane Institute that he forgot his principles.

Taylor Kinsolving—He shot one photograph too many.

Simon Mortimer—He was on board to ensure that everything went his way.

Prologue

From the **Portland Ledger**
April 1994

THE LEGEND OF THE ALEXIS MOON, FACT OR FICTION?
Answer Might Be Found
In Salvaging of Sunken Ship

Portland, Maine, April 25—The legend of the sailing vessel the **Alexis Moon** has lived on in the imaginations of history buffs for the past century and a half and is the stuff of which movies are made. What was the real outcome of an alleged high-stakes game of cards played aboard the **Alexis Moon** as it lay becalmed off Marauders Point in the year 1842?

The answer may lie at the bottom of the sea on a letter-size sheet of gold. The tablet, in the form of a deed, settled the fortune of Captain Alexander Devane on his first mate, Zachary Martineaux, if he lost the game.

Fact turned to legend when the ship foundered off the coast of Maine in a sudden squall, all hands but one lost. Was the game played and a fortune lost? Did Alexander Devane incise his signature upon the sheet of gold? The outcome of the game hinged upon the word of Breeford Kealy, sole survivor of the wreck. It was in Beatrice

Martineaux's ear that the dying Kealy whispered what has become lore: Captain Devane lost the game and signed over his ship and fortune to her brother, Zachary Martineaux.

"The gold tablet is down there, and we're going to find it," an ebullient Zack Martineaux announced today at a press conference held at the Marauders Point Diving Club. After several false starts over the past two years, Martineaux, a direct descendant of Zachary Martineaux, has been able to obtain enough financing to begin salvaging operations on the remains of the Alexis Moon. His search for financing ended when he signed a contract with Krashaw Salvage for excavations to begin in June.

"All systems are go," he said jubilantly. "The truth about who should have inherited the estate of Alexander Devane has been a long time coming."

Questioned about how finding the gold tablet might affect the fortunes of the Alexander Devane Institute, James Harrison Selden, president of the college, was quoted as saying that the Martineaux claim is an old one and cannot be taken seriously. He offered irrefutable proof that the original insurers of the Alexis Moon, Leigh's of London, paid the claim without question to Alexander Devane's heir, his brother Franklin. Franklin, who never married, used his inheritance to found and endow the Devane Institute in 1844. The college, which offers free tuition to its students, is one of the most highly regarded institutions in the United States.

But legends die hard, and this gold tablet lies one hundred feet below the surface of the ocean, covered by the silt of a century and a half. There are those who say legends should never be rewritten.

Chapter One

Portland, Maine
June 1994

Bree Kealy stirred in her chair, opened her eyes slightly and saw that the fire had turned to embers. She should really get up and go to bed. Instead, she reached over and pulled the plaid throw up under her chin.

They said Alexander Devane's ghost still walked the high cliffs at Marauders Point, searching for his *Alexis Moon,* cursing the wind. She would go there soon, call him, curse the wind with him, wait for the *Alexis Moon* to come sailing on the horizon, a proud black ship. But now, halfway into sleep, all she wanted was that lovely, beautiful, familiar dream. She stirred once again, remembering. Along the edge of the dream, something had begun to cast a subtle shadow. She closed her eyes. Perhaps not this time. Perhaps not ...

THE WATER WARMED under a noon sun whose rays penetrated the limpid abyss. She floated through the gentle current, eyes wide to the treasures of the underworld around her, a school of silvery minnows darting in and out of a reef cave, the fast, opulent passage of a stingray, a shark smoothly intent upon his journey.

She did not wonder where she was or how she came to be there. Clad only in a gossamer gown that clung to her body and revealed every curve, she moved steadily toward the place where Alexander waited.

A touch upon her waist set her heart to beating wildly. She was drawn swiftly into Alexander Devane's arms. She thought her heart would burst with happiness when she caught the look of desire in his emerald eyes. His chest was bare, his white breeches were tight and revealing, his muscled body glistening and taut.

Ahead lay the three-masted black clipper ship Alexis Moon, bow steady, sails unfurled rap full, all-a-taut and fully rigged, as though poised for flight. A thrill of recognition traced her bare arms, but her happiness was only momentary. The waters around them churned, turned dark and threatening. Panic engulfed her. Alexander set her aside, his body tensed, his eyes searching, fixed upon the unknown enemy. He advanced on the shadow, but it coiled and disappeared into the depths of the great clipper ship.

Alexander followed, prowling the decks and passageways of the ship, his tight and muscled body straining. He twisted through the passageway into cabins and then out again. She longed to learn what bedeviled him. His discovery of the Alexis Moon was an encounter that would bring him no peace.

Bunks were made ready for sleep. Brushes and silver jars sat upon trays, trunks held clothing still unpacked. All was in readiness for the long journey ahead.

In the saloon, tables held abandoned crystal glasses, Great sconces grasped candles waiting to be lit. An abandoned violoncello and pianoforte stood in a corner.

They were in a room of carved mahogany panels, with a corner bunk covered in an embroidered spread, and a table set for a game of cards. A half-filled decanter of wine sat on a silver tray with crystal goblets. The cards lay facedown—a game in progress that had been abandoned. A chair seemed to have been toppled, as though in a moment of haste. Alexander scowled. He reached out and dashed the cards to the floor. He turned toward her, his eyes dark and dangerous now.

Bree drew back, her heart banging against her chest. Her fear was not directed at him, but at something far worse. She went toward him, drew her arms about him, and wrapped her legs around his body. With an expert touch, he lowered her lacy silk strap, and then his mouth found her pebbled nipple. She was swept along on a wave of desire as his lips sent a trace of fire down her body. A great hunger roared through her that only one person, the man in whose arms she lay, could satiate. She arched toward him, surrendering. She wanted to hold him forever, to be encased in this closed world, without the specter that even now seemed to surround them. His hands caressed her body, and as he fitted himself to her, she could feel his manhood pressed against her thigh.

But there were shadows around every corner. He came toward them, a swarthy, bearded stranger moving in on them, knife in hand. She pushed away, pointing in horror. Alexander whipped around. He grabbed his assailant. The water throbbed as they fought, the knife in one terrible moment hitting home. A curve of blood oozed from Alexander's arm. Bree reached for the decanter, advanced on them, but the assailant swam swiftly away.

Alexander moved after him, but then stopped. He came back to Bree and, with a gentle smile, removed the decanter from her hand. He smiled and, ignoring his wound, pulled her close. He brushed his lips against her hair, against her neck, and held her. His lips came down on hers, hard and insistent, as if by his power he could translate what he needed into deeds.

And yet, even as his hard male body encircled hers, she felt him change. In another moment, he gently pulled away, holding her at arm's length, gazing keenly into her eyes.

His words were whispered against her lips. "I cannot rest. I need you now, my beloved Bree. You see that I cannot live without you."

FAST-MOVING CLOUDS swept across a bruised late-afternoon sky. All around her, the air tingled. A storm was about to break, but Bree took it as an omen, a celebration. Somewhere offshore, beyond the Cyclops's eye of the lighthouse, under a century and a half of shifting sand, lay the *Alexis Moon.*

"Alexander," she called, "are you here? Are you truly here?"

For a moment, standing at the edge of the cliff, Bree wanted to float off into the void, to enter that realm where time and space were one. She waited on a held breath, savoring the magic. But she heard only the noise of the wind through the trees, the sound of waves breaking against the cliff, the rousing cry of a tern overhead.

Surely he was there, watching for ghostly signs of the *Alexis Moon,* as they said he did on nights such as this. "Alexander, you must hear me. They're going after the *Alexis Moon.* They'll destroy your legacy, the one good thing left of you in this world."

Her words were cast back at her, as though not even the gods believed in the power of faith.

"Where is it, then? Tell me." For as easily as she could believe he was there, she at once understood what he had been looking for. The gold tablet.

"I'll find it for you," she called. "Just give me a sign."

Then, just when she was about to admit the folly of her errand, she felt a light brush against her shoulder. She turned, filled with anticipation and joy. No one was there. She had been caressed fleetingly by a leaf, or a butterfly blown off course. Coming to Marauders Point had been an exercise in illusion, in trying to make real the stuff of dreams. She didn't believe in omens, curses, legends, *dreams*. Oh no, not she. She dealt in facts, always had.

She had come on a fool's errand. What a perfect little idiot she was. Dreams occupied one's head, one's unconscious, they randomly came and went. They had their own rules, but they didn't predict the future or relive someone else's past. And if they invited one along for the ride, the ride was *in the dream,* not in reality.

A clap of thunder rolled overhead, a summer storm flexing its muscles, about to break. A heavy wind railed through. Bree watched in horror as the waves below seemed to rear up in fury before smashing against the cliff.

This very sea had swallowed the *Alexis Moon* and every hand on board but one. It was no less relentless today than it had been a century and a half before.

"Alexander!" She shouted his name, waiting defiantly at the edge of the cliff, hands clenched. "All right, you don't exist!" she called. "I was a fool for believing in you! I am not in love with you, so get out of my dreams!" The sky crackled and was lit for a split second by a slash of lightning.

"That's it," she said. "Go ahead, make your silly point. Why not show me the pot of gold at the end of the rainbow, while you're at it?" A second angry slash split the northern sky.

She dug her fists into her jeans pockets. Oh, Lord, if someone was watching, he'd send for the paramedics. The first drops of icy rain slashed at her arms. She had to get back to Gull House before the storm hit. Soon the lightning would be overhead, and out here on the bare rock, she was a prime target, the tallest object in sight. She didn't believe in omens. She believed lightning struck in high places, like Marauders Point.

She hurried down the twisting trail to Gull House, and hit the wooden porch just as a solid sheet of water came pounding down. The air steamed with an earthy smell. Heavy-laden branches of the great northern oaks and huge spruces that dotted the front lawn down to the cliffs bowed and danced. Now that she was out of danger, Bree found the sound of rain battering roof shingles exhilarating. If she hadn't known this was the Maine coast, she'd have believed she was on a tropical island.

She pushed open the screen door and went into the inviting, antique-filled lobby, where she found a dozen or so guests waiting out the storm. She was immediately struck by the friendliness of the place. Someone was playing the piano—a Chopin nocturne she had tried unsuccessfully to master back in her college days. A couple of kibitzers in the corner watched a chess game in progress. The smell of freshly brewed coffee mingled with the scent of damp upholstery.

"You just missed it," someone said to her, offering a smile and nodding toward the rain-streaked windows.

"Sheer luck," she said, heading for the staircase. In spite of the friendly smiles, she didn't want to stop, didn't want to talk to anyone. She wasn't ready to trade reasons why she had come to Marauders Point, where she came from or how long she'd stay. Not yet, anyway. Not until she could figure out a plausible reason for being here alone, on an illusory quest for someone she didn't believe existed but insistently haunted her dreams. Captain Alexander Devane of the *Alexis Moon,* dead these many years.

In her room, she closed the windows, drew the curtains against the storm, and without undressing lay down on top of the coverlet, her head pounding.

"Why *my* dreams?" she said softly to the air. "Come to me and tell me. Why me?"

Chapter Two

June 1994

The man who called himself Alec Devon was kept awake during the entire flight from Hawaii to Los Angeles by the comely movie actress sitting next to him, who thought he was somehow entertained by her adolescent self-love. Admittedly, he liked the cut of her jib, although her eyes were without real expression. She did not interest him, and when, as the plane began its descent, she handed him her telephone number, Alec Devon took it with a murmur of regret.

"My abject apologies," he said, "however, I'm going straight to New York without a layover. I don't know when I'll be out this way again."

"Never mind," she said. "I believe in kismet. Here you are from Australia, and here I am, fresh and rested from a vacation in Hawaii. I expect to be in New York early next month. Where can I..."

"I'm sorry," he said, "I'm catching a connecting flight to Maine."

"Well, you certainly seem a man in a hurry. What's so important about Maine?"

"I have a ship waiting for me there."

"A ship. Well. That sounds interesting. I *love* ships." As did Alec, who was most at home on the sea, and ever had been. But these amazing mechanics, he thought, this winged creature, this invention now almost a century old, had its occasional uses.

Faced with no further explanation, the actress tapped her slip of paper. "Next time you're in L.A., give me a ring." She was a woman without any doubts about her talent for entertaining.

Alec smiled vaguely and tucked the paper into his pocket. He wasn't looking for entertainment, but if someone had asked him what he *was* looking for, he'd have been hard-pressed to explain.

Bree Kealy. Bree Kealy. He closed his eyes briefly. *Find her.*

He boarded his flight to New York and fell into a light sleep, aware of the business talk around him. Stocks, bonds, movie deals, what she said and what he said, numbers tossed about, numbers in the millions, words that meant nothing to him. In New York, he made the direct connection to Portland. At the airport, the first thing he noticed upon disembarking was the seal of the city of Portland, and its motto:

Resurgam. I shall rise again.

He found the limousine waiting for him, and was driven through dark, unfamiliar streets to the Regency in the old port. He reflected that only the cobblestone streets were unchanged. He scarcely recognized the old port, filled as it was with a kind of glistening charm never accorded it in the first half of the nineteenth century.

He found his hotel room at ten o'clock, after twenty-five hours of straight travel and several hours of light, broken sleep. He stripped, took a shower and then, without unpacking, lay down. Tonight, almost cer-

tainly, he would sleep. Tonight he would have no more
dreams....

ALEXANDER DEVANE *gazed upon the men sitting round
the card table, the quartermaster, who gathered the cards
in with exaggerated gravity, Breeford Kealy, bosun, sup-
pressing a yawn. And Zachary Martineaux, first mate,
whose glistening eyes and smile, at once cunning and
smug, now revealed to Alexander the rude truth about
himself. This Zachary Martineaux was a man Alexander
had never known. This Zachary Martineaux hated him
with the kind of hatred that had festered long and hard.*

*How had it come to this? They had been friends from
childhood, comrades in a dozen battles, amiable rivals
over beautiful women from eastern bazaars to the west
coast of Africa. They had laughed together, been drunk
together, seen good times together, as well as bad. He
swallowed the bitter taste of bile in his throat. To have
lost everything—and what he had believed was friendship, as well.*

*Zachary reached for the thin gold sheet upon which
Alexander had just scrawled his name.*

"A document I will cherish," he said.

*"To have had such a valuable document at hand,"
Alexander answered in an even tone, "with all my earthly
goods writ down, under the seal of the House of Devane. You were very sure of yourself."*

*"You must remember, my sister's good name was also
at stake."*

*Yes, of course, Beatrice. By losing everything to
Zachary, he had lost Beatrice, as well. Indeed, how had
things come so far that he had agreed on a whim to marry
Beatrice, whom he had never loved?*

Suddenly the cabin felt close, humid, the air filled with a kind of weight he had never known before. He pushed his chair back, got blindly to his feet and rushed over to the porthole.

Pulling it to, he drank in the fresh sea air like a glass of spirits. A chill touched his face, as harsh as a whisper from the grave. The weather will turn soon, he thought, and wondered how he could complete the two-year journey to Java and back with another man at the helm. He loved the Alexis Moon *more than he had ever loved any woman, and his mind whirled with his loss.*

One more game, and he would have it all back. Just one more. He could almost taste the winning of it. Yet he knew it was to no avail. He had but one thing to offer, his life, and for the moment that life was worth nothing. No, he had learned a bitter lesson. Neither was constant—neither victory nor friendship. He was no more now than a hired hand.

Alexander turned back to Zachary Martineaux. He straightened and raised his hand in a military salute. "Captain Alexander Devane at your service, sir."

Zachary, an arm carelessly drawn across the back of his chair, shook his head. "Captain?" Zachary's triumphant glance took in the other players, as though they, too, had something to celebrate. "No, not Captain, I'm afraid."

At his words, and the cruel humor that lay beneath them, Alexander felt a terrible rage roar through his veins. He would have Zachary's head on a sword. He took a step toward him, but reason intervened. He could not blame Zachary for bleating like a newborn lamb. He was captain no more. He had, in a moment, given that away, too.

Zachary's thin lips stretched in a smile. "I'd say you have little enough time to pack your belongings and remove them to the first mate's quarters. Now, if you'll excuse me..." Zachary left the sentence unfinished. He bent, smiling, over the gold tablet. The shadowed cabin seemed to hunker down around him.

Alexander, fists clenched, turned toward the door and stormed out. He knew then that, before the voyage was over, he would kill Zachary Martineaux, or be killed by him.

He came out upon the deck of the Alexis Moon in a night that had turned so black he could scarcely see the clouds, pregnant with rain, that raced down from the north. Winds billowed the sails and sent the ship scudding through heavy seas. Alexander Devane could almost smell the approaching storm.

He welcomed it. Let it toss the ship, and all hands aboard, to the bottom of the sea, where peace lay for them all. Alexander could not live with the shame. He took in a charged breath, then tipped the bottle of brandy to his lips. There was no pain with brandy. Before the night was through, he would finish the bottle, then fling it to Neptune, and perhaps his own misbegotten life with it.

Gone, the Devane fortune was gone, with the turn of a card. How could he have been such a fool? If he could pay with his life to undo his sins, he would gladly die. He grasped the rail, about to offer his body to the welcoming sea, when a hand clamped down upon his shoulder.

He turned swiftly, his face suffused with rage.

"Captain, may I have a word with you?" Breeford Kealy stood before him, smelling of whiskey.

"What are you doing here? Get some sleep, man, clear your head before the weather turns."

"Aye, Captain, so I will." Still, Kealy did not move.

"I am not your captain," Alexander growled.

"Sir, Captain, hear me out."

Off to the starboard side, Alexander could see the dark shade that was the last sight of land. Something was not quite right, Alexander thought. Had everyone gone mad? The sails were set in disarray, as though in mourning for the dead. Did the crew already know they had a new master?

"What is it?" His tone turned soft when he saw the look of dismay upon the bosun's lean face. Kealy was too free with the whiskey bottle at times, but no better man existed on board the Alexis Moon.

"It's not my habit to tell tales, Captain, but this I cannot let pass." Kealy nervously looked around.

Alexander listened for the shouts of his crew as they trimmed the sheets. His men. No, not his men. *"What is it? Speak up,"* he said.

Kealy put his face close to Alexander's. *"You are our captain still. I can tell you, because I know the truth. He did not think I saw him, but the deck of cards with which you played—"*

"What about them? I brought them aboard myself, and opened them myself."

"You did not play with an honest man."

"Are you telling me the cards were marked?"

"Here." Kealy dug into his pocket and pulled out an ace and a deuce. *"I took these without his notice."* His hand traced the edge. *"Marked with a pinprick, while you availed yourself of food and drink."*

Alexander took the cards from the bosun's hands. The tiniest of marks, such as could be felt only by someone looking for them. Yes, he had drunk too much, even *during the game, so sure of himself had he been. A white-hot poker of pain jabbed at his innards.*

He let the cards fall to the deck.

Kealy picked up the cards and put them in his pocket. "He did not think I saw him," he said.

In a leap, Alexander took the companion ladder below and made his way to the captain's cabin. He did not knock upon the door or stand on ceremony, but put his heel to the wood and crashed it in. He found Zachary at the table with his quartermaster, the cards still on the table.

Zachary started to his feet when he saw Alexander, pushing the table away so that it came crashing to the floor, the cards upon it skittering.

"Mr. Devane..." the quartermaster began.

Zachary bent to retrieve the cards, but Alexander put his foot out, pinning Zachary's hand. "Leave them be."

Zachary straightened, face grimacing with pain. He whipped out to his officer, "Get the bosun, have him bring some men."

Alexander picked up the ace of hearts. He had only to draw his finger across the edge to discover the pinprick. "Swine," he said, throwing the cards down. "I'll have the tablet now."

Zachary's smile was thin and cold. "You've had too much to drink, my friend. I cannot guess what you mean. Come, I don't hold grudges. Let us play again." He bent to retrieve the fallen cards. But when he stood, he had his gun in hand.

"Sit down, Alexander. The bosun will be here presently. I hope you like the accommodations in the brig."

Alexander remained standing, allowing himself a smile. It struck him now that he had maintained good *relations with the crew. They would neither shackle him nor put him in the brig.*

Then, as though the silence of the skies had been broken forever, a great thunderbolt was loosed. He thought the universe was breaking in half.

The ship heeled to starboard. Zachary reached out to steady himself, his guard down for an instant. Alexander moved quickly, slamming his fist into Zachary's face. As Zachary fell back, the gun in his hand exploded, tearing a long, searing line across Alexander's arm.

Alexander lunged toward him, but felt the ship heel, unleashing everything that wasn't tied down. He threw a pitying glance at Zachary, who lay on the floor, grimacing in pain. The bosun wouldn't be coming back with the crew. All hands were needed on deck. Alexander left the cabin. Rain poured down in great sheets. The seas were high enough to spill over the bulwarks, the ship listing as the helmsman tried to run before the gale. Alexander had not hceded the warning signs of the approaching storm, so engrossed had he been in his rage with Zachary. He should have been at the helm. Now all was lost, including his own soul.

"Bear away!" he shouted, his words shredded by the wind. He found Breeford Kealy at the helm, his face streaming with water, his hands steady on the wheel, as though he might yet steer the ship safely back to port.

"Abandon ship!" Alexander cried. "Man the lifeboats!" The air was filled with the heart-wrenching cries of men dragged overboard and tossed to the ocean like so many crumbs.

"Alexander."

He whipped around. Zachary stood there, gun in hand. "The Alexis Moon no longer belongs to you." He smiled, holding up the gold tablet. "I give the orders now. Sail ahead!" he cried.

"You fool! Save yourself while you can!" Alexander dived toward him, the gun blast missing him by a hair. All reason was gone, every ounce of energy and strength he possessed directed at destroying his old friend. The gold tablet slipped from Zachary's grasp, skittered across the deck, hit up against the bulwark, and slid aft, where it stuck tight against the rudder housing. Zachary, a frozen scream on his face, slid down the deck, arms outstretched.

Suddenly the ship rocked savagely as the turbulent waters rose up and over its sides. The air filled with the screams of men scrabbling unsuccessfully for some handhold to save them. Lightning struck the main mast and toppled it. The crash sent seamen sprawling overboard. Zachary tried to get to his feet. He reached out to Alexander for help. Alexander scrambled toward him. He wouldn't see a life lost if he could help it, but Zachary, picked up in a great wash of water, was gone in an instant.

With a terrible, piercing crack, the *Alexis Moon* broke in two. Her sails thundered down around them. Alexander felt the deck shift beneath his feet.

The awful significance of what he had done struck his heart at the very moment the sea claimed the *Alexis Moon*. He had held the fate of his men in his hands, all the while waging a personal vendetta against Zachary Martineaux.

As the cargo bays filled with water, Alexander stood upon the heaving deck and called to heaven.

"Forgive me!" he cried. "Forgive me!"

Chapter Three

Devane House had not changed much. Despite a new addition in the rear, the old red-brick structure retained its fierce charm and eighteenth-century grandeur. The house had been his mooring, as it had been his father's, and his grandfather's before that. And in a moment's folly he had turned a card and discarded his inheritance as easily as he might have a mistress with whom he had grown bored.

And now, after many lifetimes of wandering, of being able to call no place home, the forces controlling his destiny had allowed him this chance. If he failed, he knew he would forfeit his life, permanently.

Time had been his enemy. His eyes had beheld the passing of the years, his soul the secrets of the grave. He had roamed bottomless seas and been caught in the webs of foreign tongues and merciless intrigues. He knew the darkest sides of life, the sides that no man was meant to know, and witnessed treacheries he was fated never to change. He had wandered so long, he was weary with it.

Mist swirled around him. He stood in the ballroom of Devane House. The music began, a lively frolic, the latest from Vienna, as though he had stepped back into that fateful year of 1842.

That last evening before he departed, never to return, he had opened the great ballroom to the men of the *Alexis Moon* and their loved ones. Now he saw them again, each treasured face, as they whirled to the music. Beautiful women in flowing gowns laughed in the arms of their men. They could not see the end, for these very men would soon lie cold and dead in the arms of Persephone.

The mist parted. The music stopped. He was alone, yet felt as though someone had opened a Pandora's box of recollections and faded pictures. Talk, arguments, decisions, words spoken in haste, in anger, in love, all came back to him in a rush of shadows, sights and sounds. He struggled to regain his senses, as lost here as anywhere in the world.

BREE KEALY sat in the archive room on the third floor of Devane House, unaware of night falling around her. While she taught marine biology at the institute, she had lately begun to prowl the Devane archives after hours. She was searching—fruitlessly, it seemed—through old files, trying to understand how Captain Alexander Devane had lost his ship off Marauders Point, a spot he knew well and had sailed safely through more than a dozen times.

She was deep in the diaries of his brother, Franklin, when a crack of lightning overhead made her jump. She checked her watch. Ten o'clock. She hadn't realized it was so late. As the first drops of rain pelted the windows, Bree quickly shut the diary, grabbed her bag and remembered that her umbrella, of course, was at home.

Then, to make matters worse, the lights went down for a few seconds, to flicker halfheartedly on again the moment she stepped out into the hall. Suddenly Devane House had lost its familiar warmth and congenial air.

The third floor stood in a strained light that made shadows both black and ominous, as though a harbinger of bad deeds about to happen. The chill in the air didn't help calm her as she started down the wide central staircase, nor did the surprising, almost appreciable silence in the hall that seemed to carry weight and substance.

Even the massive central hall chandelier, the pride of the Devane Institute, gave off a peculiar glow, flickering points of pale light that sent gloomy shadows chasing up and down the stairs. Bree, who liked a scare as well as the next person when it was dished out in a movie, found the pyrotechnics at Devane House extremely unnerving. The air seemed thick with the kind of electricity that sent dogs to barking and humans to the madhouse.

"Hello? Anybody here?" She waited. "No? Okay, I'm out of here." She was a risk-taker, a deep-sea diver, someone who enjoyed testing boundaries, but this strange atmosphere sent chills up her arms.

Halfway to the ground floor, she glanced at the familiar, reassuring portrait of Captain Alexander Devane, which hung across the huge central hall above the fireplace.

Sea green eyes, black hair ruffled in a painted wind, straight, sharp nose and a well-trimmed beard... The captain would not look out of place here, tonight. He'd cut quite a figure, she thought wistfully. Alexander Devane had been generous toward the city of Portland on the one hand, reckless and hard-drinking on the other. His widowed mother had spoiled him, his younger brother, Franklin, had adored him. He was a study in contrasts—handsome, mysterious and fascinating.

She had failed to call him into being at Marauders Point, but she could not forget her dream. Now, she thought, show yourself to me, now.

Every inch of the portrait had been devoted to making the captain look alive, charismatic and ready for adventure, even after the passage of a century and a half. A crazy notion struck her that he was gazing at her, his eyes meeting hers across the years.

"Why were you born too soon?" She stopped. Had the question come out of her mouth? Was she mad? Suppose one of her students heard her mooning over a man dead one hundred and fifty years?

You're in love with a portrait, a legend, a man whose bones lie on the sea floor at Marauders Point, she told herself. Common sense told her that if she ever, ever met a man like Alexander Devane, she wouldn't be able to bear him for ten minutes. He'd be an aggressive, overbearing misogynist. In a word, he'd be everything a modern woman would despise.

She was spared expecting an answer from the good captain when the hall went completely dark. "Oh, damn," she called, "who did that? I'm still here. Put those lights back on."

She waited a moment, stranded on the staircase in an intense kind of dark she had never experienced before. She remained stock-still, holding her breath, unable to move even if she had wanted to, trying to stave off a wave of panic as whole acres of goose bumps covered her arms. *Oh, Lord,* she thought, *the ghosts of Devane's past are on the rampage.*

"Bree."

She gasped and felt her knees buckle. Above the great marble fireplace, Alexander Devane's face was lit momentarily by an unnatural light.

"Bree, I'm here."

Her heart stopped for an instant and then broke free, clamoring in her chest. The lights came back on. She whirled around in a fury, to find a stranger stepping out of the shadows.

"Who the hell are you?" she said hotly. "You scared me half to death."

He made no effort to come closer. "I did not mean to frighten you," he said quietly. "Surely you know me." He put a placating hand out, as though to assure her of his good intentions.

"Should I?"

He glanced up at the portrait. "Do you not recognize Alexander Devane?"

She followed his eyes, and had to admit that the man standing before her, his stance tall and straight, seemed of the same mettle, self-possession masquerading as arrogance, a fierce temper just below the surface. His eyes were sea green, his black hair was tied back. He was clean-shaven, with a cleft chin and the beginning of a dimple in his right cheek. His proud physique and hard muscles were visible through his denim shirt and tight jeans.

She shook her head, realizing suddenly that she no more expected Alexander Devane to materialize than to travel back to the nineteenth century. "Are you mad?" she said, amazed at how composed she was. "Are you playing some kind of game? If so, I fail to get the point."

He looked curiously at her. "Play games? Is that what you think? I'm afraid this is no game, Bree."

If he was trying to convince her he had traveled through time and stopped for a change of clothes, he was out of luck. Then the truth of their encounter struck her.

Damn, he had been at Marauders Point and heard her when she cast her foolish cries to the wind.

"Oh, I get it," she said. "Okay, right, you're Alexander Devane. Now, if you'll excuse me, I'm going to call the guard and have you thrown out."

He glanced once more at the portrait, then back at her, the intensity of his gaze disturbing. "Bree, I have come for you. Surely you know that." He took a step toward her.

"I'd stop right there, if I were you."

He held his hands up. "As you wish, madam."

What could she be thinking of? He was a perfect stranger, trespassing on private property at an ungodly hour of the night. "You're trespassing. You know that, don't you, Alexander? You're not part of the staff. Unless," she added, although she did not believe the idea for a moment, "you're the new guard."

His smile reached his eyes. "Perhaps that's what you would call it. Let's say I am guarding the fortunes of the Devane Institute."

Her mind worked quickly. His accent, old-fashioned and formal, was unlike any Maine accent she knew. This man wasn't a guard. He looked like a man whose life had gone far beyond the ordinary, who had learned more of life and deeds than any man should know.

"Bree, how I got here is of no consequence. You and I know each other as intimately as ever a man and woman could." He took a step toward her. Bree gripped the banister.

"Stay where you are," she said, unable to keep the sudden fear from her voice.

He did not advance a step farther. "I was a fool to come, then."

"I'm calling the guard," she said, making a dash to the door.

"Come, girl, it's late. I'll be taking you home."

He reached the door with her. His hand closed over hers on the knob. She could feel his breath upon her cheek, and the warmth and strength emanating from him. Her reaction to him sent an erotic shiver down her spine, a reaction that only fueled her rage. "Who the hell do you think you are?" she said. "Take your hand off me!"

He lifted his head and smiled, not quite kindly. "Dammit, you know who I am, madam, but it will give me great pleasure to show you."

"I'll scream. There are guards everywhere."

"They won't hear you."

She had no time to react. He reached for her and pulled her into his arms. His lips came down on hers, softly at first, and then, as though the mere touch made him lose control, harder, deeper, crushing. She felt her breasts tight against his chest, her nipples aching with a familiar longing.

The shock of recognition was so great, she felt her knees buckle. It was in her dreams that she had experienced such sudden, urgent passion. Her *dreams*.

She reared back in a fury, her face flushed, her body still responding to his touch. How could he know so much about her? She pushed him away. "How dare you!" She raised her hand and slapped his face, turned, opened the door and stormed out into the wet night.

Chapter Four

Bree ran a hand through her shoulder-length light brown hair, squinted her blue eyes at her hands and decided that the chip in her nail polish would never be noticed by J.H. With a brief sigh, she knocked at his office door.

A summons this late in the day usually meant bad news. A cut in funds, parents complaining about insufficient attention to their brilliant offspring by one Professor Bree Kealy, another class she might consider squeezing into her schedule in the fall term... She braced herself for the worst.

"Come in."

Bree took in a deep breath and bravely opened the door to J.H.'s lair, a large antique-filled corner office that was the envy of everyone at the college. Its desirable view was of the east lawn and the bay in the distance, now shaded by dusk. She was surprised to discover that J.H. had a guest, a well-dressed stranger who turned to look briefly at her. He was small and muscular and reminded her of a pug about to take on the world. Parent complaint, she decided, running the names of some possible miscreants through her mind.

"Ah, here you are." J.H. rose perfunctorily from his chair, and gestured to her to come forward. "This is Mr.

Simon Mortimer from Leighs of London," he said. "Professor Bree Kealy. Marine biology. She'll be going along."

Mortimer extended a hand. His smile transformed his face. Decidedly not a complaining parent, but going along where?

"Delighted." He took her hand between his and looked closely into her eyes. "Then we'll be seeing a lot more of each other," he said, in a charming British accent.

Bree returned his smile, glancing over at J.H. for an explanation. Then it struck her. Leighs of London—insurers of the *Alexis Moon*.

"Well, my dear, we'll meet again soon," Mortimer said, giving her hand an extra little pat before releasing it.

Bree murmured the safest words she could think of. "Very nice meeting you, Mr. Mortimer."

He leaned across the desk and shook hands with J.H. and, with another friendly smile at Bree, went quickly out, closing the door behind him.

"Doesn't seem a bad chap, considering. Have a seat," J.H. said.

Bree obeyed, pulling up the leather chair Mortimer had vacated, her mind a hopeful blank.

"You know Zack Martineaux," he said without preamble. J.H. was a tall, lean man with white hair and an intimidatingly willful gaze from clear, light blue eyes. That gaze was now on her.

"Zack and I belong to the Marauders Point Diving Club. I haven't seen him in a long time, though."

"You were in the same graduating class here," J.H. said.

"That was almost ten years ago, but I can't say I really know him any more than the next person. I might even add that I think he's rude, self-serving and obnoxious. Do you mind telling me what Mr. Mortimer—"

"Robin Krashaw apparently doesn't count those as faults when it comes to her salvage operation," J.H. said, interrupting her. "And where the devil did he come up with the money to hire her?"

"Zack is a very convincing salesman. Of a sort," Bree added after a second.

"I wouldn't doubt there's something very shady about this whole nasty business." A hint of wishful thinking colored his voice.

"The minute the wreck was located, we knew it was only a matter of time before Zack moved in. It's a juggernaut, J.H. If Zack didn't go after it, someone else would. About Mr. Mortimer—"

"Zack has claims on the *Alexis Moon*. You know what that means for the institute if they find the gold tablet."

Bree gave up on the question of Simon Mortimer. The discussion about the salvage operation was not a new one. Ever since the first findings, a couple of years before, the possibility of salvaging the ship and discrediting Devane had hung like a black cloud over the institute.

Once the salvage operation was begun, Leighs of London would have a vested interest in the wreck of the *Alexis Moon*, if not of the Devane Institute. She chanced the question. "Is this business of the *Alexis Moon* why Mr. Mortimer was here?"

J.H. frowned. "Hell, he's going along on the salvage operation."

"You mean..." Bree began, and then stopped, a flood of joy raging through her. Was that what J.H. meant, that she was going along, too?

"Incidentally, Bree, I want you to treat Simon Mortimer with respect. Leighs of London will undoubtedly come out of this business a winner. It will be a lot better to have them on our side."

Bree could scarcely take in his words. The *Alexis Moon!* She was going along! But why? What was J.H. up to?

"Simon Mortimer made no secret of the fact that his company plans to share in the profits," J.H. went on in a doleful voice. He swung to his feet and began to pace the office, hands dug into his pockets. "There's a similar case in the courts right now."

"Well, any money derived from the operation wouldn't belong to the Devane Institute, any way you look at it," Bree said.

"The decision in favor of the insurer might not affect Devane, if Martineaux doesn't find the gold tablet," J.H. said. "The point is possibly tying the college up in the courts for years. It'll certainly cut into our fund-raising efforts."

"So you believe the famous gold tablet exists," Bree said. She was bursting with the desire to know whether he really meant her to go along on the operation, but knew enough not to change the subject.

J.H. shook his head. "Does the gold deed exist? That's not what I said. We all know it does. The question is Alexander Devane's signature."

Ask the man who kissed me last night, she wanted to say, remembering with a little shudder the feel of his lips against hers. He thinks he's Alexander Devane.

"I was merely speculating what could happen *if,*" J.H. continued. "The Martineaux are scoundrels, and always were. That's what worries me. You know what I want you to do, don't you?"

"Go along on the salvage operation." She tried not to jump for joy, although she supposed she ought to explain that she had no more clout with Zack than anyone else. Less, perhaps. Now that he was riding high, he'd have every reason to be annoyed with her. Zack had always wanted to date her, and she had let him know from the beginning that she wasn't interested in him. But that was beside the point. He'd be salivating at the idea of taking the Devane Institute on. "I'm not sure what you want me to do about Zack," she said to J.H. "Get down on my knees and beg him to back off?"

J.H.'s smile had not an ounce of charm in it. A sense of foreboding came over her. *He'd like Zack dead,* she thought. The Devane Institute meant that much to him.

"We're not begging your friend for anything," he said impatiently. "I have a much simpler plan."

She held her breath.

"The nephew of the owner of Krashaw Salvage is married to Mrs. Plattman's son-in-law's sister," J.H. said, referring to an important member of Devane's board of directors. "Mrs. Plattman made a telephone call, and Krashaw was very amenable to having a marine biologist on board."

"That's wonderful. I don't know how to thank you, J.H."

"I'm not asking for thanks, Bree, just your unconditional cooperation."

Although she understood him well enough to know that he expected hard work and dedication from his staff, the notion of being chosen for the salvaging team was so heady, Bree at first paid no attention to his caveat.

"You're going to make certain that our friend Zack is not about to pull a fast one with that supposed deed."

"What do you mean, a fast one?"

"He might seed the wreck with a copy. It would be worth the investment, don't you think?"

"He wouldn't," she said, horrified at the notion. "Nobody would do that. Zack may be a jerk, but he wouldn't do anything dishonest. At least, I don't think he would."

J.H. shook his head, as though marveling over her gullibility. "There's every reason why you're right for the job, but being naive isn't one of them." He came back to his desk and began to fiddle with some papers on it. "You're going along because it fits in with the kind of research you're doing. You've had experience on deep dives. And you have Devane's interests at heart."

"But I'm being asked to spy on Zack Martineaux."

"We don't want to be drawn into any expensive lawsuits with him."

"I can't imagine he'd want that, either."

J.H. sighed in a dramatic way, looking first up at the ceiling, then at Bree. "I sometimes think the best thing that could happen would be for someone to find the tablet and bury it deep beneath the seafloor. So deep, it would never come to light."

So that was the reason for his generosity. She drew a breath, her disappointment every bit as deep as he wanted her to bury the tablet.

"Bury the damn thing deep," J.H. said to her.

"You know divers work in teams, J.H. The tablet won't be lying there with a sign on it saying Pick Me Up."

"Your chance is as good as anyone else's." J.H. picked a business card off his desk and handed it to her. "Miss Krashaw expects to hear from you. Call her, make an appointment."

Bree took the card and let herself out of the office. She had called out to Alexander Devane at Marauders Point to give her a sign. Was this it? Not a stranger masquerading as Alexander, but this, an invitation to explore the *Alexis Moon,* and to bury the gold tablet?

Did he, too, want the tablet buried so deep beneath the seafloor it would never come to light? When she passed his portrait in the hall on her way out, she whispered, "I promise."

FRANCINE KEALY LIVED in a co-op high rise overlooking Boston harbor. Bree doubted her gadabout mother would be home, but the phone was picked up on the second ring.

"You're home. Wonderful," Bree said.

"Only because I have half a dozen dinner guests," her mother said in her matter-of-fact voice, as though she and her daughter lived no more than ten minutes away.

Bree could hear people laughing in the background. Her mother's parties were always lively and full of good talk, and she felt a moment's regret that she could not be there for it. "Want me to call you back?"

"No, sweetie, they can wait. You know I'm always happy to hear your voice."

Talking to her mother unfailingly gave Bree a lift, and her one sadness was that they lived so far apart. But, excited as she was about calling, she also knew just how sticky the conversation could become. "Mom, you'll never guess what's happened," she began.

"You're going to be married."

"I stepped right into that, didn't I?" Bree said, with a little laugh. "Nope, something a lot better." Her mind slipped to the stranger, his look of shock when she had slapped him. He had not come after her, and for an instant she had felt a certain regret.

"There's nothing better than finding someone to love, Bree."

Bree felt a lecture coming on about the virtues of marriage and motherhood, and hurried to head it off at the pass. "I'm going along on the salvage operation to the wreck of the *Alexis Moon.*"

There was a long moment of silence from the other end. She could hear the sounds of her mother's guests talking, and then another burst of laughter.

"Congratulations," her mother said dryly. "How did you manage it?"

"I didn't even try. J.H. decided for me."

"Well, maybe it's not a bad idea, Bree. Perhaps now you'll be able to let Alexander Devane's bones rest. You know that's what you'll find, don't you?"

It was Bree's turn at silence. They would disinter him, she thought with a little shiver, find his bones, the silver buttons on his coat, perhaps his pipe, the decanter from which he had taken his wine, the quadrant through which he must have sighted a thousand times. Disturbing his grave was an indignity no man's memory should be made to suffer. And she would be right there when it happened.

"This salvaging operation involves more than that, Mom." She was aware of the defensive tone of her voice. "The salvaging of the wreck means lawsuits, if that gold tablet is found."

"Yes, of course. I'm sorry, sweetie, but you know how I feel, how your father felt, that you've always dwelt too much on the fate of the *Alexis Moon* and Alexander Devane. I always hoped when you and Chuck Wellman were going together..." She stopped in midsentence.

"Mom, it's okay, everything's fine. I'm going along as a marine biologist. It's research, that's all." She left out the part about keeping an eye on Zack. The less said, the better.

"Wonderful. Glad you've got all that business out of your mind. I don't hold much truck with the past. I'd have sold all those things in the safe for you and put the money toward your college tuition, if your father had let me. He didn't believe in ancestor worship, either, but he wanted you to decide."

"What stuff?" Bree asked, surprised.

"Family heirlooms. You know, the things you keep in safes because they mean you belong to a very old family. Nonsense. We all belong to very old families, but there it is, the Kealys have always been very proud of their past."

"Mom, what heirlooms?"

"Your dad and I thought you were too involved in the past, Bree."

"It all gets down to Alexander Devane, doesn't it? I'm not living in the past. I'm as modern as you are."

"I know," her mother said, in a soft, loving voice. "The trouble is, you live in the present, but you dream in the past."

Bree gasped at her mother's remark. She couldn't know how close she was to the truth. "Have those heirlooms anything to do with Breeford Kealy?"

"We figured one day you'd grow out of this passion of yours, and then we'd pass them on, for what they're worth. Some gold pieces belonging to your great-grandmother. Breeford Kealy's pocket watch, and those ghastly playing cards they found in his pocket—just two of them, and ace and a deuce."

"Playing cards?"

"Apparently someone sent along Breeford's clothes and the contents of his pockets to his wife when he died.

They've come down as family heirlooms. Now they're yours."

"Playing cards," Bree said again.

"An ace and a deuce. Don't tell me they mean something to you."

"Good heavens, Alexander and Zachary were playing cards when the ship went down."

"You know that to be a certainty, Bree?" Her mother's tone was acerbic.

Bree sighed, feeling inordinately embarrassed. "No, of course I don't, but we have, sort of, Breeford Kealy's word for it."

"Darling Bree, everyone in the family knows, and it was handed down like one of those heirlooms, that Breeford was a drunk and a gambler. And that he told Beatrice Martineaux about the tablet is also apocryphal. That's exactly what she would say. It was to her family's benefit to say so."

Bree was surprised that her mother could argue so passionately about something in which she had not the slightest interest. But then there was no doubt that the legend of the *Alexis Moon* was part of Kealy lore, and her mother, whether she was interested or not, had heard it more than once.

"They have little pinpricks in them," her mother said. "That's easily the most fascinating thing about the cards. The kind of pinpricks you'd find in a game of poker that was fixed."

"I'd like to see them," Bree said, unable to keep the wonder out of her voice.

"Anytime, love. When are you coming to Boston?"

"I don't know," Bree said. "I'll have to plan. Look, I'll let you get back to your party."

When she hung up, she sat for a long time thinking.

An ace and a deuce. Were *they* the signs she'd been looking for?

Chapter Five

Robin Krashaw gazed with undisguised curiosity at the man standing before her. Her office was small and jam-packed, just the way she liked it, but Alec Devon, with his powerful physique and hard muscles, seemed to take up all its space, and then some.

She had always been a sucker for big, handsome men who looked smarter than they should be. His hair was black, long enough to tie back with a rubber band. His eyes were an extraordinary green that reminded her of distant seas.

With a stab of yearning, she realized he was the kind of man she would have bedded in her youth with much gusto and no regrets.

She shifted in her chair. Now, why should this man bring back feelings she hadn't had in decades? Ah, she thought, there's always a little bit of youth left to stir one's emotions.

On with it, she told herself, he's young enough to be your grandson.

She straightened in her chair, picked up his papers and perused them again. Of a tight, leery disposition at best, she had to wonder at his credentials, which seemed too good to be true. Devon struck her as a man with a purpose. He had come a long way to ask for a job. Still, while neither physical appearance nor guessing at motives would affect her judgment, the word of the man who had recommended him did.

Then there was the matter of his speech—cultured and a bit old-fashioned. "I can't quite place your accent," she said.

"I don't wonder," he said. "It's a mix of all the out-of-the-way places I've ever set sail in."

"That'll do it every time," she said, not quite convinced, but intrigued nevertheless. "Have a seat." She pointed to a wire-backed chair that leaned on two feet against a file cabinet. Devon grabbed the chair, turned it so that the back faced Robin, and straddled it.

"Now," he said, giving her a direct look and a quick, open smile that dared her to distrust him, "what do you want to know?"

Well, she thought, for all his formal speech, he wasn't a man to stand on ceremony. "You wouldn't mind telling me exactly where you're from? Just simple curiosity on my part."

He gave a short, gruff laugh. "Well, I've spent more time down under than anywhere else."

"Ah." She sat back, satisfied. "Australia. I should have known." He had the look. Cocky, deeply masculine, and self-possessed. And what better place to learn the fine points of diving than the Great Barrier Reef? "Ian Richards says you're the best." Now everything fitted into place. Richards was captain of a vessel that did a fair amount of underwater exploration in the Pacific, and Alec Devon had been aboard every one of his operations for the past six years. "Why exactly have you parted company with Ian?" She looked at the letter that Ian had sent to her, but in his usual taciturn way, the good captain had given no explanations, merely praise for Alec Devon.

"My main interest has been in salvage operations on nineteenth-century wrecks."

She gave him a puzzled look. "Nineteenth-century? That sort of narrows it. Why not eighteenth, or seventeenth, for that matter?"

He shrugged, as if every man were entitled to a peccadillo or two, no matter how odd. "Let's call it a hobby, the sailing vessels of the nineteenth century. Especially those old clipper ships. Technical marvels, they were. I've been waiting for one as intriguing as the *Alexis Moon* promises to be." He gave her a dazzling smile. "I'll make no bones about it, madam, I am here because it is precisely where I wish to be."

"Ian says you have an uncanny feel for where the bodies are buried."

She caught a slight darkening in his eyes at her remark, almost immediately gone. He had a temper, she thought, trigger-quick, but one he was used to controlling. "Figuratively speaking," she hastened to add, and then realized that he was running the interview, not she. "You've been of immeasurable help around these old wrecks, am I right?" She pointed to Ian's letter. "According to the good captain, that is."

"Sheer luck, Miss Krashaw."

"It's more than luck, sailor. Deep-sea diving takes brains, tenacity and courage."

"I have no argument with you there."

"I need to hire the best. As it is, I have my crew, a trustworthy lot, but I lost one of them last week when he decided that salvaging in the Caribbean is more his style. Good luck to him. The *Doubloon* is state-of-the-art," she went on, "a Coast Guard cutter I bought and had remodeled for salvage work. One hundred ten feet long, displaces one hundred sixty five tons. She's moored at the end of the dock. It includes an underwater robot I call *Juno*." She made no effort to keep the pride out of her voice.

"Juno, the queen of the gods," Alec Devon said. "You might have done better to call her Venus. Some say she sprang from the foam of the sea."

Robin blinked. She knew everything there was to know about underwater salvaging, but that didn't make her an expert on Roman myths. Nevertheless, Devon's arcane knowledge and the easy way he used it impressed her.

"I've made a study of the *Alexis Moon*," he said. "I've read every word printed about her, enough so that I feel I have been aboard her and sailed her to Australia and back."

"Ian Richards says you're familiar with computers— the kinds of programs we're using."

"Enough."

"He said you're an expert."

"Computers break down," he said evenly.

"We have backup."

"I prefer my own eyes and ears, but they seem to have gone out of fashion these days."

"You have no use for gadgets, then."

"I don't believe you'll need the *Juno*. The wreck of the *Alexis Moon* is not so deep as you think."

"We've mapped precisely, to the inch, just where the wreck is, and how deep," she said huffily. "Zack Martineaux has spent the last two years planning this little jaunt. Just what do you think you know?" The precise location had been fudged in an attempt to discourage other salvage operators from moving in on the wreck, but she'd be damned if she'd let him know he was on the mark.

Alec idly picked up a paperweight from her desk and studied it. "I've told you. Historical sites interest me. I've made a study of the more unusual ones. The *Alexis Moon,* laden with goods for the Far East, was struck down scarcely before she had begun her journey. Given the weather conditions, the currents and tides, and the words of the one surviving sailor, without sonar or magnetometers, I could have picked the spot where she went down." He turned the paperweight upside down. Inside, a tiny whale, placed in a globule of liquid, moved as he shook it.

"Pity Zack didn't know you two years ago. It would have saved him a pretty penny. As for the word of the one surviving sailor, he was too busy whispering lies into Beatrice Martineaux's ear to pinpoint the exact site."

Alec smiled. "Lies? That's the first I've heard of them."

"Everybody in town has an opinion about *that,*" Robin said with a disapproving air. She sifted through his papers. "I've got your application, but no résumé."

"Ask away, ma'am, I'll answer any question you raise." He carefully replaced the paperweight on her desk.

"Don't make the mistake of thinking I'm an easy mark," she said. "There's nothing more important to me than my ship. And when I take on a project, you'd better believe I'm about as tough as they make them. And I only employ the best."

"You're looking at the best, ma'am. I've sailed the seven seas, and know my way around any ship that's been built by man." He got restlessly to his feet, focusing his

eyes on her with a dangerous glint she was certain had
broken a dozen hearts.

"I command the *Doubloon,*" she said. "The diving
master is Zack Martineaux." She caught the faint black
glower once again, this time not quite so easily erased. "I
run a tight ship, and I brook no nonsense. If you can
work with my crew, you're hired," she said, and stuck
out her hand. "Welcome to the *Doubloon.*"

He met her eyes squarely, seemed about to say something, but held his tongue. He grasped her hand and
shook it firmly. Odd, she thought, she had the feeling
that, if given his druthers, he would have brought her
hand to his lips and kissed it. *Ma'am.* She liked that.

She had no doubt that he had an agenda all his own.
Nor did she doubt that he was an adventurer, and maybe
even reckless, but the notion worked well for her. She
liked a man who was adventurous, who would take
chances and not make a fool of himself. She could not
imagine this man ever making a move that wasn't backed
by strength of character.

Then again, maybe Alec Devon spelled trouble. But
Robin Krashaw had never taken honors in spelling.

THE *DOUBLOON,* spanking-white and sleek as a dolphin,
rode the water high. Her slanted red-banded funnel
seemed to heel into the wind that came off Casco Bay. A
twenty-five-foot runabout was hoisted on the aft deck
along with a lifeboat. Bree guessed the tarpaulin-covered
object that looked like a giant sausage to be the submersible, *Juno.*

She felt a thrill of anticipation as she headed toward
Krashaw Salvage, housed in a large old brick warehouse
on the docks, where once exotic spices and whale oil had
been off-loaded. Now, one would be more likely to find

sealed containers lined up for shipment overland, with no hint whatsoever of their contents. She thought of the *Alexis Moon* docked in place of the *Doubloon,* masts draped with unfurled sails, disgorging its booty from the Far East, of the scents and colors that seemed much more in keeping with the old wharf than modern ships and trucks.

Robin Krashaw's office at the back of the warehouse was reached through a large open area smelling of urethane and varnish, in which several boats of varying sizes and types were in varying states of repair.

Bree found her way back to a half-open, grimy window to the right of an open door. Inside, at a huge desk piled with papers, sat a small, sturdy middle-aged woman with a cloud of short blond hair. Robin Krashaw, she hoped. A man stood at the desk with his back to Bree. She wondered fleetingly if he was as handsome as he was broad shouldered. Tall, muscular, with black hair ponytailed, he wore a light linen jacket and jeans. A thoroughly modern hunk, she decided.

Since Bree had arrived on time, she had no qualms about knocking on the office window. The woman looked up, waved her in and scrutinized her with bright-eyed curiosity. "Bree Kealy, right?"

Bree nodded. Her eyes, however, were on the man who had turned toward her. The moment she saw his face, she gasped. Impossible. Her world seemed suddenly to tilt dangerously. The remembrance of his bruising kiss had not gone away, and now, looking at him, at his wondrously shapely mouth, she could understand her reaction to his touch. Oh, she thought, groaning inwardly, she had *slapped* him, and here he was at Krashaw Salvage. Perhaps, at this moment, he held her life in his hands.

His eyes caught hers. He drew his hand to his cheek at precisely the spot where she had slapped him. Bree felt heat rise to her face, but realized suddenly that he had revealed no other sign that they had ever met. She glanced confusedly back at the woman behind the desk. "I'm sorry if I'm interrupting anything," she said in a faltering voice. "Robin Krashaw?"

"The same. You're right on time."

Bree knew she shouldn't, but she turned once more to the stranger. No, not stranger. The ponytail should have tipped her off.

Their eyes met, yet his expression shut out even the faintly curious glimmer anyone might have revealed at an interruption. She bristled at his snub, no matter how subtle. How dare he pretend that nothing had passed between them, not even a stolen kiss?

"Okay, Devon, you're on," Robin was saying, smiling at him. "We'll talk details later. Don't disappoint me."

He touched his forehead in a salute. "My dear madam, you won't be sorry, I guarantee it."

The same voice, she thought, the same accent, the same warm timbre.

"Oh, Alec Devon, this is Bree Kealy. She'll be on board, too. She's a marine biologist."

"Alec Devon," Bree said, pronouncing his name carefully.

Robin Krashaw beamed at them. "He's just come in from Australia," she added. "Worked with Ian Richards."

Bree knew the name of Ian Richards, and that put the lie to his claim that he was Alexander Devane. Devon came over to Bree, took her hand and drew it to his lips.

"Bree Kealy." He seemed to roll her name over his tongue, as though tasting each syllable, yet he still gave no clue that they had met before. "A marine biologist. I've met more than one in my day."

He continued to hold her hand, but in another moment Bree snatched it away, feeling Robin Krashaw's disapproval staining the air.

"Okay, Devon, we've got work to do here," Robin said, stirring noisily in her chair and clearly feigning disinterest in the way they stood and examined each other. "Show up Monday—early."

"I'll wake up with the dawn," he said, flashing a smile at them both as he went out the door.

"Damn fine-looking man," Robin said, the moment he was out of earshot. "The good Lord certainly knows how to empower some creatures. I saw the way he looked you over. Hand-kissing... Now, where in hell do you suppose he picked that up?"

"Some old Errol Flynn movie," Bree said, pretending insouciance and giving a small laugh she didn't quite feel.

"I don't go for hanky-panky on my watch."

"You don't have to worry about that," Bree said, wondering if she could trust her own words. "This trip means a lot to me. I have nothing on my mind but the *Alexis Moon*."

"Good. That's what I like to hear. Pull up a chair, Kealy. Let's get down to business."

The chair was already in place, squeezed between the desk and a huge ship's anchor that engulfed half the available floor space. She had the feeling that Robin took the time to examine her from head to foot, from her rust linen suit to her brown high heels and bag, and came up wondering about a marine biologist in power clothing. Robin herself wore jeans and a denim shirt over a white

T-shirt. Her frizzy hair gave her the look of Little Orphan Annie at last showing her years.

In spite of the woman's overbearing manner, Bree liked Robin Krashaw, and returned the hearty handshake offered her across the desk. She noted the absence of a wedding band. "Good to meet you, Ms. Krashaw."

"Name's Robin."

"Mine's Bree."

"Sounds like nobody in Portland is named Mary Smith anymore. You're the relative of the infamous Breeford Kealy, I gather. So," Robin went on, "what's your specialty? Coffee? We only drink it black here."

"Yes to the coffee, and tenacious sea creatures are my specialty."

Robin went over to a coffee machine that was the only polished appliance in the room. She poured a cupful and handed it to Bree. "Tenacious sea creatures. Looking for the glue that will make you a millionaire?"

"I think they already found that," Bree said. "No, I'm curious to learn more about sea animals that think home is where the feet stick."

"And you'll find all of them on the wreck of the *Alexis Moon*."

Bree shook her head. She was being tested, all right. "I'd like to make certain that they stay where they've set up shop."

"Well, they're down there, that's certain." Robin pointed to a series of photographs hanging on the wall opposite her desk. "We took some pictures of the wreck. Ever see them before?"

Bree was out of her chair in a shot. "Just reproductions in the newspapers. That was what, a year or two ago?"

"Two. Zack got me when I was feeling charitable. We were headed out that way to test new underwater photographic equipment."

Bree looked in awe at the eight-by-twelve color photos. The clarity was amazing. There were a dozen pictures in all, each of a different site. She saw the broad outlines of the prow, a cannon covered with algae and debris, unidentifiable beams. The *Alexis Moon* had become a rich stew of seaweed and sand and algae. And the ship was decidedly not standing upright, sails unfurled.

"How far down?" she asked.

"Hundred feet at its lowest point."

"Much easier to get to than people thought."

"The moon's a lot closer when you've got the right instruments for getting there."

"And now you have them."

Robin gave her a proud smile. "You bet we do. This job for Martineaux is our first going after an untouched wreck. We do charters mostly, out to the *Andrea Doria* regularly, for one. Any questions you want to ask?"

"Hundreds." But her mind had already wandered to Alec Devon. She could not believe the coincidence. Portland was a small city, but not that small. The fact that they would be together on the *Doubloon* stunned her. He had already stirred longings in her that were dangerous. She had no idea how she would be able to keep herself at a safe distance from him in such close quarters. She realized that Robin seemed to be waiting for questions. Bree thought hurriedly. "Date of departure?"

"One week from now. I understand you have your calendar clear."

Bree nodded. She did now. "Will there be a lab for me to work in?"

"You set it up, you stock it."

A lab of her own! Sudden joy washed through her. She'd do more than make certain the *Alexis Moon* did not yield some of its darker secrets, she'd be its watchdog and the cool, impartial scientist who believed marine life should also have a stake in how shipwrecks were salvaged. And she'd stay away from one Alec Devon.

"And if your tenacious sea creatures are on Zack Martineaux's famous gold tablet—?" Robin let the question hang in the air.

Bree turned away from the photographs and went back to retrieve her coffee cup. She weighed the idea of pretending ignorance, but anyone associated with Devane and J.H. would have to be involved. "The president of Devane assures me the tablet, *if* it was on board, was never signed. Alexander may have been reckless, but there's no hint that he was ever stupid."

Robin smiled. "He let his ship founder, didn't he? Well, I hope for Devane's sake he's right. The town needs the institute, and who knows what Zack would do if he's proved to have ownership. Maybe just change the name to Martineaux Institute."

Over my dead body, Bree thought, but all she said aloud was "Years of litigation."

"Litigation isn't my affair," Robin said sharply. "The salvors are being paid a straight salary because of it."

So Zack expected trouble after all.

Robin checked her watch. "Suppose you save your questions till the next time. Tell me then what your plans are, and make sure everything's delivered on time."

"Do you have any idea how long the operation will last?"

"This charter is by the month, with two months contracted for." An unexpected gleam came into her eyes, as though she were holding something back.

"Welcome aboard," she said, getting up.

"I'm thrilled to be part of the salvage team. Thanks for letting me come along."

"Pleasure to have you. Just watch your rear at all times. I'm not a mother hen, and I expect the entire crew to be professional. That's not a wading pool out there."

"Can't spell it out better than that." Bree returned her coffee cup to the tray that held the coffee machine. She read in Robin's words a warning about Alec Devon, as well. Robin had nothing to worry about. Alec Devon was an opportunist and a liar, as far as she could see.

"Come on, I'll give you the tour of the *Doubloon*," Robin said. "Show you your quarters."

Seeing the *Doubloon* under a strong noon sun, Bree thought there was something about the ship's absolute whiteness and its oddly hooded look that was ominous. Perhaps she hadn't been able to shake her dreams loose. Of course. That was it. She thought of the black, gold-trimmed *Alexis Moon,* in full sail. She was a modern woman in every way, appreciating the beauty of the past but in tune with the twentieth century.

Alec Devon stood a dozen yards away, his back to them. He gazed up at the ship, as though taking its measure inch by inch. Bree stopped, fascinated, her breath drawn in and held. From the way he stood, she could all but feel his blatant sensuality. She had to fight the notion that he could, even with his back to her, make her heart turn cartwheels.

"Where's he from?" she said to Robin, who stood quietly at her side, gazing at him, as well.

"Your guess is as good as mine. He says from down under. Out of a pirate novel, I'd say."

Bree was silent. No, not a pirate novel. But not from a painting that hung in Devane House, either.

"I hired him, but I have a feeling I've just hired myself a mess of trouble." She turned to Bree. "You got a guy?"

"Well, no. I mean, not at the moment." She waited to hear Robin tell her once again that hanky-panky was off-limits once they were on board ship. Bree realized that she could make all the promises in the world and mean them, but that this man could turn her into jelly in an instant.

Alec Devon saw them and came over. His walk was easy, a man in control of every muscle of his body. Bree didn't want any complications, either. Zack was enough to worry about. And she wasn't ready to put up with Alec Devon's waylaying her in every nook and cranny and kissing her, delightful as the prospect was.

"I like her lines," Alec said, with a nod at the *Doubloon*. His eyes slid from Robin to Bree, sweeping over her body, and taking in her long legs with the kind of contemplation Bree imagined he had just bestowed upon the *Doubloon*. She should have prickled but didn't.

"Yeah, she'll do the job, all right." Robin looked as though she wanted to pat her ship on the prow. "Consider yourself lucky to be one of the crew, Devon."

"About as lucky as I will ever be," Alec said, his eyes still upon Bree.

She would not prickle, she would not react... She was in the process of trying to convince herself she was in control when a car came slowly down the wharf and stopped. A young man with a shock of red hair stuck his head out the window. "Robin Krashaw?"

"You're looking at her." Robin excused herself and went over to him. Bree was summarily left alone with Alec Devon, who stood regarding her with a bemused expression.

She waited a moment, hoping he would explain himself. When he remained silent, she looked up at the sky. "Nice day. I mean, they said it was going to cloud over later. Maybe rain tonight." She thought of racing over to Robin, of asking to be excused. She felt alternately tongue-tied and garrulous, and all because this man had taken her in his arms, suddenly, spontaneously, and kissed her. As if she had never been kissed before.

"You're every bit as beautiful with the sun shining on ye, as in the night halls of Devane House," he said at last.

His remark, instead of flattering her, had the same effect as being doused with the icy waters of the Atlantic. She felt her hackles raised and said angrily, "Then *ye* admit ye was in Devane House the other night. Why the pretense back in Robin's office?"

"I saw the look in the woman's eye. We have work to do, you and I. The less she knows, the better. It does not concern her."

"We?" She squinted. "Wait a minute, you're not still claiming to be Alexander Devane?"

"You seemed sure enough of yourself when you called me at Marauders Point."

She clenched her fists, feeling her fingernails dig into her flesh. She felt a long, slow flush creep along her skin.

"Who are you, really?" she said, in a low, careful voice.

"You know quite well," he said evenly.

"An impostor, is what I think."

"Now, Bree, you no more believe that than I do."

"Prove it, then."

"I thought I already had."

"You kissed me," she said, in a low, even voice. "That only proves you've got a lot of nerve."

"And you have a good right hook for so frail a woman." He put his hand to his cheek and gave her a sudden, lopsided grin. "Although I doubt I will again put it to the test."

"Hey, you two!" Robin stood at the car, waving them over.

"I'm afraid this is neither the time nor the place for any further discussion of the matter," Alec said.

"That's right." Bree started toward Robin at a near run. "There is no time or place," she threw back at him. She reached Robin without looking back.

"This is Hank Jonas of CNT-TV," Robin said, waving at the young man. "He's going to interview me, and Zack if he ever shows up. Park over there," she told Jonas, and in the next breath beckoned Bree to follow her. "Might as well get the marine biologist point of view," she added, heading down the wharf to the *Doubloon.* "And Devon, too. He's supposed to be a top-notch diver." She looked back and frowned. "Where the devil is he?"

Bree looked around. *Devil* was right. Alec was bent over the car door, talking to the television reporter. Making points, she had no doubt.

"Give him a minute, he'll have Jonas eating out of his hand," Robin muttered. She led the way to the *Doubloon,* still muttering, with Bree following.

Chapter Six

"Coming?" Robin was looking back at her curiously from the deck of the *Doubloon*.

"Sorry." Bree hurried up the ramp. She forced herself to admit that nothing mattered but the opportunity given her to join the salvaging operation. She must concentrate on the voyage ahead. The Alexander Devane of her fevered, foolish dreams didn't exist. The sign she had asked for was not in the flesh and blood person of Alec Devon. Alec Devon, by coincidence, resembled him, but she mustn't let her imagination run wild. Ghosts did not exist. Alec Devon apparently did.

"Suppose I show you your cabin," Robin said when Bree, with another apology for her slowness, joined her on the deck.

On the way to Bree's lab, Robin pointed out the chart room, command post and mess. The ship had its own decompression chamber, which, Robin said sternly, they hoped never to use.

Two decks below, she opened the door on a small, empty cabin that would house Bree's lab. A door led from the lab to a cabin that held a bunk, a small desk and dresser.

"Great," Bree said, and meant it. She hadn't expected to have a cabin to herself, and she knew others in the crew would undoubtedly be bunking together. "A cabin of my own. I've been on dive boats before, and usually shared bunk space."

"All yours," Robin said. "Not everybody's so lucky, but we figure the closer you are to your specimens, the happier you'll be."

"Oh, I'm happy, all right."

"Desk and chair courtesy of *Doubloon*," Robin said. "And I can get my carpenter to put up shelves, tables, whatever. Nothing fancy, there's little enough room, but I figure you know what you need, I don't. Everything satisfactory?"

The only trouble Bree could foresee was in delivery of her refrigeration unit. Tanks, dissecting tools, sampling bottles and audio equipment were readily available in Portland. Microwave equipment was manufactured near Boston, and if need be, she'd ride down and pick it up herself. "Can we string some water pipes in?" she asked.

"Already in." Robin opened the door leading to a small closet. "In here, sink, toilet, washstand, shower down the passageway. We think of everything."

She led the way out before Bree had a chance to take measurements. Back up on deck, they found the reporter and his crew waiting. Bree breathed a sigh of relief when she realized Alec was nowhere in sight.

"Stick around," Robin said. "After I'm finished with him, you can come back to my office, and I'll put you on the line to my carpenter."

"Maybe I'll go back to the lab. I'll need measurements of my quarters," Bree said.

"Okay," Robin said. "I'm about to give the grand tour to CNT. We'll stop by to see you."

When Bree got to her lab, she found Alec waiting for her, leaning against the door, his muscular arms akimbo.

"Welcome aboard the *Doubloon*," he said.

"Robin has already performed that duty, thank you. And now, if you don't mind, I have work to do." She glanced nervously down the passageway, like a teenager caught in the locker room with the school jock. "You make yourself at home anywhere, don't you?" she said. "How did you know where to find me?"

"I followed your scent. Attar of roses. I am familiar enough with it. We brought the valuable commodity back with us from our journey east."

"Aboard the *Alexis Moon*, no doubt."

"I captained no other." —

She looked sharply at him. How differently she would talk to him if she could believe it to be true. Instead, with no attempt to hide the scorn in her voice, she said, "I can't waste time talking nonsense." She opened the door to the lab. "If you'll excuse me."

He followed her in and closed the door behind him. She whirled around and found him smiling at her, the look in his eyes one of pure desire. Just who did he think he was? Besides Alexander Devane, that is.

"If you don't mind..." She stormed past him and yanked the door open.

"But I do mind. I said we needed someplace private to talk. This will do well."

"It will not do well at all. Don't shut that door, if you value your life."

"Oh, I value my life prodigiously, thank ye. And I have already had a taste of your right hook."

"Good." She could not help smiling. "And I'm not certain just what life you're referring to, Mr. Devon, if that's your real name."

"You know my real name. You called me, and I came to you."

"Alec Devon? I never called you."

"Captain Alexander Devane."

"I don't like being made a fool of."

"Make a fool of you? Now what would possess me to do that?"

They stood no more than a foot apart. Bree felt that if she could just concentrate on the deep cleft in his chin, she might sail safely past wanting to be taken into his arms. Where in the archives, in Franklin's diary, had Alexander been described physically? Nowhere, she thought. Franklin had been obsessed with his brother's life, but had felt no need of describing him.

"I'm a scientist," she said. "I don't believe that a man who went to the bottom of the sea one hundred fifty years ago has come back to life in this century."

"But I have, Bree, and I am here."

In an instant, before she had a chance to pull away, his mouth was on hers, warm and insistent. "This is my proof. Now tell me you deny that I am Alexander Devane."

She was aware of her blood thundering through her veins, heated to the boiling point. If a memory of a kiss in a dream could be made real, she had her proof. But it can't be, she told herself. The man was mad, a complete stranger passing himself off as Alexander Devane, dead this past century and a half. Did he think she was born yesterday? As his mouth sought hers once again, she gathered enough strength to push him away.

"I think you ought to go," she said quietly. Her hands shook as she pulled the measuring tape from her bag.

"You're trembling," he said.

"What did you expect?"

"That you would believe me."

"Please go." They stood for a long moment, gazing at each other. She thought, with an almost imperceptible intake of breath, that he was trying to hypnotize her into compliance, so clear, green and fathomless were his eyes.

"You were at Marauders Point," she said. "You heard me make a fool of myself. I have no excuse for acting like a madwoman, but I'm not mad, and if you think you can play games with me, you're taking on the wrong person."

Only the sound of voices from down the passageway broke the uncanny spell. Robin came bustling into the tiny cabin, with the reporter, cameraman and sound technician in tow. With them were Zack Martineaux and a tall, thin man wearing a camera around his neck.

Robin, who apparently never stood on ceremony, waved her hand around, making introductions. She explained that Bree was a marine biologist affiliated with the Devane Institute. The gentleman with the camera around his neck turned out to be Taylor Kinsolving, one of the crew, also a photographer. Zack squeezed into the cabin, pushed his way over to Bree, took her hand in his and planted a kiss on her cheek. "Do my eyes deceive me? Am I to be blessed with your presence aboard the *Doubloon,* O beautiful one?"

Zack had changed since the last time she'd seen him. He had grown a beard, for one thing, and his unruly brown hair was worn a little long. She thought he had put some weight on, or perhaps, with his stocky, muscular build, he had just been lifting weights. His dark, restless eyes constantly seemed to be searching for something he knew he'd never find. Zack had always frightened Bree, and now, in the crowded cabin, he seemed more menacing than ever.

She had always thought him a man who operated without boundaries, without the customary stops that guided the actions of normal people. Some women at school had found him exciting, but Bree had suspected a cruel streak in him that was barely kept in check. He also did not know how to take no for an answer.

"How are you, Bree?" he said, brushing his fingers lightly through her hair. "Never in my wildest dreams did I think I'd see you on board the *Doubloon*."

"All you had to do was ask," she said. She glanced at Alec, puzzled to find him staring at Zack as though he had seen a ghost.

Zack's eyes slid to Alec. "You're right, I should have."

"Okay, everybody, tour's about over." Robin clearly wanted to control the interview. She said a few vague words about the lab and then abruptly headed back down the passageway, calling out to everyone to follow her.

"Marine biologist," the reporter said to Bree as they filed out. "I thought this was a salvaging operation."

"It is. I'm a diver with an interest in the marine life around deep-sea wrecks."

"Interesting," he said, beckoning to his technician to bring the mike in closer. "Do you expect to find anything unusual around this one?"

They had reached the stairs leading up to the deck. "I hope so," Bree said preceding him up.

"Like what, for instance?"

"My specialty is anemones. Maybe a new form."

The reporter chuckled. "If you do, name it after me."

Bree knew that Alec was directly behind her. "If I did, I'd name it after the owner of the *Alexis Moon,* Alexander Devane."

Zack, who was ahead of her by several feet, stopped and turned back. "Bree, if you want to name it after the owner of the *Alexis Moon,* the correct name would be Zack Martineaux."

She heard Alec growl. He pushed past her in the narrow passageway and grabbed Zack's arm. "Zack Martineaux." He stood for a moment with his eyes boring into Zack's. Then, just when Zack was about to speak, Alec said, "Your ancestor was first mate aboard the *Alexis Moon.* He was paid well for his services, and his share of the trade was fair by any man's currency."

Zack blinked. His face had grown a deep red. "Who the hell do you think you are?"

"A historian with an interest in the truth." He dropped Zack's arm, brushed past him and took the steps up to the deck two at a time.

"Historian?" Zack said, his mouth open. "Is he crazy? Where'd he come from?"

Robin laughed. "I hired him, and if that's what the man said he is, that's what he is."

They were on deck by now. Bree saw Alec climb up to the bridge. For a man who had just been hired, he certainly seemed to take the *Doubloon* for granted. She was about to go after him, to tell him to stop needling Zack, when the reporter stopped her. "The Devane Institute," he said, "they have a vested interest in this salvage operation, haven't they?"

"I really think you ought to talk to our president, James Harrison Selden."

"Right. Good idea, give the story even more depth. Well, that's about it," the reporter said. "This is good footage. Maybe we can get a hitch out to the wreck, get some pictures underwater for follow-up," he said, turning to Robin.

"No." Robin's tone was inordinately abrupt, and she seemed to regret it at once, for she softened her next words. "You come out anytime and watch the dive on our monitors, but frankly, diving a wreck a hundred feet down takes experience. The bends. Sharks. Any number of things, just waiting to get the novice. You know, we can't be responsible."

"Right. Gotcha," the reporter said amiably, as though he'd suddenly realized he could hire a seasoned diver, but that they cost money. He next turned to Zack. "You expect to find the gold tablet, Mr. Martineaux?"

Zack, glancing quickly at Bree, said, "It's there, and I'm going to find it."

"Too bad we can't pick out a time on it," the reporter said. "Maybe we could stage finding it."

"Come on," Robin said. "When we find the tablet, you'll hear the noise clear to California. I thought you said the program was going to be on tomorrow night."

"I'd like to make a continuing story of it, Robin."

Robin bent her head in acknowledgment. "Suits me fine."

Bree remembered the playing cards her mother had told her about. If the reporter wanted color for his story, she could certainly supply it. The mike was still on when she said, "I own a couple of playing cards that were aboard the *Alexis Moon* when it went down."

The reporter was light on his feet. He caught her innuendo at once. "The legend of the *Alexis Moon*. Are you telling me those cards might have been used in that infamous game? Wait a minute, wait a minute," he added, signaling to his technician to come in closer. "You're saying that a pack of playing cards that went down with the *Alexis Moon* are in your possession?"

She saw Alec step out of the bridge, a frown on his face. "It's not a pack, it's an ace and a deuce, and they were in the pocket of my ancestor, Breeford Kealy, when he died, complete with little pinpricks, the kind made to fix a game. They're heirlooms."

Alec came storming over to her and grabbed her arm. "The lady does not know what she's talking about," he said. He stared murderously at the cameraman.

"Hold it, Devon." Zack stationed himself between Alec and the TV crew. "I don't know who you are or what you're doing on board the *Doubloon,* but if I were you, I'd take my hand off the lady's arm."

"Wait a minute," Bree said. "I can take care of myself."

"I can see what a noble job you do of it." Alec began to steer her away. "I believe the lady has an appointment," he said.

Robin, who had been watching the proceedings as though dumbstruck, called out, "Hey, Devon, where do you think you're going?"

He didn't bother answering. When they were out of earshot, he stopped and gripped both her arms, as though he wanted to shake some sense into her. "Dammit, woman, what do you think you're doing?"

Her hand balled into a fist. "What am *I* doing? What are *you* doing?"

"Where's your confounded automobile?" he asked.

"None of your business." She pulled her arm away and went storming down the ramp. He caught up with her.

"Where are they, Bree?"

"What are you talking about?"

"Dammit, woman, I want them."

"The cards, I presume. Not where you'd ever find them."

"I'm sticking to you like rabbitskin glue until you produce them."

"They're mine. They're my inheritance."

"Those cards belonged to Alexander Devane. They did not belong to Breeford Kealy. I saw him return them to his pocket shortly before the ship went down."

"Oh, my God." She stopped and looked at him. "You saw him tucking them into his pocket? Now I've heard everything." She began walking down the wharf toward her car. "How can anyone who looks so smart be so *weird?*"

"Bree," he said, coming after her. "Don't try to be logical. Depend upon your heart, and trust me."

"I don't know what books you've been reading," she said, "but none I ever read said anything about the playing cards. They were found in my ancestor's pockets and belonged to him."

"The playing cards belonged to Alexander Devane. They were printed to order in England and contained a painting of the *Alexis Moon* on the back."

"I see. Then it was Alexander Devane who put the pinpricks in them. Well," she said, "we'll see."

He swiveled her around to face him, a light of nascent fury starting in his eyes. "You don't have them in your possession, do you? Where are they?"

She released a deep sigh. "Your hands, Mr. Devon."

He took his hands away at once, as though scorched. "I don't believe the cards exist," he said. "And, but for the look of curiosity on your face, I would believe you have something on your mind about this salvaging operation that bodes no good."

With that he turned and walked away, back toward the *Doubloon.*

Bree looked after him. Playing cards. No one could prove they were used aboard the *Alexis Moon* during that last game, *if* there was a last game.

"Bully," she said out loud. She hoped Robin would fire him.

Chapter Seven

The following day, Bree was loading supplies from her lab onto the *Doubloon* with the help of a couple of graduate students. She would have no difficulty with the delivery of the additional supplies she had ordered, with the exception of the microwave. She'd have to go down to Boston to pick it up. And there were a couple of reference books she wanted to buy, as well. The trip to Boston would fit in with her plans to visit her mother. And while she was there, she'd pick up the cards, the ones with the *Alexis Moon* on the back—if Alec had known what he was talking about. She carried in her underwater camcorder and carefully placed it beneath her bunk.

She paid off the graduate students, thanked them, and set to work stowing what she could. Robin had mentioned that the crew, both salvors and staff, numbered twenty. Bree was curious about them. A couple were local divers, members of the Marauders Point Diving Club, but others came from California and Florida. Then there was Alec Devon. She wondered how she would handle seeing him everyday for the next two months. She had to admit to herself that he clouded her thoughts, made her dizzy. When she was near him, she thought of nothing but the touch of his lips, the feel of his arms around her. The bully.

She was about to lock up when Zack knocked at the open door. He stepped uninvited into the cabin and looked greedily around. "Hey, you really mean to settle down to work."

Bree wanted to say something about his not coming into the lab unless invited, but decided to be diplomatic, at least for the time being. "You didn't think I was coming along for the ride, did you?"

"I thought you wanted to be with me."

"Oh, right, Zack. It slipped my mind."

"I just came in to warn you," he said, grinning as though he were about to confide a joke.

Bree frowned. He was about to bring up the subject of the gold tablet. "Warn me? About what?"

"Look," he said, affecting an air of earnestness, "we're going to be working together. Let's see if we can't operate on trust. Trust is the *numero uno* thing on dives, and you know it as well as I."

Trust. Alec wanted trust, and so did Zack. "Is that all?"

"I want you to tell me you feel safe diving with me. I have to know who's with me and who's against me on this trip."

She was astonished at his remark, and let him know it. "For and against? What the devil does that mean? Who's the enemy, exactly?"

His face darkened. "You know why you're on the salvaging team, and so do I. The college wants you to keep track of what I'm doing. They think I'm up to something funny."

"Look, Robin invited me . . ." she began.

"Right. And Robin was approached by somebody on the school's board of directors."

Bree flinched. Why had Robin discussed her with Zack? Well, that did it. She apparently couldn't quite trust Robin, either. "Zack, you're paranoid. I'm here as a marine biologist with an interest in seeing that the ecology of the wreck is left undisturbed where possible. You know my feelings on the subject. Who's your enemy? The whole board of Devane, or can you be more specific?"

"It's down there," he said, coming closer and breathing in her face. "Gold bullion, and a thin tablet of gold with Alexander Devane's handwriting on it, ceding his entire estate to my ancestor. Devane Institute is hoping I'll never find the tablet, Bree. Don't act so innocent with me."

She reared back. "I'm not crazy about your tone, Zack, but I'll let that pass. I do know this much. I doubt the Devane Institute wants its name changed to Martineaux, if that's what you mean."

"The place is going to go under," he said. "If it were up to me, I'd deep-six it."

"Strange thing to say, Zack. Devane gave you a good education."

"I could have gone to Harvard."

"But you wouldn't look a free education gift horse in the mouth, would you, Zack? As for trying to find the tablet, all I can say is, good luck."

He seemed not to have heard her, so intent was he on pursuing his hurts. "If you're not it, then there's somebody else on board this ship who's going to see that I don't finish the operation alive."

His remark surprised her. "Zack, don't be melodramatic," she said. "Diving is dangerous enough, without any additional fears."

"You haven't answered my question. Are you with me or against me?"

She went over to the door and stepped outside. She waited until he was forced to join her, then locked the door and pocketed the key. "I wish you luck, Zack. It's been your dream, finding the gold and the tablet. That's about all I can do, wish you luck. Someday soon, tell me exactly what your plans are if the tablet does show up. Meanwhile, the only side I'm on is my own." She began to walk briskly down the passageway. Zack came up to her and drew an arm around her shoulder.

"That's my girl. Neutral if she has to be."

She turned swiftly, knocking his arm off. "I'm not your *girl*, not by a long shot."

He laughed, hurrying down the passageway, still chuckling.

She peered into the control room on her way out. Robin was there, talking on the ship-to-shore phone. She saw Bree, smiled and beckoned her in, putting her hand over the mouthpiece. "It's being shown every three hours on the quarter hour."

Bree drew her brows together. She had no idea what Robin was talking about.

"CNT-TV. The interview. They're showing it every three hours on the quarter hour, which means you could try to catch it at 4:15 this afternoon. There's time. Don't forget."

"Great."

"Everything okay?" Robin asked.

Bree looked at her and wondered about her connection to Zack. Why tell him that the real reason she was on board was to spy for Devane? When Bree spoke, her tone was cool. Robin was another person she'd have to steer clear of. "Everything's okay," she said. "Just brought in some supplies."

Robin nodded and returned to her call. Bree checked her watch. If she hurried, she'd be home in time to catch the program on CNT-TV. She was still wondering what in the world she had said to the reporter that could have ticked Alec off like that.

"Peace?"

Alec. Bree turned, color warming her cheeks. She had been dreading this moment, dreading what her reaction to him would be. She had a foretaste of what the next two months would be like, finding him around every corner. She knew she should hold her temper, but the last time they were together, they'd engaged in a test of wills. Now he wanted peace. On his terms, no doubt.

"Do you have to sneak up like that?" she said. "And the only 'peace' I want from you is the kind I feel when you're not around. So keep out of my face."

"Keep out of your face? By the devil's tail, woman, speak English."

His knowing smile unnerved her. She headed straight for the stairs leading to the top deck, knowing he would follow. On deck she saw a couple of people she didn't recognize, but she waved at them anyway. They waved back. Alec came up to her and took her arm.

"I'll go where you go, Bree, whether it be in your cabin or on board the *Doubloon* with all the world watching, but talk we must. You know that as well as I."

She turned to him abruptly, her heart softening at his words. "The truth, and nothing but?"

He nodded, his eyes holding hers in their green depths. "I can tell you what I know, who I am, and all I ask of you is trust." He took her hand in his and drew it to his lips.

That word *trust*. She should give it a lot more freely than she had before. A rush of emotion overcame her. She knew what he wanted to tell her, and she realized she was all but ready to believe it. "Come on," she said. "Robin said the CNT-TV report is going to be on at 4:15. We can watch on my television set. Let's see what damage I've done."

"Television," he said with a scornful laugh. "That evil piece of colored glass does enough damage on its own."

"That colored glass can be very instructive."

"Life is instructive. You have to live it, not watch it bottled up in glass."

She went down the ramp and pointed to the car parked in front of Krashaw Salvage. "Do you have a car? That's mine over there."

"I don't hold much with automobiles," he said.

"I'm afraid a horse and carriage won't get you very far in these parts. Come on." When she retrieved her car keys from her bag, he took them.

"I may not approve of automobiles, but I don't approve of women driving them, either."

"Oh, I see. You think we're not capable."

"The only trouble I see ahead of us, madam, is just how capable you are. Surely you can't object if I have rigid notions of what is feminine or not."

"Go right ahead and drive," Bree said, laughing. If Alec Devon was putting on an act, he was doing a mighty fine job of it. She went around to the passenger's side. "Exactly what kind of license have you got?"

He didn't miss a beat. "International."

"My, that is convenient. Try not to drive like a cowboy."

"I cannot say how a cowboy drives, Bree, but you're precious cargo."

Ten minutes later, Bree was tapping her fingers with impatience. "Who taught you to drive, President Tyler? Just how familiar are you with horseless carriages?"

"I have the fortunate knack of being able to pick up mechanical knowledge quickly. And I am carrying a delicate piece of porcelain," he said. "I have no intention of seeing her broken into bits because I like speed and power."

"But I'm no delicate piece of porcelain. How could I be a deep-sea diver, if I did not like to skirt the edge of danger?"

"I cannot fathom what you're about," he said simply.

"Maybe I can't, either. Turn right at the next light. That's about as far ahead into the future as I want to see at the moment."

Bree had a bright, airy co-op apartment in a small complex in the city's east end, close to the promenade. It was furnished almost completely in pale sand colors, with abstract paintings on the walls. The effect was cheerful. She was glad she had managed to clear it of clutter that morning, in an effort to get ready for the trip.

"This be home," Alec stated, looking around, his expression once again a near blank, as though he dared not express his true opinion.

"This be home. Have a seat. Wine?"

He shook his head. "We have some serious conversation on our menu, Bree. I want a clear head."

"Coffee." She checked her watch and then switched on her television set. "Ten minutes. I'll start the coffee. If the program comes on, call me."

He sat down on the couch and began to frown at the screen. She smiled and went into her kitchen. She knew she shouldn't, but she felt happy and at peace. His word. The bubble might burst any moment, but for now she just wanted to think about the man who sat on her couch, whose touch could melt her heart.

She was back in ten minutes with a tray holding coffee and a couple of sandwiches. The television set was still on. Alec lay full-length on the couch, fast asleep, with one arm behind his head. She stood quietly at the entrance to her living room, holding the tray in her hand. His lips were parted, but he was breathing quietly, steadily. His long, lean body was still, yet she could not help but think of a panther concentrating intently upon his prey, pretending unconcern. Looking at him this way, she had no doubt this man had ties to the Devane line.

Alexander had never married, although it had been said, particularly by Beatrice Martineaux herself, that he was to marry his first mate's sister when he returned from his journey. But Alexander could have sired a dozen sons the world over. Perhaps Alec Devon was a descendant, with more on his mind than time travel.

The commercial was over, the news program came on, and she recognized Hank Jonas, sitting at a desk, wearing a suit and tie. She went over to the coffee table and put the tray down. Then she bent over Alec and lightly shook him awake.

"What?" He sat up abruptly, his eyes focusing on her at once, a man used to danger, she thought, who always slept with its possibility on his mind. His expression softened at once, and he was about to reach for her when she put her hand to her lips and pointed to the screen. She retreated to a chair safely distanced.

"The legend of the *Alexis Moon*. Is it just that, a legend, or is there some truth to it?" Hank Jonas was saying. "Successive generations of one family have dreamed of salvaging the wreck of the *Alexis Moon,* which sank off the coast of Maine one hundred fifty years ago. Now, thanks to modern technology, that dream may come true."

"Ha!" said Alec Devon to the screen. "Go right ahead, perpetuate the lies."

"The question is, who was the owner of the *Alexis Moon* when it went down, Alexander Devane and his brother, Franklin, or Zachary Martineaux, who was first mate of the vessel?"

A picture of the *Doubloon* appeared on the screen. Over Hank Jonas's words, Alec said, shaking his head, "So this is what the invention of television is for, to encourage the spreading of lies."

"Let the man talk," Bree said, her eyes on the screen. Robin was giving a quick tour of the reconditioned Coast Guard cutter, and then, suddenly, there they all were in her lab. She saw herself as though she were looking at a stranger. Good Lord, had she put on that much weight?

Alec, however, turned from the screen to gaze appreciatively at her. "You're a lot more buxom than I took you for," he said with a grin.

"Never mind. They say you always look ten pounds heavier in a photograph."

"That's a curious enough fact."

"Shh," she said, leaning forward. They were now on the deck, and there she was, suddenly talking about the playing cards. "I own a couple of playing cards that were aboard the *Alexis Moon* when it went down."

It suddenly hit her why Alec was so angry. "Oh..." Bree groaned. "How could I have been so stupid?"

Jonas had jumped in at once. "Are you telling me those cards might have been used in that infamous game?"

She remembered Alec coming off the bridge, a frown on his face. But instead of drawing back, she had gone breathlessly on. "It's not a pack, it's an ace and a deuce, and they were in the pocket of my ancestor, Breeford Kealy, when he died, complete with little pinpricks, the kind made to fix a game. They're heirlooms."

The screen switched to Jonas in the studio. Alec was on his feet, standing over her. "Where are the cards?" he said, making no attempt to hide his fury.

"Not here." She was suddenly frightened, not of what she had revealed, but of the look of rage simmering in his eyes. She got to her feet, checking the distance through her foyer to the door. Just what had she let herself into, bringing him to her home?

He gripped her arms. "My dear woman, have you no idea of the danger you put yourself in with your boasting?"

"Boasting? I own an important bit of history, and I see no reason to keep it a secret. You call that boasting?"

"Does it not occur to you that they are the cards used in the game between Zachary Martineaux and—" He stopped cold when Bree pulled away from him, a look of shock upon her face. He was about to disclose something she did not want to hear, because she could not believe it.

"How—how do you know a game was played on board the *Alexis Moon?*"

"How do you imagine I know?" He stood there, fists clenched at his sides while she retreated to the farthest corner of the room.

She was a long time answering. The notion still made no sense, in that thoroughly modern room, with its abstract prints upon the wall, and sunlight streaming through to expose every shiny, innocent nook and cranny. "You can be making it all up," she said in a weakened tone.

"You don't believe I could come down in time for you," he said. "And you believe me afflicted with a touch of madness."

"Yes." The word came out in a whisper.

He stood his ground, unmoving, fists still clenched at his sides. "Are you frightened of me, Bree Kealy?"

"Yes, I think I am."

"Have you no faith in me?"

Bree stirred uncomfortably, but if he wanted the truth, she would have to tell him what she felt. "I'm sorry, Alec, but you came into my life at Devane House, and..." She stopped, thinking of how she had savored the kiss of the stranger who appeared in the night and seemed the embodiment of her dreams.

"There it was," he said quietly, "the *Alexis Moon* upon the seafloor, in a watery dream, my clipper ship in full rig. And you and I, hands entwined, floating toward it."

Bree gasped. It couldn't be. He was telling her dream. She stared at him, feeling the chill of fear deep into her bones.

"You believe it every bit as much as I," he said.

She spoke as though the words formed of their own accord. "Danger... I could not put a name to it, but it was there, shadows all around us. You were searching for something, but I could not help you. Then, suddenly, someone approached, a knife in his hand. You fought him off, but he came at you again."

She went to him and put her hands on his arm. "Your left arm, just above the elbow, a deep slash." She shuddered, remembering how his blood had stained the water. He did not move while she raised his shirtsleeve. She touched the thin, curved scar. She felt tears fill her eyes. "You told me you needed me. I thought it was a dream."

He put his lips to hers and held her in a long, hungry kiss. "It was no dream, Bree."

"They said your ghost walked Marauders Point. I went there and called you. Did you hear me?"

He shook his head slowly, a smile creeping into his eyes. "I heard you call, Bree, and as you see, I have answered."

She smiled through her tears. "Maybe we can believe in only one phenomenon at a time." She reached up and traced her fingers along his cheek, feeling his warm flesh. "No, you're not a ghost. You're very real. The trouble is," she went on, almost reluctant to say her next words, "Alexander Devane's bones lie one hundred feet below the surface of the sea, in the wreck of the *Alexis Moon*. We have the word of the only survivor that everyone else perished with the ship."

Alec drew away from her. She could see a glint in his eyes that was both disappointment and anger repressed. "He was wrong, my dear Bree. I did not die."

"You did not die. You have been here all along."

"Bree, do you know the man I was?"

"I thought I did."

"I was a fool, a spendthrift, reckless with my birthright. Worse, through my intemperate ways, forty men died before their time. I caused their deaths, for I had given up control of my vessel through drunkenness and rage."

She felt her heart turn over. "The game was played, and the gold tablet signed."

But he went on as though he had not heard her. "I did not die, but well I might have, for I have been given no peace, no happiness, a man cursed, without a country, without friends or love, or a place to rest."

He grasped her hands, as though touching her, holding her, gave him an anchor in reality. "I have wandered, a sleepwalker, through time, unaware of the passage of days, of years, the man I have always been, searching for atonement. I am the same man who cried out to the gods to forgive me, except I know this. To retrieve my soul, to make redress for the unhappiness I caused to so many through my wanton ways, I am here, now."

"The gold tablet," she said gently. "You want to find the gold tablet with your signature upon it."

"Yes, I do not deny that."

"And to destroy it forever. Is that for your sake, or for the Devane Institute?"

"What do you think?"

She realized that Alec's goals and J.H.'s were the same: to save the Devane Institute by destroying the gold tablet.

"I studied at the Devane Institute," she said. "It was endowed by Franklin Devane to give the children of Portland a chance at a higher education, tuition-free. If the gold tablet is found with Alexander Devane's signature on it—"

"Mine," he said.

"The school, and everything Franklin stood for, may be in jeopardy."

With every syllable she spoke, strong, ineluctable emotions passed across his face. "If I do not succeed in this, then I have failed in my every purpose for traveling through time."

His words cut through to her soul. "I can't lose you," she said, the words tumbling out before she could stop them.

He gathered her in his arms. "Then help me, Bree. Help me."

She reached up and touched his brow, a shiver of sexual response drawing through her as she feathered her fingers along his check. "You know I will."

He kissed her eyes, her nose, her mouth. "Be my eyes and my ears aboard the *Doubloon*."

"Even if it means being dishonest?"

"Too much is at stake, Bree, to engage in discussions of that kind."

"I have only your word for it that you're Alexander Devane," she said, wavering once again, as though what he asked of her proved she could not even trust the truth about him.

"I'll have your proof, Bree. The cards, an ace and a deuce, have a painting of a clipper ship on the back, a clipper ship as close to the *Alexis Moon* as the artist could make it. My initials, *AD,* are in each corner of each card. On each card, there is a pinprick in the upper right-hand corner."

While he spoke, she felt a long shiver run down her spine. She could call up her mother and ask her to describe the cards, but if they did not match, she thought, she could not bear the disappointment.

"I have never seen the cards," she admitted at last. She caught the look of undisguised anger in his eyes. He might always give more than his share, she realized, but he wanted no one to block his plans, either. "I never saw them," she said. "My mother has them."

"Damn." He released her and, in one swift movement, balled his fist and slammed it into the wall. Her favorite print, framed delicately and expensively between two layers of glass, shook and slid sideways on its hook.

"Wait a minute! What do you think you're doing?" She dashed over to the print to set it straight.

"Where's your mother? Isn't she home?"

"She's a gadabout. I don't keep track of what she's doing, any more than she keeps track of me. Where did you learn your manners, anyway?"

"A gadabout? I should think your mother would concern herself with what her unmarried daughter is doing at all times of the day. If the cards are here, why do you not have access to them?"

"My mother has them, in a safe, in Boston, and I have never laid eyes on them."

"In Boston?" He frowned. "What are they doing in Boston?"

Bree was beginning to lose patience with him. "My mother lives in Boston, Alec—Alexander, whoever you are."

"At this moment, Alec. Why does she not live here?"

"Good heavens, she works in Boston. I work here. We're not in each other's hair. We live independent lives. Now, will you calm down? I'll get the cards, I promise." Then she remembered something. The Portland Historical Society had a couple of rooms devoted to the contents of Devane House. If they had a pack of cards that had belonged to Alexander Devane, she wanted to see them for herself, now.

"Come on," she said. "If you ordered more than one pack of cards with a clipper ship on back, we may be able to see it at the historical society."

MRS. DOOLITTLE, who volunteered at the Portland Historical Society, on Congress, looked from Alec to Bree and back again. "Now why would anyone care about a pack of cards that belonged to the Devane estate? I've been a volunteer here more years than I care to mention, and never heard that question before, about a pack of cards that's been gathering dust for a century. Now it's twice in one afternoon."

Mrs. Doolittle was narrow of build, with a stern, impatient expression, although Bree knew from experience that it was all surface. In fact, there was nothing Mrs. Doolittle, who had been her history professor at Devane, loved more than passing the time of day, and she could be broken down with a smile.

The question didn't faze Bree one bit. She smiled. "We were on CNT-TV today. I happened to mention that my mother has a couple of cards that were in the possession of my ancestor when he was rescued from the wreck of the *Alexis Moon*." She looked at Alec, to find him frowning. He obviously still hadn't come to terms with the information age. Or with the fact that the future was now, and everyone was going to be famous for fifteen minutes.

"Where are the cards?" Bree asked. "Can we see them?"

"Not on display, Bree, but I'd suggest you come back tomorrow. We're closing now," Mrs. Doolittle added, with a stern look at her watch.

Bree was all set to leave when Alec spoke up. "Five minutes, my dear Mrs. Doolittle. That's all we ask of your worthy time."

Mrs. Doolittle turned a smile on him. "Well, if it's only five minutes. Come along." She grabbed a set of keys and led the way through the warren of rooms that contained the history of Portland in books and memorabilia.

While the Devane Institute had its own archives, many bits of Devane memorabilia had ended up in the possession of the historical society. They were on display at the rear of the old Victorian house, in what had once been an open veranda. Bree had often browsed amid the bookshelves and glass cases.

"The cards are in storage," Mrs. Doolittle said, producing a key and unlocking a door. "There's a limited amount of space," she said, "unfortunately."

Bree had stopped to look at the contents of a small vitrine that she had examined before and been curious about. She pointed to a charming heart-shaped box. She had always wanted to see what was inside. "That's so pretty," she said, beckoning to Alec. "What do you suppose it looks like inside?" A small label ascribed the locket it contained to the mother of Alexander Devane. She saw him start, then pale.

Mrs. Doolittle had opened the door and was waiting for them. "Five minutes," she said. "Bree, you should know better, you've been here often enough."

"I was just curious about the locket," she said, still looking at Alec and the fixed expression he wore.

Mrs. Doolittle came impatiently over, opened the cabinet and picked up the box. Its velvet casing was long faded. She handed it to Bree. "Really, Bree, you could have asked me any other time."

Bree heard Alec take in a sharp breath. He put his hand over hers before she could open it. "A heart-shaped gold locket, engraved with the initials *A.M.D.* Alexis Moon Devane, mother to Franklin and Alexander."

She opened the box and found the locket. She picked it up with shaking hands. The small gold piece opened easily. Inside Bree found a lock of very fine black hair.

"Alexander's."

"Franklin had pale yellow hair," Alec said quietly.

"It's a lock from when Alexander was a baby," Mrs. Doolittle said.

Bree touched the small, delicate curl, then closed the locket, laid it carefully in its case and handed it back. Bree reached out and took his hand, then, to distract him, pointed to a small metal object identified as a seal.

"And that?"

"The Devane seal," he told her.

"Have we come here to see the cards?" Mrs. Doolittle said impatiently.

"Oh, yes, please," Bree said, although she couldn't help adding, "In the vast scheme of things, I guess the cards don't add up to very much."

"I wouldn't say that," Mrs. Doolittle pointed out. "They came in recently with other contents of the Franklin estate that your president wanted us to take over."

"Really?" Bree had never heard of J.H. unloading some of the school's hoard of antiques.

"Apparently Mrs. Plattman purchased them, then donated them to the Portland Historical Society." She led them to a small storage closet lined with shelves upon which lay dozens of small antiques and books. "The pack is right over here on the third shelf..." She stopped and looked confusedly around.

"Good heavens. They're gone."

THEY WERE SITTING over dinner at a small, sunny restaurant in the old port that offered hefty hamburgers and home fries with steamed vegetables. Alec, whose appetite was prodigious, not only wolfed down his share, but the remains of Bree's half-eaten portion, as well. The disappearance of a pack of cards, on the surface, might mean no more than vandalism. Someone collected antique playing cards, and the Devane set looked so good. Mrs. Doolittle admitted to not knowing exactly when they had been taken. She had turned her back on her visitor when someone else came into the room, and had not checked to see if they were still there when she locked the door.

"Those cards may not have anything to do with the *Alexis Moon*," Bree said.

Mrs. Doolittle, who had described her earlier visitor as young, burly and nondescript, had said he had neither a black beard nor dark hair, as far as she could tell, because he wore a baseball cap. With or without dark hair, Zack was out of the running.

"I didn't even know the cards existed," Bree said, "and I've always considered myself an expert on life aboard the *Alexis Moon*. Except, of course, that card games figured in these long voyages," she added. "I mean, I knew Alexander Devane was a gambler."

"Say it, Bree." Alec's expression was somber.

She looked at him curiously. "Say what?"

"You're still treating me as separate from Alexander Devane. You refuse to accept who I am. Say it."

She had nothing to say in her own defense. She found him startlingly attractive and sexy and very masculine. He was polite and elegant, well-spoken and just about everything she wanted in a man. That he might also be a dissembler worried her. She wanted proof, and perhaps that proof lay in her mother's safe. It certainly no longer resided at the Portland Historical Society.

"I think I believe you," she said. "I want to believe you with all my heart." She put her hand across the table and touched his. "I'll help you, if that's what you want. I'll help you find your gold tablet before Zack does."

He cupped her hand in his and kissed each finger. "And together we explored the *Alexis Moon,*" he said in a quiet voice. "Doesn't that mean anything to you?"

"Do I believe in the transference of souls? I just don't know, Alec. Help me to know." Her question was heartfelt. She had dreamed of Alexander Devane. This man, this Alec Devon, showed that he shared her dream, or she—his.

"We can't get very close to the truth," she said.

"We can try."

She put her napkin down. "We'll go back to my apartment. We can phone my mother from there. She'll describe the cards to you."

"Fair enough."

Ten minutes later, she handed him the keys to her apartment. "I hope my mother's home," she said.

But when he opened her door, she gasped. There would be no calling her mother that night. Her telephone had been ripped from the wall—the only overt damage done to her apartment. Someone had been there, and had been relatively neat about searching it. But search it he had. And a pack of contemporary playing cards lay scattered on the floor, as though they were a warning to ante up, and soon.

Chapter Eight

Bree ran into her bedroom, opened her closet, pulled out a small overnight case and tossed it on her bed. The trip to Boston would have to be made a little earlier than expected. She'd show up at her mother's at midnight, but it couldn't be helped.

She grabbed some lingerie out of her dresser drawer and then looked up to find Alec leaning against the bedroom door, his eyes upon the flesh-colored bra and panties she held.

She tossed them quickly into her case and for a moment stood defiantly there, wondering if the butterflies she felt in her stomach were reflected in her cheeks. Alec wasn't the first man in her life, so why was she acting like a teenager? Why did she feel like some little nineteenth-century maiden, menaced by the master of the household?

His eyes traveled over her body. Then he gazed past her to the bed. "What do you think you're doing?" he asked.

She cleared her throat, hoping to sound more in control. "Excuse me, I didn't know I had to explain myself to you. But if you must know, I'm going to Boston."

When she saw him scowl, she added hastily, "I was planning on going in a day or two, anyway. This just pushes things up. Do me a favor, Alec, call the police, tell them what happened. And keep after my mother, too. Tell her I'm on the way. Ask her to describe the cards, if you want. Oh, and tomorrow, explain to Robin and J.H. that I'll be back tomorrow night. Just let me finish packing, and I'll give you their numbers.''

He came into the room. "Spare me the telephone numbers, Bree. I'm going with you." He went over to her bedroom door and found her nightgown hanging there. He ran it through his fingers before lifting it slowly to his face, to bury his nose in the silken material. His blatant sensuality took her breath away. Alec smiled at her and tossed it in the overnight case. "What else?" He glanced around the room.

"That does it," she said hotly. "You're *not* going with me." She grabbed a T-shirt and another pair of jeans and a linen jacket.

"Is that your uniform, the same clothes men wear, even for a trip to Boston?"

"What has Boston got to do with the way I dress? This is positively unisex, and everybody dresses this way, from kids to seniors. We're equals, Alec, you and I."

He laughed. "If opposites are equals, then perhaps you have an argument." His eyes took in her body once more, as though he could feel her flesh beneath her clothes.

"Alec, I'm in a hurry. My mother may be in danger, and I don't need you along to tell me how to behave. You're too damn distracting, as a matter of fact." She returned the same slow look he gave her. His tight jeans were molded to his body, and she saw the soft bulge at his crotch. Oh, hell, she thought, if I don't leave soon, I'm going to be in a lot of trouble. She threw in a robe and her slippers. Although her mother had entreated her often enough to leave a suitcase in Boston with her overnight things, Bree had never managed to get one together.

Alec was in her bathroom now, searching among her shampoos and lotions. "I suppose milady is required to use all of these."

"Git," she said, coming into the bathroom. "I keep a special case for these trips."

"Git?"

"You really have been out of it, haven't you?" she said.

"I must have been, since you and I scarcely speak the same language."

"If language speaks for the pleasures of modern living, you're darn right we don't." She grabbed her makeup kit and a sweater and snapped her case shut. "Can I drop you off at your hotel?"

"You won't drop me off. You'll take me there, wait until I check out, and then we'll continue on to Boston."

"We're not continuing on to Boston together. I don't think I can explain you to my mother. I'll take you to your new home, wherever that is."

"I'm going to sleep aboard the *Doubloon* from now on." He took the case from her and led the way to the door. "Unless, of course..." He stopped and smiled back at her.

"No chance whatsoever, Alec." At the door, she had difficulty fitting her key into the lock. "Whoever broke in knew just how to slip a lock," Bree said. "I paid a lot of money for that deadbolt."

Alec took her keys from her, and managed to lock the door. "He won't be back."

"Meaning he's figured out if I don't have them, someone else in the family does, and that someone else is my mother."

At her car, which was parked at the curb, Alec went around to the passenger's side and opened the door. "Get in," he said.

"No way, Alec. I'm driving."

He held up the keys. "Get in, Bree. I have no taste for argument. Boston is a hundred miles distant."

"Will you stop treating me like a child?" she said. "I've driven that distance dozens of times. You don't even have a license the state police would accept, do you?" She made a grab for the keys, but she was no match for him. For a moment, she stood there, feeling her breath coming in short spurts. He merely wanted to protect her, she knew that, yet there was nothing gallant in the way his eyes swept over her, as though he wanted to touch her, to possess her soul.

"I am not going to let you wander about Boston alone," he said. "Ye know that. Fortune wants us together, Bree."

"Nevertheless, I'll drive. We're arguing about feminine verses masculine, while my mother, who lives alone, may be in danger."

He dropped the keys into her hands. "Madam."

It was nearing ten when they arrived at his hotel. Bree took the time to call Boston while she waited for him to check out. Her mother was not home. Bree left a message on the answering machine, telling her to open the door to no one and that she'd be arriving near midnight. Her mother had a guest room, and Bree wondered if she should suggest that Alec stay the night on the living room sofa. Her mother would like Alec, even though Bree had no intention of telling her the truth about him. Perhaps it would be better not to show up with Alec at all.

But then again, she did not want him wandering around Boston alone. She did not even try to work out the logistics of forbidding a man who had wandered the centuries to do what he possibly knew best. As they settled in the car, Bree had to admit to herself that she was glad he was with her.

Her car, which was a two-door sports model, was not built for hunks, she thought, but then, Alec could always stay home. She put the key in the ignition and turned it. "Well, let's make tracks."

"I beg your pardon."

"We're on our way." She thought that if she weren't so apprehensive about her mother, she would think of the trip as a great adventure. She glanced at him through lowered lashes, and felt a long-repressed charge go through her. She had to get a grip on herself, or he would take over every moment of her life.

"Remember," she said. "No back seat driving."

"I have no intention of sitting in the back and driving," he said, looking behind him, as though expecting to find a wheel there.

"It's just an expression, Alec. Buckle up." She put the car in reverse and roared backward, catching Alec off guard. He grabbed his seat and glared at her.

"Hell's bells, Bree, are you trying to kill me?"

"I'm going to burn rubber on this trip down, Alec, I'm warning you."

"Burn rubber?"

"Don't ask for a translation." They were on a secondary road with only two traffic lanes, but because of the late hour, traffic was light. She knew enough of the road to avoid its bumps and cracks, but Alec nevertheless felt required to direct her every minute of the way.

"Come along, woman, change into the passing lane, but slowly. Are ye sure you're comfortable for the long trip? It seems to me you sit a little low. Can you see ahead properly? Just a minute, don't cut him off. Watch up ahead, there's a hill. No way of knowing what's coming up."

"Alec, I know what I'm doing," Bree said. "Are you going to keep talking all the way into Boston?"

"Aye, if I have to."

The connection to the main road leading to Boston was a mile ahead. She began looking forward to three-lane highways where she could pick up speed.

"I hate to think of what you'll be like on deep dives, Alec." She swerved to avoid a bump in the road, and almost hit an oncoming car.

"Blood and guts!" Alec roared as he reached for the wheel. The car caromed onto the embankment and skidded to a halt.

"Don't ever do that again," Bree said, hearing the hysteria in her own voice. "You could have killed us."

"You forget, Bree. I am here for a reason. I have work to do."

"Oh, I see, the gods have given you a stay of execution. But what about me? They couldn't care less what happens to me."

He put his hand on hers. "Then perhaps you had better let me drive. You're safe as long as I am."

"Why doesn't that make me feel any better?" She put the car in drive and pulled out, still looking at Alec. From behind she heard a sudden screech of wheels, and felt the jolt of a collision.

"You stupid idiot!" The roar came from the car behind. "You blind or something? Don't you watch where you're going?"

"I'm sorry," Bree called back. She reached for her driver's license. One more incident to hold them up.

Alec, however, wasn't having any of it. "By the devil's beard," he said, hauling out of the car and making a dash for the car behind.

"Alec, don't!" Bree yelled, but he was already in the process of yanking the driver out of his car.

"Don't you know how to speak to a lady?"

"Hey, hey, take it easy, Mac." The driver tried to pull out of the grip Alec had on his collar. "She was in the wrong."

"That doesn't give you the right to use insulting language. I'll have an apology from you."

"Are you crazy? That stupid cow—"

Alec had him by the throat, his eyes blazing. "Crazy, is it? Man, crazy is the least of what will happen to you if you don't apologize."

Bree raced over to him. "Alec, let him go. He's right. I didn't look where I was going."

"That's a thin excuse for bad manners." He shook the man, a cat testing its prey.

Bree tried to loosen his grip. "Alec, let go. It's against the law to threaten people this way."

"Hey, lady, is this guy nuts? Get him off my back."

"Just one word of apology, sir."

"Okay, okay, no harm done."

Bree hurried over to her car. "There's hardly even a dent, Alec. For heaven's sake, calm down."

"What is the word I'm looking for?" Alec said to his prisoner.

"Okay, I'm sorry, I'm sorry."

Alec loosened his grip and stepped back. "You need some lessons in manners, sir."

The man straightened his shoulders and stepped into his car. "Nuts," he said out of the open window. "You're both nuts. They let anyone drive these days." He turned on his ignition, backed out and sped away.

Bree stood there shaking her head at Alec as he watched the car disappear down the road. "You know what you did was wrong, don't you?"

He turned to her. "Was it? He was an uncivilized lout."

"We have no laws in the United States against being an uncivilized lout."

"Perhaps there should be, then."

She began to laugh. "It was funny, wasn't it? You came to my rescue, and you know something? I liked it."

He came over to her, placed an arm about her shoulder and gently rubbed the back of her neck. "I think I could spend the rest of my misbegotten life protecting you, and I would enjoy every minute of it."

She had no idea how to control her emotions when he touched her. She found herself responding, moving up against him, pressing her body to his. She turned and let him hold her, her breasts hard against his chest. For a blinding moment, she totally forgot where she was, who she was.

But then, as Alec put his cheek against hers, reality struck. They were standing on a busy road. The whizzing cars speeding past were like so many noisy windstorms.

"This is crazy, you know," she said.

She realized in a moment that he, too, cared nothing for where they were, or who might observe them. Without warning, he leaned over and put his lips against hers in a hard kiss, his tongue searching, then retreating.

"It's crazy. These are private moments, for the bedroom. Come on," he said, taking her hand. "You have spirit, and I admire that in a woman." He led her back to

the driver's side. "Now handle this machine with care,"
he said once they were back on the road, "or I might have
to do away with the next poor devil you crash into."

Smiling to herself, she thought how she had not wanted
him along, that she did not quite know how to explain
him to her mother. "Mom," she imagined herself saying, "meet my miracle man."

"My stomach is growling," Alec said, an hour into the
trip.

"Okay, I want to see if I can reach my mother. There's
a place called the Red Rooster about a mile down the
highway. The food is typically New England, plain and
simple."

The Red Rooster Inn boasted a long mahogany bar,
which was still crowded with a friendly, laughing crowd.
There were smells of baking and beer, mixed with other,
undefined odors that Bree found pleasant and welcoming.

"I'm going to try my mother," Bree said. To her great
relief, her mother answered on the first ring, and said
right away that she had heard Bree's message.

"You're on your way down? Darling, there's nothing
to worry about. I have someone here with me. I'm perfectly safe."

"Oh?" Bree's mind began working overtime. From the
tone of her mother's voice, she knew the someone was
not Mrs. Smith, who lived next door.

"When will you arrive?" her mother asked.

"Midnight, or thereabouts." Bree knew her voice had
gotten smaller. One day soon, she was going to have to
admit to herself that her mother was a busy, independent woman who might have a lover. And to think she
was worried about explaining Alec Devon.

"Well, we'll be here," her mother said.

"Oh, incidentally, I have someone in tow, someone who wants to talk to you about the cards."

"See you soon, darling. Just watch your driving."

She found Alec waiting for her in the restaurant. Their table was at a rear banquette. She slid in beside him. He plucked a daffodil from the small vase on their table and handed it to her. "I wish I had a garden filled with blooms for you."

She put the cool, palely fragrant flower to her nose, but all she could think of was her mother alone at night with a stranger. "Guess what?" she said, and, without waiting, launched into what she decided was her worst fear. "My mother has a boyfriend, a lover, just from the sound of her voice. I think she would be just as happy if I turned around and went back home."

"What do I hear?" he asked, with a bemused expression on his face. "An independent daughter of an independent mother has old-fashioned notions about how her mother should act? Don't come to me for advice, my woman."

"But she's my mother," Bree said.

"I agree, then. Her behavior should be seemly. She must move back in with you, where you can each act the way a woman in society should act."

"Why are we sitting here, anyway?" Bree said. "My mother could be in danger, and we're worrying about our stomachs."

Alec gave her a lopsided grin as he signaled the waitress. "If your mother is in danger from this lover of hers, I'll need a little fuel to stoke my furnace."

Bree picked up the menu and hid behind it. "Yeah, right."

"WELL, I ALMOST GAVE UP on you. What took you so long?" Bree's mother's gaze swept briefly over her daughter and then took in Alec, standing beside her. She stepped aside and beckoned them in, her eyes still upon Alec. "Come in, don't just stand there, you two."

The moment she was in the foyer, Bree looked around for telltale signs of her mother's friend, but since she wasn't certain what she was looking for, she found none.

"Aren't you going to introduce us?" her mother asked.

"Right. Mom, this is Alec Devon." It struck her now, as Alec and her mother shook hands, that she had never realized how beautiful her mother was.

Her silver hair, usually worn in a short, severe bob, had grown in a flattering inch or two and been shaped into a simple pageboy. She was a tall, slender woman with a charming smile that she was now bestowing upon Alec.

"Well, I'm pleased to meet you, Mr. Devon." She creased her brows for a moment. "You look somehow familiar. Have we met?"

The portrait, Bree thought. "We're both part of the diving crew," she said hastily.

Alec had taken up her mother's hand and raised it to his lips. "I see where Bree gets her beauty, ma'am."

Her mother had the goodness to blush at the compliment. "Are you hungry?" she asked. "I wish I'd had more notice. I'd have prepared something." She led them into the living room, where two half-empty wineglasses sat upon the coffee table. "Pity my friend couldn't wait. He had an early appointment tomorrow morning."

Bree breathed a sigh of relief, although she felt it her duty to say something about his leaving her mother alone. "He could have stayed until we got here," she said.

"No, Bree, he couldn't. I can take care of myself."

Alec laughed. "Those words could well have come from your daughter's mouth, ma'am."

"I really don't want to be an object of discussion," Bree said. She took her bag and headed for the guest bedroom. However, she turned at the door to find both Alec and her mother staring after her. "Alec can sleep on the couch," she said, "if that's okay with you." She paused, realizing her mother expected her to share the guest bedroom with Alec.

THE NEXT MORNING found all three of them at the local bank, in a tiny, claustrophobic cell without windows. A metal box was brought to them, and its contents revealed.

"Mom, you know I love old jewelry," Bree said, reaching for a gold necklace, momentarily forgetting the cards.

"Here," her mother said to Alec. She handed him an envelope that contained the two cards. Bree put down the necklace when she caught Alec's grave expression. She had heard her mother and Alec talking late into the night and known they were discussing her. She wondered what her mother had left out. They were now on a first-name basis. Francine and Alec.

Alec had taken Bree aside while her mother was preparing breakfast. "I told your mother I'm a historian," he'd said. "I figured it was better that way."

Bree had let out a sigh of relief. Her mother trusted Alec Devon, obviously, enough to invite him along to the bank for the viewing of the cards. If wonders never ceased, and Alec was one of them, then so was her mother.

"What do you think?" her mother asked.

Alec turned the cards over. "The *Alexis Moon*." He pointed to his initials in the decorative border. "*AD*. The packs were ordered by the score."

"The same ones?" she said.

"Why should possession of these cards put my daughter or me in danger?" her mother asked.

"Francine, I do not know contemporary law, but when the prize is so valuable, every pebble can seem like an immense rock barring one's path to victory."

"There were no witnesses to the game," Bree pointed out.

"Breeford Kealy," her mother said promptly.

Bree's eyes opened wide. "Breeford Kealy? You said he was an old drunk." She picked up the gold necklace. "You, who thought I had an unnatural passion for ancestor worship."

"This is not ancestor worship," her mother said. "This is setting the record straight. If a card game was played aboard the *Alexis Moon,* then these might be the marked cards used." She took the necklace and drew it over Bree's head.

Alec tucked the cards into his jacket pocket. "If I may," he said.

"You must ask Bree. They belong to her."

"No," Bree said. "They're not mine. They belong to the Devane estate."

Chapter Nine

By late afternoon, their errands finished, Bree and Alec headed out of Boston, the back of the small car filled with supplies for the *Doubloon*.

They decided to break the journey back with a side trip to Cape Ann, on the Massachusetts coast, since they could not make it back to Portland before dark under any circumstances.

Alec, who sat behind the wheel, cast a sly glance at Bree. "With any luck, the Blind Raven Inn will still be there."

"Could be," Bree said. "Never heard of the place, but Massachusetts has an extraordinary number of old buildings that predate the Revolutionary War."

"If memory serves," Alec said, "and if time has been good to the place, we can spend the night."

"Oh, time can be good even to human beings," Bree said, smiling at him. "My mother certainly believes you're quite a man."

"Charming woman, your mother."

"Like mother, like daughter," Bree said. "It was very nice of her to remove her boyfriend from the premises before we came. Very delicate indeed. That brings up another subject. The case of separate rooms. One for you. One for me. And no connecting doors.''

"I hope the good landlord will oblige.''

"Grease his palm. He'll oblige.''

"With butter? If that happened to me, the greaser would find himself on the floor.''

"Alec, you're hopeless.''

"Let him grease his palm himself.''

The mist rose phantomlike across the horizon as the day reluctantly began to fade to night. Ahead, the empty road seemed to lead to nowhere, its straight yellow line swimming in and out of his vision.

Then, unexpectedly, there it was, the sign pointing left, leading to the ocean. The Blind Raven Inn. He felt his heart lift. He made the turn, and a half mile down, found the inn. At the entrance to the drive, another sign swayed in the breeze, bloodred letters against a black ground. Beyond lay the inn, lights blazing from curtained windows, and smoke billowing from chimneys.

"Charming,'' Bree said when they stepped from the car. "And the night's cool enough for a fire. When did you say you stayed here?''

"Long ago, when kerosene brightened the rooms, and not the incandescent bulb, which hides nothing and destroys any mystery.''

"And did you come here with a woman?''

He took their cases from the trunk and led the way to the front entrance. "My memory is not that clear.''

But the Blind Raven Inn was, of course, exactly as Alec remembered it from when he and Zachary had stopped on a return trip from Boston, where they had gone on a business matter. Several lifetimes ago, he had crossed its threshold, in the company of this friend of his, with whom he had caroused more times than he could count.

He could almost hear the raucous cries of the inn's patrons, hardy fishermen and whalers, home from long journeys or, like him, about to set out upon one. He could almost hear their merry laughter, smell the running malt, and see the wenches who served them.

He was Captain Alexander Devane, sitting content with his back to the wall, ale in hand. However, his enjoyment of the moment was tempered by the company of Zachary Martineaux. Much had been soured between them. Now his first mate stood in the midst of the crowded bar, an arm around the lady of the inn, sharing a cup of malt with her. Her husband, behind the bar, looked none too happy about it, although the lady herself appeared to be having a good enough time.

Alexander Devane thought about the bet he and Zachary had made just before the *Alexis Moon* docked in Portland harbor. Zachary was a fool to contemplate winning. He played cards with a deadly concentration that sapped his senses and wrote every emotion on his dark, unhappy face.

And Alexander Devane knew this much. He had no need of the Martineaux fortune, piddling as it was, nor of Beatrice. The promise to wed her if Zachary lost was as empty as his promise to stop wenching or drinking. No, Zachary would lose, and he, Captain Alexander Devane, would accept none of the winnings.

He raised his mug, then, and ordered the landlord to serve drinks all around. Zachary had his glass refreshed, and called out to him. "Be generous with your gold, Captain. You will never have the opportunity again."

And now he was here at the Blind Raven Inn with Bree Kealy. He wondered if she understood that she was his one great hope for salvation. In a watery world, where every movement would be monitored from above, or by other salvors, he needed an ally. With Bree at his side, he would find the gold tablet and destroy it forever.

Now they had the night. He had claimed her in his dreams, had taken her into his arms and caressed her smooth flesh until she moaned. He had known her breasts, her thighs, the moist, intimate part of her. All this in a dream. This night, he would claim her in the flesh.

BREE WAS ENCHANTED by the Blind Raven Inn. They had stepped into another time zone, where the owners believed in the therapeutic value of candlelight and blazing log fires, a well-worn bar and highly polished wooden floors.

"Has it changed much?" Bree asked Alec as they went up the narrow stairs to the second floor.

"Not a whit."

"Full of memories for you?"

"More than enough."

They were shown the only two rooms available in the busy seaside inn. The manager apologized, with a wink at Alec, for the connecting door between, but by now Bree was entranced. Her room had a four-poster bed covered with a hand-sewn coverlet that was faded with age, but nonetheless beautiful. The fire blazing in the fireplace took the chill off the air. And before she could unpack, a pot of tea and some scones were brought up on a silver tray.

She stripped, showered quickly and came back wearing the nightgown he had so unceremoniously tossed into her overnight case. She was restless, and not at all sleepy. Why hadn't she suggested a nightcap? She took a scone, bit off a small piece and wandered about the room, tea-cup in hand. She pushed aside the white lace curtains and stood for a while watching the sea and the white breakers that moved in and disappeared under their own foam.

Except for electricity and a modern bathroom, she could have been back in Alexander's time. She closed the curtain and continued her wanderings, examining the primitive paintings on the walls, and old framed needlework. She touched the antique dresser and wondered if he had used this very room—and with whom.

She reached out to try the knob of the connecting door, but drew away. Suppose he heard? Suppose it was open? Just pretend it's a wall, she told herself. She could hear no movement from beyond, and imagined that Alec had stripped, showered, then thrown himself across the bed. She knew what his body would look like, all muscle and hard flesh, his manhood strong and proud. She knew because they had dreamed together, made love together. He knew her body every bit as much as she knew his.

Perhaps he had already fallen asleep. Perhaps, in fact, memories had crowded in upon him like avenging angels, and he lay there suffering.

She was about to throw caution to the winds and knock on the connecting door when she heard him moving about. She heard a door open, then softly close. She went quietly to her door, opened it and looked out. She saw him heading down the stairs. Restless, she thought, just as she was. Restless in a different way, pursued, perhaps, by memories. Would he walk off his demon down by the ocean's edge, in the eerie silence of the night?

She closed the door and retreated to her bed. She, on the other hand, could not sleep for thinking of him. A moment later she got up, went over to the window and looked out. Sure enough, Alec was there, hands dug into his pockets, heading along the beach.

She watched him for a while, wondering whether she should go down and join him. His broad shoulders were squared against the ocean breeze, his stride was long and bold. If he didn't watch where he was going, he'd end up back in Boston. At any rate, she'd never catch up with him. She drew away from the window, and without really thinking about what she was doing, went over to the connecting door and turned the knob. It was unlocked. He had undoubtedly greased the manager's palm. She should be furious, but curiosity got the better of her. She opened the door and stood there, looking around. The room was dark except for a bed of red embers in the fireplace and the moonlight slanting through the lace curtains. One glance at the bed, without so much as a wrinkle in its coverlet, told her that he had not thrown himself upon it, tossing in an orgy of memory.

So much for her own overwrought imagination. Even so, she hugged herself as a shiver passed through her body like a warning. She went into his room, directly over to the window. He now stood unmoving on the jetty, looking out to sea. From the angle at which he stood, she doubted he would be able to tell which room was his.

She let the curtains fall back. At his bedside table, she switched on the low-voltage lamp, casting a soft yellow glow around the room. She could smell his undeniable masculine scent.

His knapsack stood upon the luggage rack. Like her, he had packed lightly. She checked quickly through the luggage, touching each item of clothing as though it were his flesh. She found the envelope that held the two playing cards, but no other token that might show he was a man who had come through time.

On the dresser, she picked up his wallet and leafed through its contents. He was a man of mystery who seemed to have no worries about cash on hand. Apart from that, she found a business card, which told her nothing except that he frequented a dentist in Hong Kong. His last appointment, she noted, would not have been met.

She had no idea how long she had been there when she heard his key in the door. She sprinted for the light switch and succeeded in turning it off in time. Damn, without even thinking about it, she had shut the connecting door. As she raced for it, she prayed the lock hadn't slipped. Before she could reach for the knob, Alec was in the room, lunging for her, cursing under his breath. She went down with all his weight on her. He pulled her arms behind her and shoved his knee in her back.

"Who the hell are you?" he said in a hoarse breath.

"Get off me, you oaf."

"Bree? What the devil!" He hesitated, but didn't free her.

"Yes, it's me, now let me go."

He held her pinned, her arms in a vise. "You came looking for me, admit it."

"I did not. You were down on the beach, I saw you." Oh, she thought, giving up her struggle, now she had done it.

"What were you looking for, then? The real Alec Devon?" His tone turned mocking.

"As a matter of fact, yes."

"And did you find him, Bree?"

"If you don't get off me, Alec Devon, I'll scream."

"No, you won't. You want this as much as I do. Else why would you be here?"

"I don't, I don't," she whispered. "It was all a mistake, honest."

"You're not a lady who makes mistakes." With a laugh, he turned her over and fastened his lips to hers, his kiss molten lava that set a slow, heated flow of desire coursing through her body. Almost involuntarily, her arms circled his neck, and in another moment he crushed her close. She was totally unprepared for the passion and power of his kiss, and the way his body moved relentlessly against hers. She knew then that she had been anticipating this moment throughout the long day. But whatever she had dreamed of or hoped for, she was not prepared for the unleashed force of his need.

In her dreams he had been gentle, with time and tide dictating the course of his lovemaking. She felt the familiar heat of his body, the sinuous feel of his flesh against her hands, as he brought her to new heights of ecstasy. He was ruthless, greedy, his mouth seducing hers, and she felt herself responding in a way her dreams had not prepared her for.

"Not like this," he said huskily.

He wrapped his arms around her and lifted her to the bed. He pressed himself to her, moving against her, even as he reached for her gown and removed it. In another instant, he had his own clothes off and was coaxing her to respond. He touched her as if he knew every sensitive spot on her body, as though he had been on this journey before, and knew the landscape well.

"Remember," he whispered, locking his mouth to hers. She seemed to burn and blister under his touch. He found her secret, vulnerable place. She cried out, willing him to stop, knowing that if he did she would die.

He kissed every tender spot and she arched her head back as his lips found her eyes, her mouth, her throat. Holding her hips, he lowered his mouth to her breasts and found the quivering tips. She drew in a sharp breath, and he felt her shiver under him. His mouth traveled her body, darting here and there, warming every crevice and teasing her toward a scream. Her thighs were soft and warm under his tongue, and then, with precision and ease, he found the core of her and felt her trembling need, even as his own desire peaked. She called his name, and he rose to meet her.

And then he was in her, moving with the sheer, unrelenting force that had overtaken them. He was deep inside her. With a groan of surrender, Bree gave up everything as his mouth plundered hers with a frenzied kiss. With a convulsive shudder, she arched against him. As if that were the signal he had waited for, he thrust once more before his own impassioned release.

The world stopped spinning, and reality returned. Alec lay on his side, holding her in his arms, his head buried in her hair. She heard his soft breath, and thought he was falling asleep.

"I came into your room," she said in a low voice, "because I wanted to learn more about you."

He stirred. "And did you?"

She smiled. "More than I ever dreamed."

Chapter Ten

Fast-moving clouds darkened the morning sky. The weather forecast had called for high seas and strong winds for most of the day. As the *Doubloon* moved out of Casco Bay into the heavy currents of the Atlantic, Alec Devon figured they'd be kept from getting much work done at the wreck. But schedules were schedules, weather was a fickle woman, and everyone aboard the cutter had been acting skittish, from Robin to the cook.

Once the cutter moved out of Portland harbor into Casco Bay, the crew began to straggle below, with the exception of Bree. She had wandered over to the bow, and now stood hugging her jacket close, her hair whipped by the winds ripping down from the north. Alec, observing her from the bridge, where he stood with Robin and the helmsman, thought how the woman touched his very core. His mouth hungered for her. Under his breath, he cursed the journey, because it interfered with his desire to be with her, to feel her flesh against his own.

Robin poked him. "Alec, what's Bree doing out there?"

He came to his senses. Unmindful of the buffeting winds, Bree gazed ahead, as though somewhere on the lowering horizon she discerned their future together.

"Better tell Bree to put a life jacket on," Robin said to him. "If she insists upon playing the *Doubloon*'s figure-head, that is."

"Wave washes her over, she won't need a life jacket," the helmsman commented. "We'll slice her in two."

Alec gritted his teeth and left the bridge, feeling as if he had slammed into a hurricane. He could all but feel the resistance of the cutter as it plowed through the surf. What the devil *was* the woman trying to prove? That she was as tough as any man?

She was holding on to the rails, smiling, when he reached her side, her face and hair wet from the salt spray. "Are you mad?" he shouted above the noise of ocean and wind. "Have you no idea how treacherous the seas are?"

"It's wonderful." She turned to him, her eyes bright and dancing, her hair tossed about her like a flame. If only they were alone, he thought, he would take her in his arms, kiss the light in her eyes, and the salt spray off her cheeks.

"My father used to take me sailing when I was a kid. I cut my teeth on this kind of crazy weather. We're part-ing the waves, Alec. Watch it. I love that feeling of raw power all around me."

"Love it somewhere else. Come on."

She drew back in surprise. "You're afraid I'll get sea-sick. Cute." She seemed unaware of the danger that crackled in the air. "I never get seasick."

He had no more patience with her. The cutter heeled to port suddenly, as though slammed by a huge fist. Without another word, he hauled her over to the ladder below. "Better check your lab supplies. They'll be all over the cabin by now."

"Right," she said, her eyes widening. "Oh, my God, broken glass. Thanks, Alec. What a start to a trip." She ran quickly down the stairs.

When he came back to the bridge, shaking his head, Robin said, "She has this idiotic smile on her face. I've only seen that smile on women in love, or women who are being carted away to the loony bin."

"Maybe a little of both," Alec said. He had no wish to discuss Bree with Robin, or with anyone, for that matter. As the journey progressed, he knew, it would be harder and harder to keep from touching her. He had the good sense to know that in the cloistered setting of the *Doubloon,* it would take no time at all for every feeling, every mood, every touch, to be fodder for rumor and innuendo.

His only goal should be to find the tablet, he thought with an aching heart, and then he might shout his love to the world.

If Robin had any ideas about them, she masked it well enough. He was turning over in his mind her assumption that Bree was acting like a woman in love or a madwoman when she said, "Hey, Alec, don't sailors have some kind of line about bad weather, good seas ahead? Come on, make me feel good."

Alec relaxed. Bree was the last person on her mind. He could think of a dozen axioms offhand, but couldn't speak them in the company of Robin Krashaw. "Sailors, madam, have an entire warehouse of sayings about rough seas and bad weather."

"I'll tell you one," Sandy Mace, the helmsman, commented. "We should have waited a day."

"You don't wait a day," Robin snapped. "That's not how we do business. We're setting up shop today. A hundred feet down, you'll never know whether the sun is shining or not, or how high the seas are.''

Like the other members of the *Doubloon*'s crew, Sandy was a diver, as well as a sailor, but he was also cautious. "We're hitting fog," he said, motioning ahead. The horizon had turned fuzzy.

"So what? What's that thing for?" Robin pointed to the radar screen.

"Right," Sandy said. "Thanks to radar, ships don't sink anymore."

Robin turned to Alec. "Man's a manic-depressive."

"Number one," Sandy said, "since you never marked the wreck with buoys, we're going to have a hell of a time dropping anchor anywhere near it."

"We have a magnetometer for that, Sandy. We know where the wreck is, we're not flying blind."

"And this tub is going to bob around like a rubber duck in a Jacuzzi. You're not diving today," Sandy finished. "Are you?"

"Don't count your chickens before they're hatched," Robin said.

Alec, whose mind was not on choppy seas, left them to their argument and went to the chart room. It was empty, except for Zack, poring over the map of the wreck with one of the divers, a burly redhead from Florida called Billy O'Brian. Zack looked up, and he and Alec exchanged brief nods. Too much his ancestor, Alec thought with that edge of irritability he felt each time he saw the man. Zachary Martineaux, without the gregarious nature that had fooled him for so many years. He continued down the passageway to the divers' room, looked in, found half a dozen of the crew hanging around with mugs of coffee in their hands. He could have used a cup, but did not fetch one. Instead, he went down to the lower deck.

He refused to admit to himself that he needed to see Bree, and that it was to her cabin that he was heading. He could no more get their lovemaking out of his mind than he could the feel of her flesh under his hands.

He even made a pretense of walking down the empty passageway beyond her cabin, but abruptly turned back. Both lab and cabin doors were closed. He stood listening for a moment, remembering her admonition that morning, just before they'd left for the *Doubloon*.

"Robin made it very clear about what she expects from us, Alec. You're going to have to keep your distance for the next two months, you know that, don't you?" Her face had been very serious, but glowing, and more beautiful than he had ever seen her, from the love they had just made.

He had smiled, resisting the temptation to take her into his arms once more, only because the *Doubloon* was scheduled for departure at eight. "I don't know anything of the kind. Half the crew is going to end up in bed with the other half before the *Doubloon* returns to port."

"I can't take responsibility for what the rest of the crew does. I just know what I promised."

Now, standing before her cabin door, Alec thought that he wasn't a man to stick to foolish promises. Two months without her in his arms—she could no more believe in the possibility of that than he. A kiss would change her mind. He knocked lightly on her cabin door. She was slow to answer, and he tried to control his impatience. He knocked again.

"Just a sec," she called out, and then in a moment she was there, smiling as if she'd expected him. Empty words, empty promises, he thought with a grin.

She wore shorts, a halter and no makeup, and once again he was struck by what a fine-looking woman she was. Her hair was still damp, either from the sea spray or from a fresh shower. Instead of greeting him with a kiss, however, she let him in with a sigh of forbearance. "I knew you'd come."

He reached for her, but she took a step back, her hand out as though to ward him off. "I'm glad you did so I can remind you that my quarters are off-limits. Alec," she said, sighing again, as though she knew her words fell on deaf ears, "you promised you'd stay away."

"I promised nothing," he said.

"You promised with your silence. At least that's what I thought. Maybe you'd better go, then."

He shook his head and closed the cabin door, slipping the lock.

"Ooh," she groaned, "what am I going to do with you?"

"Do you really want me to spell it out?"

"I can spell, thank you very much." She ran the tip of her tongue over her lips in a nervous movement. He watched the pink tip dart out and slowly moisten her mouth. His groin tightened with the need to feel those lips on his and the desire to take her in his arms.

"Robin be damned." He pulled her close. "Dammit, woman, you want this as much as I do. You're mine, and I'll see you as often as I like."

"Don't *dammit, woman,* me. I'm not yours," she said quietly, struggling to get away.

His lips came down on hers with a fierceness he knew she'd fight against, and he admired her all the more because she did not disappoint him.

She moaned deep in her throat, then pushed her hands against his chest. "Alec," she said, her breath short, "you don't know how to take no for an answer, do you?"

He released her. "I don't remember asking a question." Her face was flushed, her eyes were brilliant with the kind of light that told him he had won, no matter what she might say.

"No, you wouldn't ask a question, would you? Listen to me," she said, in a low, biting tone, "you may have overpowered women with your damn sexiness in your own time, but that doesn't work in the late twentieth century. Lovemaking is consensual in the late twentieth century, and for the time being it's shut off. You can't strong-arm me every time you get a hankering. It just doesn't work that way."

"But it does," he said. "Nothing has changed. I can see the way your breasts heave under that strip of cloth you're wearing. You want me every bit as much as I want you."

"Hell's bells, Alec, don't you understand? I have a job to do and so have you. I promised I'd help you. Isn't that enough?"

"If I hadn't held you in my arms, yes," he said, "it would be enough. But I've felt your body yielding under me and trembling with need." He took her into his arms. "I've got the memory of your perfume in my nostrils, the taste of your flesh still with me."

She did not move from the circle of his arms. "Oh, Alec, don't you understand? We have to keep you here, you and I, that's what's important. The rest can wait." She looked at him imploringly. "We can never appear to the rest of the crew as if we're in collusion. We're here to find the gold tablet. We *must* find it. I can't bear to think what would happen to you if we don't."

Alec released her reluctantly. "The lady argues with a lawyer's tongue," he said. "But I assure you, my dear Bree, you and I will not wait two months. We will not even wait a day."

She shook her head. "We'll see who wins that little argument." She pointed to the door with a smile. "Out."

When he returned, still grinning, to the bridge, he found Zack there, as well as Robin, with a frowning helmsman who looked as though he might break down and cry.

Robin scowled when she saw Alec. "Where the hell have you been?"

He turned to Sandy. "What's the problem?"

Sandy cast him a glance of disbelief. "What's the problem? Man, you must be carrying some ballast. Rough seas, man, thick fog, in case you haven't noticed. I say the current's too strong, and we ought to set anchor right here."

For the first time, Alec was aware of the pitch of the cutter. Hell and damnation, was he so besotted with Bree Kealy that he ignored the very world around him? Dammit, she was right. They had started on a great journey, and freedom was in his hands, if he could but keep his mind on the work ahead.

Fog had indeed rolled in, woolly and quiet. The sight of the cutter heading through icy gray waves that heaved as though about to give birth to a great monster exhilarated him and threw him into action. The sea parting with mile-high waves wouldn't have stopped the men of the *Alexis Moon* from staying its course. This poor helmsman was a confounded pup with no steel in his veins.

"Better get below," he said to Sandy, grabbing the wheel.

Sandy cast a hopeful glance at Robin. "Go on," she said.

He left in a hurry, passing Zack, who stood at the door to the bridge and had heard the whole conversation. "Wind's died down," Zack said. "Too bad. It would have blown the pea soup away. Don't like the way the ship's pitching, though. We're going to have a devil of a time setting anchor when we get there. These island-class cutters do a better job if they stick close to shore."

"Never heard you complain before," Robin said, clearly annoyed. "Now that you've put up some money, you think you bought a good weather forecast with it."

"Just tell it like I see it," Zack said.

"Well, I don't want any more negative vibes, pal. Get down below, if you don't have the stomach for it."

Zack grimaced and then motioned to Alec. "I want to see him show his mettle, or learn if he's all mouth."

"Alec—" Robin pointed to the chart table "—here's the course, if you want to check it over."

Alec laughed. "I rely on me senses, ma'am, what the good God handed me at birth." And those senses told him that the sun would burn through any minute, and told him the lay of the wreck no worse than when he relied on quadrants and chronometers. A glance at the compass told him they were on the same course as the *Alexis Moon* all those years ago.

Alec was so intent on the storm that he wasn't immediately aware of the tall, rake-thin man standing on the bridge, aiming a camcorder at him.

"Just keep working," he said to Alec from behind the eyepiece.

Alec started. "Who the devil are you? What are you doing on the bridge? Get below, you fool, before the seasickness overtakes you."

The photographer smiled, in no hurry to obey, in spite of the pitching of the ship that suddenly shot him from one end of the bridge to the other. He came over to Alec, hand extended. "Taylor Kinsolving. We met the other day in Miss Kealy's lab."

"I'll have you taking no more pictures of me," Alec said. He did not remember the man, but then, his mind had been on Bree, no one else.

"Hey, take it easy, Alec," Robin said, coming over to him and nudging him with her elbow. "Taylor's a diver, same as you are. Filming's his hobby. Don't pay any attention to him."

"Fool things that insinuate themselves into your lives without your say-so," Alec muttered grimly.

"Okay, okay, I'm the invisible man." Before leaving the bridge, Kinsolving looked at Robin and gave a faint shrug, as though between them they shared a confirmation that Alec was not a man to be crossed.

"Captain of your ship, eh?" The words were spoken by a friendly, round-faced man who had passed Kinsolving on the way off the bridge. His waterproof jacket was open at his shirt collar, around which he had knotted a silk foulard. He had thinning gray hair, and gray eyes that were fixed on Alec. "That was the same attitude that got Captain Alexander Devane into trouble in the first place."

His accent was British, and he spoke in high good humor. He offered Alec a smile and a handshake, neither of which Alec returned.

"And precisely what do you know of the troubles of Captain Alexander Devane?"

"As much as any man. I'm Simon Mortimer of Leighs of London."

Alec started, then allowed himself a smile. He stuck his hand out. "Mr. Simon Mortimer. I'm Alec Devon."

He remembered Leighs of London well, and the women they had generously fixed him up with when he came to London. They'd been a hard lot to lay a claim with, and he wondered what trouble Franklin had had with them over the *Alexis Moon*.

"If Leighs had known then what a daredevil the good captain was," Mortimer said, "I daresay they'd have thought twice about insuring his ship."

Alec winced at the words. "No one knows what happened aboard, that last journey, sir."

"One man lived to tell the tale."

"To a woman whose retelling of it could have held more false tales in it than truth."

Mortimer shrugged. "Perhaps. Legends—and truths— die hard."

They stared at one another for a moment. Alec could not help but like the man, dandy though he appeared to be. "And have you come along on the operation as a representative of Leighs?"

Mortimer nodded. "Of course."

"To see that you get your just share for moneys paid out so long ago?"

"We're entitled to regain our losses, if possible, Mr. Devon."

"I have no quarrel with you there, Mr. Mortimer. Are you a salvor, as well?"

"I am," Mortimer said, with a gleam in his eye. "Five hundred dives to my credit. I mean to be there when the gold is recovered. I hope to aid in bringing it up."

"And in counting it."

"And in counting it," Mortimer repeated.

"Then I say good luck to you, my friend."

Robin interrupted them suddenly. "Look, the sun." The fog did not lift so much as come to an end. They plowed through it as though through a bale of hay. The clouds had swept past, as well, and a warm sun illuminated the still-choppy seas, casting each ridge in spangles of light.

Alec saw the distant cliffs of Marauders Point off to starboard, and was surprised at the sudden clattering of his heart. He closed his eyes briefly. The gold tablet skittered down the deck. Zachary Martineaux lunged for it, then turned pleading eyes to him for help. The gold tablet lodged tight against the stern.

He opened his eyes to find Robin grinning at him. "You've got an angel whispering in your ear," she said. "Hell, you copped a look at the charts. Come on, Devon, admit it."

"No," Zack said. "I had my eye on him all this time. He never looked at the chart. Admit it, Devon, you've made this run before."

"What are you talking about, Zack? The site isn't even marked with buoys. That's the way you wanted it. Listen," she said, clapping a friendly hand on Alec's shoulder, "some people feel the ocean the way others feel poetry, or their own dancing feet." She stopped, embarrassed by her own enthusiasm.

Alec allowed himself a smile. Perhaps, but for Bree, it might be the last smile he would manage until they found the tablet. As for the *Alexis Moon,* he'd know how to head straight for her in the darkest of nights, with the fog heavy and weighted down, the seas all atilt. He had relived again and again those last moments of his folly. He knew well enough where and why he had gone wrong. And he had, often enough in his mind, sailed his great clipper ship through the angry waters to land her safely at the farthest reaches of the world.

"It won't be long now," Robin said.

"No," Alec murmured, looking straight ahead at the horizon, "it won't be long now."

THE CHART ROOM had not been built to hold twenty people, yet the entire crew managed to squeeze in and crowd around the center table. There, Robin had laid out black-and-white photographs of the excavation taken earlier by *Juno*. Stripped together, they provided a clear map of what to expect during the first dives, when grids would be laid down.

Alec, who had studied the photographs in Bree's office, now saw for the first time what was left of his ship. She had broken in two and then lain down on the sea-floor like a dying animal, to be covered by the silt of a century and a half. Enough of her bones were visible to cut him through the heart. He looked across the table at Bree, to find her watching him, her eyes glistening. Tears. She cried for him, he thought, yet the moment their glances met, she looked away with a faint shake of her head. I'll share your grief with you, she was saying, but no one else must know.

"So that's the *Alexis Moon*," someone said, a pretty blonde Zack had said belonged to the Marauders Point Diving Club. "It's so sad, when you think..." She stopped.

"She was a great clipper ship," Bree said. "Fast, graceful."

"Majestic," Simon Mortimer said. "We've got a painting of her in our archives."

Alec looked sharply at him. He did not remember commissioning a painting of the *Alexis Moon* for Leighs of London. "Not possible," he began, and then caught himself. He found Bree gazing at him with an expression of horror on her face.

"Well, we don't exhibit it to the public, if that's what you mean," Simon Mortimer said. He seemed not to have caught the meaning of Alec's outburst. "And an early photograph. Grainy, but marvelous."

"A photograph. Man..." Vic Cramer, a twenty-year-old, experienced diver, said. "I keep forgetting the camera wasn't invented yesterday."

"She was a great clipper ship, and beautiful. I guess that was the most beautiful class of all," Robin said with her authoritative air.

Alec looked gratefully around at the salvors. They had not come to plunder his ship like so many pirates. They were dedicated men and women, as interested in history as in artifacts.

Catching Bree's eye, he wondered if she had had the same sudden thought he had, to tell them the truth about himself. They challenged the seas. He had challenged time.

"Okay, listen up, everybody." Robin tapped the table with her pencil, and Alec knew that the moment had passed. He could no more tell them he had come through time than he could explain about the tablet.

Robin regarded her crew with satisfaction—a young, attractive lot, most of them, divided almost equally between men and women. "Before we go into a discussion of the map, I just want to say this. I'm not questioning the agendas of anyone on board this ship. You could be here because it's what you do for a living, or because you like to dive old wrecks and help bring up the booty. Maybe it's because you're interested in the history of ships." She stopped and nodded at Alec, then went on.

"Maybe you're looking for something that's going to change your lives, or somebody else's life." Here, she nodded at Zack and at Bree in turn. "Whatever the reason is, leave it at the door, folks. We're a team, we've got a single agenda, and that agenda is to do everything by the book. One for all and all for one. Anybody got any objections?"

No one spoke up. Alec glanced again at Bree, but she kept her eyes on the map, as though willing herself not to make eye contact with him.

"Okay, diving master," Robin said to Zack. "It's all yours. Get this crew into shape, remind them that they're professionals and that we don't want them to make up any new rules as they go."

Alec sat back, arms folded across his chest. Zack wasted no time, the perfect diving master, instructing his crew on safety measures.

Alec pondered the bad start between them. Even now, with many lifetimes gone by, the memory of Zachary Martineaux stirred his innards. Dark bearded, heavyset, a driven man whose excessive tastes could be seen in the puff about his cheeks, Zack had his ancestor's obsessions, if not his wit. Alec also noted the way he directed his talk to the women, Bree in particular, and had all he could do to hold himself back from slamming the man up against the wall.

He glanced over the rest of the crew, the pretty women with their attentive smiles, the men with their virility showing like medals for valor. Simon Mortimer, Taylor Kinsolving, both looking a little out of place among the young folk.

He saw Billy O'Brian, who sat next to Bree, lean over and whisper something into her ear. She smiled briefly and turned her attention to Zack. Alec studied O'Brian.

He was a big, sharp-featured man with pale skin and red hair. O'Brian had the dead-serious mien of a man who thought his face might fall to pieces if he tried to smile. Every now and then he stole a look at Bree. Hell, Alec couldn't blame him. She was the most beautiful woman of all.

When Zack asked for questions, several members of the crew wanted to know when the first dive was planned. "Today," Zack said, without hesitation.

Robin looked surprised. "Listen, Zack, we had enough trouble dropping anchor over the wreck. The wind's started up again. We don't want to deep-six like the *Alexis Moon,* and we don't want any bodies floating out to sea on the currents."

"We'll find out soon enough," he said. "I'm on a budget, and we're sticking to schedule. Today we go down and lay the markers. Tomorrow we set up the lights and begin to lay down the grids. As for who's scheduled, I've the roster here." He read some names off.

Alec heard neither his name nor Bree's. His plan was to have them operate as a dive team. It might be easy enough to arrange, if he played his cards right.

He waited while the salvors filed out of the room, then caught up with Bree and put his hand around her wrist. "Thanks," he said quietly.

She waited while a couple of salvors squeezed past them and continued down the passageway. Then she said, with a carefully framed smile, "My wrist."

He drew his hand away, as if scorched. "I've held a lot more than your wrist, my dear Bree, as early as six o'clock this morning. What the devil were those messages you gave me across the chart table?"

"Alec, if I know what you're going through, I won't hide the way I feel about it. But that's it, that's all." As if to emphasize her words, she rubbed her hand along her wrist.

"I'll see you tonight in your cabin," he said.

"What? Are you out of your mind?" She stood there aghast.

"That's my girl," he said laughing. He bowed and let her precede him onto the top deck.

The seas were still rough, with a high wind blowing across the deck. The ship seemed to be straining at its anchor, as though trying to escape the waves battering its hull. The crew milled around on deck, feeling the chill in the wind that even early summer in Maine could not quite dispel. It was clear that, with heavy currents, divers trying to set the first lines could be pulled off course.

"What's all that noise?" Robin said, coming up behind them. A clamor had started on the quarterdeck, with Zack in the middle of it. They found him reaming out Vic Cramer.

Zack, hands clenched at his sides, had poked his face into Cramer's. "Listen, kid, you've got an attitude, and I don't like it."

Cramer pulled away, hands up, as though in surrender. "Hey, Zack, I don't have an attitude, I'm just not stupid."

"We'll go down when I say we'll go, or you're off this crew." Zack's face had turned a deep red. "I want those markers down now, and now is when we'll do it."

"No way," Cramer said. He was Zack's weight, and stood a couple of inches taller than he, but his manner was mild and placating.

Alec pushed his way through the crowd, figuring that Cramer had it all wrong. The young man actually expected Zack to be reasonable. Alec had once thought that he could reason with Zachary Martineaux, and Martineaux had killed a man.

"Wait a minute," Zack said, grabbing Cramer by the collar. "Day one, and I already have a mutiny on my hands."

It had gone far enough. Alec took a step toward them. "Hold it, Zack. If you want a partner down there, I'm your man."

Zack swiveled around, letting go of Vic's collar. "How about the rest of the crew?" he asked, not looking at Alec, but letting his eyes sweep over the crowd.

With downcast eyes, they almost simultaneously shook their heads.

"I won't forget that," Zack said. "Okay, Devon, it's you and me. I'm setting our lead line for getting to section A, and if we have time, I'll mark the spots where the grid goes. Tomorrow we can begin to set up the grids. Get that diving platform up!" he yelled at Cramer.

Cramer looked at Alec, who nodded his head to him to go ahead.

"Listen, guys," Robin said, clearly having a change of heart, "let's not be stupid about this."

"If I can add a word," Simon Mortimer began, coming over and putting a hand on Robin's shoulder, "Zack knows what he's doing. And time's money," he added, with a smile that said he was joking, but not quite.

"So's a funeral," Robin said. "I don't think my insurer would appreciate that."

"Dive time is twenty-five minutes. Check your computer and suit up, Devon." Zack hauled his tank over to the compressor to top it up with oxygen.

Alec had already topped up his tank, and was suiting up when Bree came up to him, looking distraught. "Do you feel this wind? It's choppy out there. The boat's dancing a jig. You can stop the macho nonsense right now, Alec. Everybody knows you're a hero.''

"Macho? My dear Bree, that word has no meaning for me, but I'll take it for a compliment. Are you Robin's emissary, or do your words come from the heart?''

"What do you think?''

He resisted the temptation to brush the hair out of her eyes. "Unlock your cabin door, tonight. We can discuss it then.''

"Oh, that's right, I forgot about you. You can go down in any kind of storm. You can walk on water. You're invincible.'' She turned and stormed away.

He smiled. She believed he was Alexander Devane, yet she did not. She would leave her cabin door unlocked.

Did she not truly believe that his life, for the moment, was suspended between heaven and earth, that no harm could come to him? Perhaps it would be better if she did not believe it. How sweet her lovemaking would be if she thought him truly mortal.

Zack was already on the diving platform as Alec checked his gauges. The ship described circles around the anchor line, pitching in the still-roiling sea. They would enter the water from the diving platform, move along the hull to the anchor line and make their way down to the wreck along the line—not an easy task, considering the movement of the ship and the sway of the anchor line in the current.

Alec responded to Zack's salute, climbed down to the diving platform and followed him through the choppy water to the anchor line.

He could not rid himself of a feeling of apprehension as the water closed around him. This was Zack's dive, but it was Alexander Devane's ship. He should have come down alone, in spite of all he knew about diving with a

partner. He should have paid his respects at the graves of
his men.

Above, the *Doubloon*'s white body lay cast in shadow,
the water framing it in sky blue. After a while, the trans-
lucent blue disappeared and turned into murk. The anchor line, which had been given play, belled out in the
strong current, but he had no fear concerning the dive.
He tried to convince himself that he could confront the
skeletal remains of the *Alexis Moon* without too much
emotion. Zack moved slowly but surely down, Alec
above him.

At thirty feet, Alec turned on his dive light, hoping for
a glimpse of the ship from above, but in the murky water, the glare was thrown back at him. Fifty feet, sev-
enty-five, then at last the seafloor. The anchor had
hooked on to a heavy beam, the first sight he had had of
his ship. But to Alec it might have been from any of the
wrecks he had salvaged in other parts of the world. He
felt no disappointment, no deep pain.

He had hoped, despite all the evidence to the contrary, that the *Alexis Moon,* like others before it, had
settled on the seafloor, waiting for him to free her.

The currents at one hundred feet flowed gently. Zack
signaled him to follow. Zack had studied the photographs and magnetometer readings until they were imprinted on his brain. The readings showed the greatest
concentration of metal in the center of the wreck. There
the first grids would be laid, where Zack felt he would
strike gold.

There they planned to tether the line that would connect the planned grid to the *Doubloon.*

His eyes began to slowly adjust to the shadows and
colors cast by his dive light. Then, suddenly, there she
was, the bulk of his ship, the rotting bones of the *Alexis*

Moon. He forgot all else. The shrieks of his men filled his ears, the roar of the wind, the noise of the great masts toppling, of sails flapping down, the thunder of the ship breaking in half, and the sound of the ocean coming to claim her. Alec felt his heart clanging in his chest.

Photographs lie, he thought. They reduce the truth to flat, tiny images that have no basis in reality. He was staring at the burial ground of his crew, and he dreaded the possibility of coming across their bones. His heart seemed to crack in two.

Zack gestured to him to get a move on. Debris, scattered about in ever-widening arcs along the seafloor, lay half hidden in the sand. The ornate woodwork of the vessel had long been devoured by an army of countless borers whose hollow remains now littered the wreck. The ship's great ribs, like that of a mastodon lying on its side, protruded from the sand.

He checked his computer. Too much time had gone by. He had oxygen left for fifteen minutes. Zack signaled him to help attach the degassing line to a heavy piece of timber, half buried in sand, that still supported an iron ring. Then they began to mark the outer edges of the central wreck, Zack working the north end, Alec the south. When he finished, he twisted around, looking for Zack.

Damn, he thought, the fellow had gone out of range of his flash. Zack Martineaux, diving master, had broken the cardinal rule of diving with a buddy; he had slipped away, dragging the free end of the degassing line with him. Alec put his hand on the line and moved along it until he saw a faint light. He found Zack sifting through some debris. Hell, what did the man think he was doing?

Zack looked up and saw him. Alec pointed to his wrist computer. Zack signed that he knew, and picked up the line. As he began to swim toward Alec, a smooth, shadowy shape appeared out of the darkness.

A lone shark. Alec gestured to Zack that there was danger behind him, but Zack was so intent upon making his way that he didn't catch the signal. Alec pulled his knife from his belt and swam toward the shark, remembering that panic was his worst enemy. He breathed in slowly, careful of the amount of oxygen he consumed.

Zack pulled up in a panic when he realized that the shark had begun to circle him. It drew in closer. Zack reached into his belt for his knife, reached out and nicked the shark's gray flesh. The shark attacked. Zack shot upright, flailing with his legs, caught now in the degassing line. Alec recognized the signs of panic.

He moved in on the shark, trying to distract it by poking at it with his dive light, hoping to scare it into flight. The ploy didn't work. The shark moved in while Zack showed all the signs of panic.

Alec attacked the creature with his knife, striking its flesh repeatedly. Another rip in its side, and it gave up, moving away and out of range. When he caught up with Zack, he had become tangled in the degassing line, and was trying desperately to free himself. He even fought off Alec's attempts to help him. They had no time to work out enmities, old or new, Alec thought. He reached out, grabbed the line and hauled Zack up, splaying the line out as they went. At fifteen feet he forced Zack to degas for three minutes. Damn him, he thought, he was an ungrateful sod, no better than his ancestor. They hit the surface with no oxygen to spare.

Chapter Eleven

"Okay, they've surfaced!"

Bree, with a sigh of relief, pushed her way to the crowded rail in time to see both Alec and Zack hoist themselves onto the dive platform, which was none too steady in the heavy seas.

"That was a crazy stunt, going down in this current," Robin said, squeezing in next to Bree. "What the devil did they think they were proving?"

Bree's eye was on Alec as he crossed the platform to the ladder leading up. "Macho stuff, I guess. Whatever it is, it's between Zack and Alec."

"Not on my time, it isn't."

The moment Alec removed his goggles and mouthpiece, Bree knew with a sinking heart that something had happened. And, from his set expression, she also knew that it had nothing to do with Zack, and everything to do with the *Alexis Moon.* Seeing the *Alexis Moon* in its watery grave had obviously taken its toll. She longed to go over to him, to smooth his brow and reassure him.

As they came up on deck, neither man spoke. Exhaustion seemed to be written into every step they took as they sat down on a bench below the bridge.

Bree saw Alec stretch around, and guessed that he was looking for her. Instinctively she knew he must not see her with her emotions so close to the surface.

As she moved away from the rail she ran straight into Simon Mortimer. He took her elbow. "Steady, my girl. Don't want you slithering all over the deck."

"Sorry," she said. "I really thought I had my sea legs." She was almost glad of the diversion, and let him direct her back to the rail. When she looked across at Alec, his elbows rested on his knees, and his head was bent, as if in contemplation.

"So the heroes return from their journey," Mortimer said. He motioned to Alec and Zack. "That Devon's a curious chap."

Bree glanced at Mortimer. He was serious. She took the easiest tack, affecting surprise that Alec was worth talking about. "Really? You think he's—unusual? I'd have said he was a hunk with nothing more to him than muscle."

"Between the ears, too, do you suppose?"

The subject needed changing. She squinted up at the sun, in a sky that had turned cloudless. "Looks as if we might see summer yet. Wind's died down."

"So it has. We could still do with a little less chop in the seas."

At that moment, Alec looked up from his contemplation of the deck, caught her eye and winked. He touched his wrist computer. She shook her head, trying not to smile. Whatever had happened at the wreck had obviously not affected his libido. *Unlock your cabin door tonight.* She read the message clearly enough. She deliberately turned to Mortimer. "Muscles between the ears," she mused. "I wouldn't doubt it a bit."

Mortimer grinned, as though he interpreted the remark to mean short, well-dressed bald men were a lot more attractive than Greek gods.

She couldn't resist another glance at Alec. He was watching her intently, clearly willing her to come over to him. She mouthed the word *no* and turned her back.

"Mind answering a question for me?" she asked Mortimer, sensing that Alec was still watching her.

Mortimer bent his head toward her, an interested gleam in his eyes. "Fire away."

"Well, it's nothing personal, just avid curiosity."

"If you're going to be curious, it might as well be avid."

"Did Leighs of London pay off on the gold tablet? I mean, was that taken into consideration during negotiations after the *Alexis Moon* went down?"

His answer apparently did not require much thought. Nor did he seem to think her question was out of the ordinary. "We used the manifesto and the value of the ship to come up with the sum paid out. There was no proof that the gold tablet was on board."

"Despite Breeford Kealy's word."

"Despite Beatrice Martineaux's word," he said.

"And so it doesn't matter whether the tablet is found— I mean to your company."

"Not a whit. How the state of Maine feels about it, I can't say. Martineaux will almost certainly claim the tablet belongs to him. He has the documentation to prove it."

"Right, documentation. I guess he has that, all right. Zack isn't looking for the worth of the tablet, so much as legal retribution."

"That's up to the courts," Mortimer said. "Beyond my ken altogether."

"This operation is no small thing to your company, I suppose."

Mortimer looked shrewdly at her. "My dear, we never undertake anything that doesn't have comparable rewards."

The word *undertake* puzzled her. She associated it with financial support. She held back from asking him. He might not tell her the truth, anyway.

Mortimer tucked his arm companionably through hers. "It looks as if the heroes are properly degassed," he said, drawing her over to Alec and Zack, now talking heatedly with Robin.

"You're making a big mistake, Robin." Zack was stripping off his wet suit, his face red with rage. "You and I have been planning this for two years."

"You're too hotheaded, Zack. The longer I live, the more I believe that you don't know somebody until you live with them, so to speak. I can tell you this much, the crew isn't going to listen to you after a while, and I won't stand for any trouble on board. You get your act together, maybe I can change my mind."

Alec caught sight of Mortimer with his arm through Bree's, and scowled. Good, Bree thought, he's back to normal and perfectly full of himself. She wasn't prepared for Robin's next remark, however.

"Devon's the new diving master. He has his papers, he's certified. Period."

"I'll talk to my backers," Zack muttered. He flushed when he saw that Bree and Mortimer had caught him in a vulnerable situation. He turned to Alec, lashing out at him. "Who are you? The devil's own man, I'd say."

Alec laughed and took his wet suit over to the hose to wash it down. "Maybe you're right, Zack. Maybe I am the devil's own man."

Bree couldn't keep it in any longer. "Alec, did you—I mean, did you both find the wreck?"

Zack burst in. "What did you think we were doing there, playing tag?"

"The wreck," Alec said simply. "Yes, I saw it."

Her heart went out to him. She wondered if anyone else could read the pain in his eyes. But only she expected to see it, only she knew the truth. She thought about reaching for him, leading him away to some quiet place where she could tell him that everything was all right.

"Going to tell everyone about your heroics?" Zack said, sarcasm evident in his voice.

"What heroism?" Alec glanced over at Bree, as though it were the last thing he wanted her to hear. "I'd expect you to do the same thing for me."

"Okay," Robin said. "What happened?"

"One shark, which was minding its own business," Zack said, "until Alec decided he was Saint George attacking the dragon."

"You what?" Bree cried out to Alec.

"You took on a shark?" Robin asked.

Alec did not bother answering. He picked up his wet suit and walked past them, not even glancing at Bree.

DINNER IN THE CROWDED mess was a raucous affair in which sea stories and encounters with sharks, moray eels and nosy sea lions bounced off the paneled walls. The crew sat at two long tables, on backless wooden benches, after trooping out of the small kitchen with their plates in hand. The smell of frying fish and fried potatoes prevailed, a foretaste of the kind of rich diet to come.

While the crew got to know one another on their first night out, Taylor Kinsolving caught the lively atmosphere on his camcorder until, with boos and catcalls, he was told to knock it off.

"Sorry," he said, with an air of apology and his characteristic habit of looking as if he were engaged in a great artistic endeavor. He sat down on a bench and applied himself to his dinner, which had already grown cold.

O'Brian, who sat next to Kinsolving, echoed Alec's complaint. "I don't like having that thing shoved in my face all the time, either." He touched his unruly red hair, as though wondering just how good he looked on camera.

Kinsolving looked sheepishly over at Robin. "Once you get hooked on these things, you can't stop," he said, with forced geniality.

"You're too sensitive, all of you," Robin remarked. "Jeez, I've got a crew of prima donnas. I really needed that."

"My old man gave me a camcorder for Christmas," O'Brian said. "Figured I'd want to film some of the dives I've been on. Not me. Time's too valuable. I'm a salvor, and all I want to do is find the booty. I cashed in the camcorder for new dive equipment. The last word in computer technology for me," he said, grinning.

"If you want to film us in action," Alec said quietly, "tell us why it's so important, Kinsolving."

"It's just a record," Kinsolving said, allowing a certain amount of sullenness to creep into his voice.

Bree was surprised at his remark. "A record for whom?"

"His grandchildren," Robin snapped. "Let's forget it. The whole subject is extremely boring."

During dessert, Zack suddenly turned to Alec, who sat across the table from him. "Hey, Devon, where did you say you got your diving experience?"

"I didn't." Alec had been talking in a low voice with one of the salvors, a blonde whom Bree thought entirely too pretty. He turned back, clearly bent on continuing his conversation with her. Bree felt her heart sink. By his own admission, he had been a notorious womanizer. Some things, she thought, die hard.

"Maybe it's time you told us," Zack said, still directing his conversation to Alec. "I'm not the only one who's curious about the new diving master."

Alec whipped around, his jaw tense. "I don't mind recounting my adventures," he said, "if everyone else is agreeable."

There was a general groaning, stopped when Robin put her hand up. "We're all in this together. Nobody questions anyone's credentials except me, and I've already questioned them. You got problems, you come to me. You, too, Zack. Alec is a master diver. That's all you have to know."

Zack eyed Alec with the kind of tenacity that Bree feared most—obsessive, with an underlying fear and hatred. "I still don't have any answers to why you came all the way from Australia to dive the *Alexis Moon.*"

Billy O'Brian piped up. "You don't blame us for asking, do you, Devon?"

"Us?" Alec looked carefully from O'Brian to Zack and back to O'Brian, who shifted uncomfortably and cleared his throat.

"Maybe Zack speaks for some of us," O'Brian said.

"Alec came here because he wanted to dive the wreck of the *Alexis Moon,* easy as that," Robin said, with an air of having finished the conversation. She drained her coffee mug and set it down. "Well, I'm for a game of cards. Any takers?"

Card games or the VCR were popular activities after dinner. Robin found three takers for a game of poker—Zack, Simon Mortimer and Billy O'Brian. She cajoled Bree into joining them, and since Alec had wandered off with the blonde, Bree agreed readily.

Robin had a table hauled out on deck, along with five chairs. The fading sun left a trace of orange on the horizon. Bree, wearing shorts, had considered changing into jeans, but the wind had died down, the sea was tranquil, and there was a thread of warmth lingering on the air. Most of the crew was on deck, sitting around, listening to Vic Cramer play his guitar, the music sweet and clear in the twilight hour.

"Kid's talented," Robin said, when Bree and the others took their seats around the table.

Just as Robin began dealing, Alec joined them, carrying the extra chair.

"Decided to join the action," he said, pushing in next to Bree. When he sat down, he was so close to her, his thigh brushed her bare leg, the roughness of his jeans faintly abrading her flesh. She moved her chair a little to the left, away from him. He spread his legs, made himself comfortable, and let out a deep, contented breath. "Nice night," he said. The feel of his rough jeans was once more against her leg.

"Just ante up like the rest of us, Devon," Robin said, scooping up the cards and shuffling them again. "Five-card draw, jacks or better, progressive."

"Suits me fine, madam," Alec said.

Bree heard the smile in his voice. Poker had been his weak spot, and even now, knowing how the game had betrayed him, it was apparent that he longed for the feel of the cards in his hands.

O'Brian cut the deck. Robin dealt the cards.

Bree played the game regularly with a couple of cronies from the college. She knew that Alec would win every hand. She did not have a poker face, nor was she good at reading anyone else's facial signals. Except Alec's, she thought. She could read every one of his moods.

"I'll open," Alec said.

"I'll see you," Mortimer said.

Zack smirked. "I'll raise you."

Bree's hand was a mess. She longed for an ace or a deuce, with or without pinpricks. She decided almost at once that she was outclassed by the others, but hung in. She did not have long to wait. Within five minutes, Alec had laid out his winning hand.

"Okay, Devon, you were lucky," Zack said, slapping his cards down.

"Luck has nothing to do with it," Robin said sourly as Alec raked in his winnings. "The man thinks on his feet."

Simon Mortimer laughed. "Even when he's sitting down."

"Especially when I'm sitting down," Alec said. He managed to drop a dollar bill on the floor, and glanced at the players. "Never let a dollar bill get away," he said with a lopsided grin, and bent to retrieve it. Bree felt a sudden shock as his fingers closed around her ankle and then slowly, teasingly, moved up her leg to her inner thigh. A cry of pleasure grew automatically in her throat that she could scarcely stifle. The nerve, she thought. She reached down, grabbed his hand and flung it away.

He sat up, showing the dollar bill. "No, indeed, a dollar won playing cards is a dollar earned."

"Okay, Devon, we get the point," Zack said. "You won. Game's not over."

"You're right," Alec said, looking him full in the face. "It's a long way from over."

"Deal," Mortimer said.

After several rounds, with Alec taking in all the winnings, Zack said, "You a professional gambler, Devon?"

"I'm a betting man, but diving is my profession."

Zack pondered his remark for a moment. "I'm betting you're after something, and you know it's there."

Bree felt Alec's leg stiffen next to hers. "Are we talking about the wreck of the *Alexis Moon?*" Alec asked.

"The gold bullion. I'll be watching you like a hawk."

Alec laughed. "Go ahead."

"No problem, man. I intend to."

"For God's sake," Robin said, "let's play poker." She dealt the hand.

Alec picked up his cards. "Couldn't say it better myself. What do you think, Bree? Am I after the gold?"

"We all are," she said, and picked up her cards. Alec had more nerve than any man Bree had ever known. And he was able to arouse her as no one ever had. The trouble was, she thought, glancing at him sideways, he didn't care if he was discovered or not. He did what he wanted to do. Nothing ever stopped him.

He caught her look, gave her his lopsided grin, and threw out a card.

"Hey, Bree, too bad you don't have that famous ace and deuce with you," Zack said. He exaggeratedly rubbed his fingers along the cards in his hand. "No pinpricks."

"I don't think a couple of cards from an antique deck would do me much good, anyhow."

"They were stolen from your apartment, weren't they?"

She put her cards facedown on the table, hearing Alec's sudden intake of breath. "Now, why do you think that?" she said.

After the faintest hesitation, Zack raked his beard with his fingers. "Hey, it was all over the news."

"Right," she said. "I forgot. That's right, they're gone."

"They were just artifacts of the age," Zack said in an offhand way. "They couldn't be used in a court of law."

"Cards? What cards?" Mortimer put in.

"I realize they have historical interest, but only to our family," Bree said.

"What cards?" Mortimer asked once again.

"Too much kibitzing in this game," Robin said. "Put a lid on it, you guys."

"What language is the woman speaking?" Alec muttered, but only Simon Mortimer laughed at the remark.

Bree picked up her cards, then put them back down. "I'm out," she said. She could no more concentrate on the game than on who would win it. Zack had made a major mistake.

Mortimer joined her at the rail. "Compared to poker with Devon, insurance is a no-risk pursuit. What's eating Zack?" He paused, knitting his brow. "What was that business about the cards?"

"Nothing, just a bit of local history having to do with the *Alexis Moon*," Bree said. She looked over at the table. "They're suckers for punishment," she said, referring to the players left in the game. O'Brian, who said he was cleaned out, declaimed loudly that Alec had cheated him. "I don't know how you did it, Devon, but I'll find out."

"I don't like being called a cheat," Alec said, in a low, steely tone.

"You're not a cheat," Robin said. "O'Brian, he's not a cheat."

"I said he's cheating."

Alec slapped his cards down and stood up, knocking the table over. "By the devil's beard, no man calls me a cheat and lives."

"Alec." Bree's warning stopped him for a second. Damn, she thought, she shouldn't have said anything. But she needn't have worried. Both men ignored her.

"What are you going to do, Devon? Put a knife in my back?" O'Brian smiled over at Bree, as though he needed an audience.

Alec shook his head. "I don't need a knife."

Knives. The next thing would be guns. And all over a card game. Bree turned to Mortimer and gave him a pleading smile. "Simon, why don't you stop this thing before it escalates?"

He shook his head. "Sorry, love. I had sense enough to get out when I saw what was happening. The man's a professional poker player, I'd stake my life on it. Well, he'll get no more money out of me."

She realized that Vic Cramer had stopped playing the guitar, and that the crew had appeared from all corners of the ship, silent shadows with expectant glimmers in their eyes.

"You think I care about your threats?" O'Brian was on his feet, and both men stood nose to nose.

"We've been on board the *Doubloon* for all of sixteen hours," Alec said evenly, "and you've managed to insinuate yourself everywhere. You irritate me. Connecting with your jaw would give me untold pleasures. I don't like to hear the word *cheating* in my vicinity, *friend*."

"Nobody wins five hands in a row without knowing something we don't, *pal*."

"Keep playing, O'Brian, and I'll win a lot more." Alec bent over and righted the table. "Now, shall we continue?"

"Give it up," Robin said. "And you, O'Brian, I took Zack's word for it that you're good at what you do, and that you'd fit in with the crew. Don't make him a liar."

Zack had the cards in his hands and was shuffling through them absentmindedly. "My word should be good enough for you, Robin."

She threw him a look of contempt. "I told you, Zack, you don't know anybody until you've really lived with him. We're together on this ship for the next two months, all of us, and I want it to be a goddamned honeymoon." She turned around and poked Alec in the chest. "And that means you, too, Devon. You're smart, obviously you're tough, and you play a mean poker hand, but when I say honeymoon, I mean honeymoon."

She grabbed the pack of cards from Zack and stormed off. Just before going below decks she stopped and looked back at Alec. "Come on, Alec, I'll buy you a cup of coffee."

Alec hesitated, glanced over at Bree, and saw her with Mortimer. He dug his hands into his jeans pockets and followed Robin below.

O'Brian stood talking in low tones with Zack for a few minutes, and then Zack went below. O'Brian clapped his arm over the shoulder of one of the salvors, a freckle-faced redhead with curly red hair. "You could be my sister," he said, heading her back toward the stern.

The redhead laughed. "I wouldn't want to be your sister for all the tea in China."

"How about all the beer in Berlin?"

Their laughter dissipated in the night air.

Bree was beginning to learn who Zack's allies were. O'Brian, for one. Simon Mortimer, for another. He could have interfered, but hadn't. Others, too, no doubt. But this was the first day out, and there was a lot of sorting out to do.

The other members of the crew slowly ambled their way below decks, until Bree was left alone with Mortimer.

She turned back to the rail. The sky was black, seeded with stars. The moon was low on the horizon. It was a fine Maine night, like the nights she had spent with her parents on their sloop when she was a kid.

After a while, Mortimer tried unsuccessfully to stifle a yawn, apologized, and said he was scheduled for an early dive. He asked her if she was going below. She shook her head.

"Well, it's time for bed," he said. "I bid you goodnight."

"Good night, Simon." She could not bring herself to turn in yet. The moon had begun its rise, turning the sea silvery. From below she heard Vic's guitar. Perhaps only a minute had passed when Bree heard a slight rustling. Her heart soared. She did not have to turn to know that Alec stood behind her. He pulled her close and pressed his cheek against her hair.

"I see your Englishman has left."

"My Englishman? What happened to your blonde?"

"Was that the color of her hair?"

"Besides, Alec, I was merely doing research for you," she said teasingly. "Are you jealous of him?"

"If I were, he'd be in the drink right now, scrambling for the dive platform."

"You're incorrigible." She thought of his hand against her inner thigh, and the electric shock that had gone through her at his touch. Incorrigible, cheeky, and able to make every nerve in her body come alive at his touch. "And what have you got to say about your behavior at the card table?"

"Winning five games? I thought my behavior was exemplary. Besides, I cannot resist a challenge."

"And that was a challenge, the way you dropped that dollar bill."

He smiled. "The challenge was in the way I picked it up."

"Try that again, Mr. Devon, and you'll lose an important part of your anatomy."

"Until we play another game of poker," he said, "why don't we finish what I so incorrigibly began. In your cabin, I mean."

He lifted her chin and was about to kiss her when a flash of light startled them. They pulled apart. A shadowed figure darted behind the bridge.

"Kinsolving," Alec shouted, barging after the figure, "you whore's offspring, I'll blow your brains out!"

"Oh, great," Bree thought. That was all they needed, pictures of her and Alec in a clinch. She was unable to finish the thought. She stopped, distracted. A shadow shifted near the lifeboat.

"Hey, who's skulking around?" she cried. "Is that you, Kinsolving?"

Perhaps she had been seeing things. Nothing moved.

"Alec?" She began to worry about the complete silence, and was about to go below when she was shoved from behind with such force she fell to the deck. Footsteps ran heavily to the stairs leading below before she could get her equilibrium. The last glimpse she had was of someone heading below deck. She could have sworn it was not Kinsolving, but Billy O'Brian.

"Bree?" Alec bent over her. "What happened?" He gathered her into his arms.

"I don't know. I was blindsided, I think maybe by Billy O'Brian. Wait." She put her hand out. "Don't get excited. Just help me up."

He pulled her up as though she might break into pieces if he let her go. "I'm sorry I got you into this. I'm going to have Robin ship you back to Portland in the launch tomorrow morning. Meanwhile, I am not letting you out of my sight."

"Leave for Portland?" She bent down to examine her shin for damage, but felt none. "Wait a minute. You didn't get me into anything. I'm here under my own steam, Alec. There's no way I'm going back to Portland. You've got a pretty old-fashioned notion of me, if you think I can't take care of myself."

He put his hand on her arm. "Bree, Zack did not waste a moment when we were at the wreck. He slipped away while I was laying down markers. The man is looking for the gold tablet. I caught him at it."

"That's no secret, Alec. The whole world knows he is."

"He wants it now."

"Meaning?"

"Meaning he knows somebody else on board has an interest in the tablet. You."

"That doesn't mean he's afraid of me." She reached up and patted his cheek. "We'll find it, I promise, and we'll bury it halfway to China. Pleasant dreams, Alec."

She turned and headed for the hatchway. Only then did she realize she had twisted her ankle. It hurt like hell, but she gritted her teeth and pretended nothing had happened. But something *had* happened, and Kinsolving might have the pictures to prove it.

She was about to turn the lock in her cabin door when it opened and Alec came in, locking the door behind him.

"Oh, Alec, please," she said. "Aren't we in enough trouble?"

"Kinsolving caught nothing on film."

"Just two recognizable bodies in a clinch, that's all. We can't trust anybody. Look what Zack said. He knows my apartment was broken into. We didn't even tell anybody."

"Ignorant move on the man's part, then. Now we know he was the culprit."

"Or knows the culprit. He might have been expecting me to react."

"He's not a clever man, Bree."

"Are you talking about him as a cardplayer, Alec?"

Alec laughed and drew his hand around her waist. "I have no desire to talk about him at this moment."

"I know what your desires are, but you can forget them tonight." She spontaneously reached behind him and pulled the band that held his hair back. There," she said, stepping back to admire him. "Prince Valiant."

"Who the devil is Prince Valiant?"

She laughed. "You are. A comic-strip character."

"Woman, you puzzle me."

"You can't stay here. It'll be a tight squeeze. And besides, it's a bad idea all around."

He began to unbutton his jeans shirt. "Couldn't ask for anything better than one bunk for two."

Bree let out a breath of exasperation. "Do you win every game?"

"You're no game, Bree. And yours is the only hand I want to win."

He held his jeans up. "Perhaps I ought to put these in the wash." He went over to the porthole, opened it, and made as if to toss his jeans out.

When Bree stopped laughing, she said, "And you know how to play your hand, don't you?"

"Desperate times call for desperate measures."

Bree threw in the towel. "Promise you'll be out of here by dawn?"

"My promise is my honor," he said, reaching for her. She came to him willingly, letting him unbutton her shirt slowly, as though he savored each revelation of her flesh.

"If you think we're going to make love," she whispered, "you're mistaken."

He expertly removed her shorts, her sandals, her lacy bra and panties. "I often make mistakes."

He closed the overhead light and led her to the bed, now bathed in the soft, cool light of the moon coming in the porthole. When he lay down next to her in the cramped space, she said, "You can lie here quietly with me, or else get out. It's really for the best."

He took her in his arms and cradled her. "My dear Bree, you are so foolish, I could cry." He kissed her eyes, her nose, and then wandered slowly to her mouth, which he took swiftly.

"Alec, please . . ." But she knew her plea had become mere words, and soon they dropped away.

It was so easy, as if all the forces in the world were now on their side. She shuddered and gave up the struggle, coming to him with a passion that told him she had been waiting for the moment as much as he.

He was gentle now, using time as if it were indeed endless. His hands slid over her body, and when at last his fingers found her flowering heat, she arched toward him.

He caressed her, held her, spoke of his need. He touched her breast, his mouth finding her throat, then he teased her by nipping at the taut pink buds. She was now meeting him with a passion she feared would tear them apart.

"Oh, woman, you don't know what you're doing to me," he moaned.

She felt the laugh rise from deep within her throat. "Oh, yes, I do, my captain."

He was over her, enveloping her. Her legs surrounded him. He held her as he entered her warmth, and she knew he held back, waiting for that deep cry from within her. She called his name, and knew he would hold back no longer. He thrust mightily into her. She rose to meet him. She knew in an instant that she would belong to him forever, that she would never let him go.

Chapter Twelve

Late the next day, while Bree was working in her lab, there was a light tap on the open door and Alec stuck his head in. "Bree, can you spare a minute?"

Bree had spent the past couple of hours with her nose in one of her source books. She beckoned him in, smiling. "You can have two. What time is it?"

"Dinner in another half hour." He came in, bent down and kissed her on the neck.

"Hey," Bree said, giving him a mock frown, "I thought after last night we agreed to keep our hands off each other from now on."

"Those were my lips." He kissed her again.

"You know what I mean, Alec."

"I know what you mean, my dear Bree, but I'll take every opportunity I can to break the rule." He glanced at the book on her desk. "What are you looking for?"

"I'm researching giant anemones. This wreck abounds in them." She marked her page before closing the book. "What's up?" She motioned to the only other chair in the small room.

Alec straddled it. He carried a clipboard in his hand, and a copy of the map they had made of the wreck.

"Zack has laid out the diving schedules. He agreed almost too readily to my suggestion that I dive with you."

Bree made a face. "Really. I had no idea I was that popular."

"Following you around while you check out sea life doesn't strike salvors as the kind of work they hired on for."

"They're looking for gold bars." Bree turned serious. "Alec, you should have a very clear idea of where they were stored, and where they ought to be positioned in the wreck."

"Let them figure it out for themselves. There's nothing in it for me."

"You wouldn't want to find a couple and sort of slip them past Robin?"

He shook his head. "I have found my share of gold before this, and been paid handsomely for it. You're all the gold I want now."

"And the tablet."

He gave her an endearing smile. "And the tablet."

"Which Zachary Martineaux bought and paid for and therefore belongs to Zack, no matter what the message on it is. And you're going to deprive him of his birthright."

"If we're lucky," Alec said.

"You know that's dishonest."

"Is it? After all, it was bought with the intent of evil."

"Which, my dear Alec, we have only your word for. The goldsmith who took the commission from Zachary Martineaux said he had no idea of its purpose."

"And Lizzie Borden said she didn't kill her mother and her father."

He looked at her in surprise. "Did you know her?"

"Never mind. The goldsmith gave Beatrice Martineaux a very clear sketch of the gold tablet, and Zack has it. He could have it copied, we both know that already."

"I have no doubt that Zack wishes to imitate his noble forebear with yet another commission for a gold tablet."

He got up and spread the map on her desk. He was about to close the door when Bree shook her head. "Better keep it open. People are used to floating in and out of here."

Alec clearly checked his annoyance. "We can always use your cabin, Bree. As a matter of fact, I think it would solve all our problems."

Bree chose to ignore his remark. She had, as a matter of fact, given a lot of thought to the fact that she had a cabin to herself. She had known that sooner or later she would find herself alone there with Alec. If it were up to Alec, she suspected, he would move in, expecting to share the single-bunk room, and damn anybody who objected, herself included. She supposed there would be a certain amount of pairing among the crew, in spite of the difficulties of finding private time. But she had made a promise to Robin, which she at least wanted to make a pretense at keeping.

Alec took over her desk. He pointed to the rear section of the wreck. "It's somewhere around there, I think."

"Zachary is betting that it's in the captain's cabin," Bree said.

"It's what I want him to think."

"Alec, tell me what happened between you and Zachary. Tell me what happened when the ship went down."

He shook his head. "In time." He turned back to the desk. "Not now. I have no patience for remembering."

She reached out and put a hand on his arm. "But you're hurting. Wouldn't it be better if you talked about it?"

"Finding the tablet is more important."

"But how can I help you if I don't know the absolute truth of what's driving you?"

He pointed to the map. "The tablet had lodged itself beneath the guardrail and the deck. It might have remained so, even as the ship foundered."

She knew she couldn't break through to him. Everything, it seemed, had to be on his own terms.

"Currents can be strong down there," he went on. "On the other hand, if the tablet slipped off and ended up under the deck—"

"It might not be found for decades," she finished for him. "But we have to look, and if it can be found, we have to find it before Zack does. That being the case, what's your dive plan?"

"Murky water, that's our best bet."

"I don't get it. If you can't see two feet in front of you, we'll have a hard time even finding the keel. For one, we're going to have to operate out of view of *Juno* and the spots they're laying around the central grid. And that's for starters. We have to be aware of sharks, loose fishnets, and other divers wondering just what we're doing."

"You leave the problems to me, my dear Bree. You just go down and do what you have to with your anemones."

Bree felt her face grow warm. In all the dives she had made over the past decade, she had never been treated as anything but an equal. She was a certified diver with a lot of dive time under her belt, and he had to get used to the idea. "Alec, we're a dive team. You can't insist upon doing anything unilaterally."

"But I can, and I am." He pulled her toward him and kissed her on the forehead, as though she were a sweet nineteenth-century child-woman who needed his masculine reassurance. "I need you as my ally, but I'm not going to put you in the way of danger."

"Alec, don't do that again," she said, pulling out of his touch and retreating to the open door. "Maybe you'd better leave. I have to clear up some stuff here." My head, for one, she thought.

He smiled, though clearly nonplussed. "Have I misunderstood you? You don't want me to kiss you?"

"Alec, you can kiss me all you like, but I won't be patronized. In fact," she said, storming over to him, "this—" she raised her arms around his neck, put her lips against his, then pulled back "—is the twentieth century." She kissed him again, ignoring his stunned expression. "This is the way we do it now." She kissed him yet again, then again, softly with her tongue tracing his lips, his teeth, and when she felt his arms go around her, and his body press close, she pried open his mouth and tasted him.

In another moment, she tore out of his arms. "Is there anything else you would like to tell me, Mr. Devon?"

The dinner bell sounded down the passageway. She folded up the map and handed it to him.

THERE IT WAS, in a cool haze of light from the battery-powered spots that had been rigged up on the seafloor, the *Alexis Moon,* a movie set, a spectral aura from a science-fiction world. Bree realized with a shock that she had hoped somehow, even if all the evidence was to the contrary, to see the clipper ship whole and in full rig.

What lay upon the seafloor was the burial ground of Zachary Martineaux, of forty innocent men, of the hopes of wives and children who had smilingly seen them on their journey. All that was left was debris, scattered about in ever-widening arcs, half hidden in the sand. The ship was a series of dark shapes, home to the wear of currents, sea creatures, fish that used the curves and crevices as home, withdrawing like fussy housekeepers as she moved in close.

Alec waved a hand gloved in neon yellow at her and pointed to his wrist computer. *Juno,* the submersible, tethered to the ship, was an all-seeing eye, manipulated from above and monitored by Vic Cramer in the control room. Bree couldn't dawdle over shattered dreams. They had no more than twenty minutes to explore the wreck before starting the slow ascent to the surface.

The salvors at work rigging up sand-removal vacuums were under the same constraints, and too busy at their work to notice what the resident marine biologist and buddy were up to.

Alec gestured toward the south side of the grid. She swam toward him, holding up her camcorder. Beyond the halogen lights was the impenetrable gray of bottom waters, beyond which lay the unexplored keel.

Bree began filming algae, bivalves and other life-forms that clung to the wreck. Soon work would begin with the sand vacuums, and she had to be assured that nothing rare or endangered would be sucked in and destroyed.

Alec was, to all intents and purposes, collecting specimens for her. Bree would stay safely in sight of the other salvors and *Juno,* and that meant that as long as she remained there, he could leave her for a few minutes. The plan was for him to swim beyond *Juno*'s capacity to catch him in her all-seeing eye and to head immediately for the wreck. Bree would warn him if someone came snooping around. There were five divers on the central grid, with some going back to the surface, others arriving as replacements.

She checked her computer. Alec had promised to return with five minutes to spare, but when she turned around to look for him, she found Taylor Kinsolving on her heels, in his distinctive black-and-red wet suit. He also held a camcorder, and she had the odd notion that he had been taping her.

Alec was still not back. Panic rolled through her, while all she could do was pretend to turn back to her work. She signaled Kinsolving that everything was okay, but he signaled that he was puzzled to find her alone.

Damn Alec, she thought. He was convinced no harm would come to him. Fishing nets, sharks and Zack Martineaux, among other problems, knew nothing about missions. She slowly moved past the lights, deliberately turning away from Kinsolving.

She did not even look back, but swam ahead, her dive light in one hand, her camcorder in the other. Taylor might come after her, but she would have to wing it. Alec would have had to do the same, but ahead all she saw was the blackness of the deep. Feeling lost, she realized she had done what no diver should do—swim into unknown territory without a buddy. A glance at her computer told her that she had eight minutes left to begin her ascent to the surface.

But all she wanted to concentrate on was finding Alec. Using her dive light to guide her along the seafloor, she began to trace what she thought might be the half-sunken remains of the ship's keel, lying on its side. It might lead to the stern, but might not. Then, just as she realized she was hopelessly lost and confused, she saw a light directly ahead. Alec. She swam toward him and he looked up. She pointed to her computer. He nodded and pointed down, giving her the okay sign. He had located the stern.

Then, suddenly, a figure came toward them. Zack, she realized at once. There was no mistaking his black dry suit, with its bright yellow top, and his bright yellow air tank. He moved steadily toward them, determination in his every stroke.

Zack gestured to begin her ascent to the surface, then headed for Alec. He had found their spot. Alec pointed to his computer and, as if he had been foraging for marine samples, held up his mesh bag and swam back to Bree. Zack knew every inch of the wreck. He'd had two years to map it and to learn every inch of it. Bree realized for the first time that Taylor Kinsolving had photographed them.

"OKAY?" ROBIN'S TERSE question when they came back on board referred to just about everything from the effects of degassing to whether Bree had the footage she wanted.

"No problem," Bree said, looking over at Alec, who had already removed his tank and was now unstrapping his weight belt. She had to get him alone. It wouldn't wait.

"Alec, what was that little bit of business with you disappearing? Bree was alone down there."

"Taylor Kinsolving had his camera dead on her. What was *that* about, Robin?"

Robin shook her head. "I'm asking the questions. Let us know ahead of time if you're going adventuring, Alec, so we can keep an eye out for you. And Zack tells me you were about to plunder the stern."

"Zack doesn't know what he's talking about." Alec shook his head, giving Bree a covert glance that told her not to say anything. She hadn't been about to, but had no way of letting him know she could draw an intelligent conclusion on her own.

"I still don't understand why Kinsolving is swimming around on his own with a camera. I thought he was a salvor," Alec said.

"I did him a favor, Alec. That okay with you?"

"No. I'm superstitious. I don't like being photographed, at least not without my permission."

"I'll tell him," she said shortly, and then turned her attention to Bree. "Bio stuff what you expected?"

"Typical diversity for this area," Bree said. "So far."

"Nothing's going to hinder our work, right?"

"I don't know, Robin." She could have kicked herself for the shortness of her response.

"Time's money."

Robin turned to the next team, about to go over the side. Bree missed noting who was behind the masks. Alec was stripped down to his bathing suit. He stood for a moment, looking out to sea. Bree, try as she might, was unable to lower her gaze from his muscular, broad-shouldered figure. She had been frightened down there, but not of being lost herself so much as of losing him.

Alec turned, caught her admiring glance and grinned. "Come on, let's eat." Although they had been underwater for a short time, the spent energy left the divers with an enormous need to take in calories and liquids.

"Sandwiches, waiting in the galley," Robin said. "Meet me here in fifteen, twenty minutes."

"Come on," he said to Bree, "let's chow down."

"Chow down? You're learning fast."

"What's he learning fast?" Robin said. "I didn't hear."

"The English language," Bree said. "You know how these folks from down under talk."

She found Alec in the galley, along with some crew members.

Damn, she thought, too late. She couldn't talk to him in front of them, and she couldn't ask him to come back out. She grabbed a sandwich. "I'll be in the control room, checking out my tapes." He'd have to get back to Robin in fifteen or twenty minutes. Bree had plenty of work of her own ahead. She went into the control room. Vic Cramer was still there, monitoring the site. She stood for a few seconds with him.

"Amazing how clear everything is," she said. She waited for him to say something about Zack chasing after them when they'd strayed from the central grid.

"Zack said he caught Alec snooping around the stern."

"We were down there to work. What's the matter with Zack, anyway?"

"First Alec swims out of range of *Juno,* and then you did. Robin had a giant-size fit."

"I know, she's right. Well, I've got some footage. I'm going to see how things turned out."

She was deep in the examination of her film when she felt a hand on her shoulder. Alec bent down. "Good color. How's it look?" Robin was with him. Bree wondered if she would ever see him alone.

"Wood's got enough holes in it to pass for sponge," Robin said. "Any area you might clear yet?"

"I need a little time, Robin."

"Right."

"I know, time is money," Bree said.

Alec pressed her shoulder. "I'll be in the chart room." Bree was trying to figure out whether that was an invitation to visit him in the chart room when he asked Robin when their next dive would be.

They were, because of the depth and the cold, scheduled for no more than two dives a day. "This afternoon, 3:30 *al punto*." Robin hurried out of the cabin.

Alec left, and Bree turned to her work. After fifteen minutes, she got up. "I could use a Coke," she said to Vic.

He nodded, still staring at the screen. Divers had to keep up their intake of liquids, and he saw nothing unusual in her remark. She got a Coke and then went into the chart room. She did not waste a moment. Alec sat at the table, poring over a site map. "Alec, don't ever do that again."

"Don't ever come after me again. It's too dangerous."

"You're placing all your trust in something you can't even name. You're flesh and blood. You can die, Alec."

"No, I can't. The trouble is, in my loneliness I often prayed for death. It did not come then, and it will not come now, unless I fail."

She bent toward him and put her lips to his. "You won't fail. But don't make mistakes, I beg you."

But nothing more could be said. Zack's voice came down the corridor. "You in there, Alec?"

They broke apart seconds before Zack came storming in. "Alexander Devane," he said without ceremony, but not without tossing Bree an angry glance. "Alec Devon. I figured it out."

Bree felt as if the floor were about to give way beneath her feet.

"What have you figured out, Zack?" she said, in what she hoped was a dismissive tone.

"Alexander Devane never married," Zack said. "If he left any progeny, you'd have a hard time proving it. Don't even try. None of it's yours, none of it."

Alec began to laugh. "You're pretty good at solving puzzles, Zack. I'll bow to your superior intelligence. None of it is mine."

Bree had to act as if their argument were none of her business. She stumbled toward the door, her mind a near blank. Zack had just missed the truth by a hair. Was it possible he would take the next step and discover Alec's true identity?

She escaped to her cabin, but was too restless to do anything except pace the tiny length from her cabin to her lab and back again. She was a scientist, but she believed in a multilayered world and the miracle of life. She believed that, with time and curiosity, the last code of how the universe began could be broken. And she believed in the miracle of life and the miracle of art and the miracle of love.

Was that why she believed with all her heart that Alexander Devane had skipped the curse of time? That he had appeared before her, as in her deepest heart she had wished he could, unchanged and full-blooded, the embodiment of youth and vigor?

There was a quick tap on her cabin door. Alec opened it and stepped in, closed it behind him and slipped the lock. "He won't guess. He doesn't have the imagination."

"He still thinks you're after the gold, that you'll somehow upset his applecart."

They stood apart, facing each other, hands clenched at their sides, as though each were fighting the same battle to keep from touching.

"I don't care what he thinks, but I need some answers of my own. Are you in love with Alec Devon, or have you always been in love with the idea of Alexander Devane?" he asked at last, as though somehow he could not quite connect both sides of himself.

The question surprised and confused her. "But you're asking if I loved a historical character who was shrouded in myth, who lived and, I thought, died, a century and a half ago."

"Love is dreaming, wanting," he said simply.

"I'm sorry." She was aware of the pleading tone in her voice. "I'm not certain I can even come to terms with what you want me to say. I never loved Alexander Devane, not in any real sense. He was . . . you were . . ." she added, correcting herself, "part of my growing up. Alexander Devane is part of the lore of the city. We took in the history of the Devanes with mother's milk. Then I saw your portrait in the great hall of Devane House and, like every other smitten young girl, appropriated it for my own."

He seemed barely able to contain his amusement. "Was I that famous, then?"

"Very."

He thought about that for a while, then said, "For failure to sail his ship clear of the storm, I suppose."

"No, for dying a hero's death."

"And who was responsible for that misinformation?"

Bree answered promptly, not quite understanding what he was getting at. "Your brother, I suppose. I know my ancestor, Breeford Kealy, supposedly said something about your gambling the ship away, but we have only Beatrice's word for it.''

"Beatrice's word. She was too much like her brother."

"Why haven't you come back before?"

"I am not a magician, Bree. I've been waiting a long time for this, for the chance to atone for what I did, for expiation. For a measure of peace."

She was living in a half-world of illusion and fact, no longer able to distinguish between them. "But where did you come from? I don't understand."

He shook his head. "From nowhere and everywhere, Bree. I can no more explain myself than can you. I thought I was dying, but I did not. When I at last regained my senses, years had passed. I know not how or why I was a thousand miles away from home. I've been a man without a home, without a country, without meaning to my life, a life that seemed to have no middle or end."

He took her hands in his and brought her over to the bunk, gestured for her to sit down and joined her.

There were so many questions she wanted to ask that Bree merely grabbed at the first one that came to mind. "Robin said that you and Zack were very much alike. Is he like his ancestor?"

Alec shrugged. "He has the family features, and seems to have his ancestor's bombast and tenacity. I don't like him, and I'm afraid the feeling is mutual, but do I feel he is Zachary Martineaux reincarnated? No. Zack is a modern man, a bully and short-tempered. He doesn't have my friend's talent for deceit."

"Perhaps he does," Bree said. "J.H. believes he's going to seed the excavation with a gold tablet that has your signature on it."

"It won't be easy."

"Not unless he has a confidant."

Alec reached for her and took her into his arms. "As long as you aren't his confidante."

"I think he's dangerous. J.H. thinks so, too."

"I can handle him," Alec said. "I'm more worried about you."

"I've known him for a long time," Bree said. "I can handle him just as easily as you can."

They remained that way, eyes locked, for a long while. "You believe me," he said, "believe that I've come a long way in space and time, that I've never had a moment's rest."

"Oh, Alec," she said, taking up his hand and resting it against her cheek. "I can't bear to think of it."

He brushed a wisp of hair out of her eyes. "It's all gone now," he said quietly. "We'll talk of it no more. Only understand this, my dear Bree . . . until I found you I did not know what it was to love."

Overwhelmed by love, she could only nod her happiness. His lips came down on hers. She knew with his kiss what she had been afraid to face before, that she was his, and had always been. She thought her heart would burst with happiness and wonder as his kiss deepened and his tongue probed her mouth. Her lips trembled, her body heated under his touch, all caution about privacy, about being aboard the *Doubloon,* melted away. Quickly, tenderly, he removed her clothes. She stood naked before him. His clothes were thrown aside, and the two were down on her bed, entwined. He was familiar, yet altogether new, each stroke she made along his silken skin a discovery. His body was taut and strong, his muscles were tight under her fingers, his flesh was as hot as her own.

He calmed her with his hands, easing her with whispered words of assurance. She knew his hunger for her was equaled by her own for him. When she was quiet, he moved to kiss her breasts, taking first one, then the other, of the taut nipples between his lips, scraping gently with his teeth until she moaned with joy.

They seemed to float between two worlds, a remembered world on an old clipper ship, and this, their bodies entwined in the present. He entered her then, and she met his thrust with a wild urgency, a needy longing to be closer and closer, to know the man she had loved with such passion in another time. Now she knew him, yet again, in her world of flesh.

After a long while, and when she thought he lay asleep in her arms, he began to speak.

"The night was so black," he began, "I could scarcely see the clouds racing against the sky. We had set sail earlier that day on a light wind, but once out of Casco Bay, the winds died down, and we were suddenly becalmed.

"Zachary Martineaux and I had made a bet on our last journey home." He paused, contemplating her face, as though memorizing it. "I think you have to know something about our relationship. We had been friends from youth, whoring, gambling, seeing the world together. We were alike in many ways, yet different enough to keep us amused with each other's company.

"What I did not suspect on that journey home, but understand now, was my friend's jealous nature. Zachary's father had served mine as first mate, and often voiced his resentment of my father, of what he considered my father's cheating ways. He expected more of the rewards of the long and profitable trips of the *Alexis Moon*.

"Apparently Zachary was more like his father than I realized. He became my first mate, and forgot his position, that I was sole master of the *Alexis Moon*. But he was good at masking his emotions, I see that now. He played a waiting game, dreaming that one day I would make a mistake and the *Alexis Moon* and all my fortune would be his.

"Things began to sour between us when Zachary killed a man in Saigon, for no more reason than irritation. The dead man was a weasel, a lowlife, but he didn't deserve death at the hands of Zachary Martineaux. Zachary showed no sign of remorse. On the return journey, we argued incessantly about his callousness.

"But I had an Achilles' heel, too," Alec said with a regretful smile. "I was a gambler. Zachary, who was cold and methodical, set up games night after night on that endless journey. We gambled as though our lives depended upon it, risking everything. I had a talent for gambling, and Zachary was a poor loser."

"You seemed pretty anxious to join the game yesterday."

He raised his hands. "Guilty, without an excuse." He found her lips, as though in expiation for his recent sins, and then released her, the memory and his need to tell her everything apparently uppermost in his mind.

"The *Alexis Moon* docked in Portland. Things between us were at their nadir. Just before we disembarked, Zachary hurled one last challenge—an all-or-nothing card game to be played on our outward journey to the Far East. Zachary's inheritance of two hundred pieces of gold that his father had left him, and the hand of his sister Beatrice in marriage, would be bet against my entire fortune, including the *Alexis Moon*.

"The challenge was issued with all hands present. I didn't hesitate for a moment, confident I would win. And yet I was tired of Zachary, tired of gambling, and promised myself it would be my last game. I tried to convince myself that it was time I settled down, and that Beatrice Martineaux would be as good a wife as any. As the ship made ready to sail once again, I discovered that the game to be played was much discussed amongst the sailors, with wagers as to the outcome.

"Because the sea was becalmed when we had scarce left the dock, Zachary and I commenced our game. I lost everything on the turn of a card, and suddenly I was a man without a ship, without a possession in the world. I thought of ending my life when your ancestor told me that Zachary had fixed the cards and that the *Alexis Moon* was still mine.

"Then the sea picked up rough. A nor'easter, from the smell of it. The ship came alive with men hoisting sail. I should have stayed there on the top deck, but instead, in my fury at Zachary, charged into the captain's cabin. He was there, not on duty as any man, captain or first mate, would be.

"I do not need to say more. Zachary held a pistol to me, and I thought no more of my men and the ship than of my own life at that moment. The ferocity of the wind took us by surprise. The ship heeled. By the time I recovered my senses, it was too late, all was gone. I saw men die, good men and true, and called to God for forgiveness, for a chance to right what I had done."

Alec stopped, spent and weary from the telling.

Bree put her hand against his mouth. "Don't speak," she said. "Don't say any more."

Chapter Thirteen

Bree, in her lab, heard the shouting topside, and the cheer that followed it. "Found it," someone shouted below.

Her heart stopped. The gold tablet. She sat rigidly in her chair, unable to move for fear. They had found the gold tablet. So soon? Her thoughts flew to Alec. Where was he? The panic began deep in her gut. If the gold tablet had been found, what would happen to him? Would he just disappear as quietly as he'd come?

She couldn't bear thinking about it. He mustn't know, not yet. If she could just keep him from the truth a little longer. She got to her feet, her adrenaline working overtime. She must do something. She couldn't lose him. She couldn't.

Footsteps clattering down the passageway toward the stairs brought her to her senses. She must find Alec. She ran out of her lab, down the passageway to the control room, throwing doors open along the way, checking each cabin as she went. But she realized almost immediately that everyone had rushed topside. No one would let an opportunity like this pass. Would Alec also be there, to face what he must?

She came up on deck to a warm, sunny afternoon, but Bree felt as cold as she had ever felt. She found the entire crew standing at the rail, some still in their dive suits, others in shorts and Ts.

She stood for a moment at the hatchway, trying to orient herself to the intense light. Then she heard Alec's voice. "Easy now, easy. She's slept a long time below, this lady."

She heard nothing in his voice that showed fear, but then, Alec was the strongest man she had ever known. He would not show fear, no matter how tough the odds were. She longed to be with him, to take him in her arms and hold him. She went slowly, heavily, over to the railing to watch them haul in the lift bag.

A hand clapped her shoulder. She turned. Zack, still in his dive suit, gave her a triumphant smile. "Saved by the bell. You never know until you find it. Now we have the pure, unadulterated proof."

Don't crow, she wanted to tell him, when a sudden cheer went up. Bree at last dared to look over the rail and saw, without benefit of the lift bag, the ship's bell being hoisted up.

"The ship's bell." She turned back to Zack, suddenly wanting to plant a kiss on his hairy cheek. "You found the bell."

"Proof positive that we're diving the *Alexis Moon*."

"But you knew all along."

"We had all the parameters right, but there's nothing like the real thing to prove to my backers that I was right all along."

She tried to push through the crowd at the railing to reach Alec's side when the bell was hauled in, but no one gave an inch.

"The *Alexis Moon*, Portland, Maine," Alec said, reading out loud. The legend was still clearly visible on the iron surface, despite the rough wear given it by the sea, and the algae that gave it a greenish cast. Finding the ship's bell was the marker that identified a wreck unequivocally.

It was brought ceremoniously over to the hatchway and placed on top. Simon Mortimer, holding a small camera, joined Zack and Bree. "This is the kind of thing we like to see," he said, putting the camera to his eye and snapping away.

Zack's expression turned to one of cold fury. "You have no lawsuit against me. I hope you understand that."

"Against you?" Mortimer looked to Bree, as though for confirmation that Zack was talking nonsense. "Leighs of London will undoubtedly be proved to have complete ownership of the *Alexis Moon* and all it contained."

"Perhaps," Zack said, backing away unexpectedly. "But costs of salvaging will go right into our pockets. Remember that."

Mortimer smiled. "Leighs of London always pays its bills, you know that."

Zack preened and then said, "Anyway, an equal part of the Devane estate did not concern the ship. I'm after the single most important thing down there, the gold tablet. Why else did you think I mounted this operation?"

"And if you don't find the tablet?" Bree asked.

His face hardened. "We'll find it."

A long striation of fear went through her. He meant what he said. J.H. was right. Zack would find the tablet, one way or the other. He was playing a waiting game. He couldn't find the tablet right off without arousing suspicion. He'd have to wait, which meant she and Alec would be able to buy some time.

Bree was emotionally drained, and would have retreated to her cabin if she hadn't caught Alec moving off to one side. Then it struck her. He had paled, and looked stricken. Alec had touched the talisman of his ship's demise. Perhaps its bell had tolled as the ship broke up, the last sound he heard. Surely the sight of this iron survivor must have broken his heart.

Bree went over to him and touched his arm, unmindful of the others present. Only she knew what was going through his mind at that moment. She longed to hold him in her arms, to tell him that he had suffered enough.

Her deepest wish was that the crew would discover no bones, no grinning skulls to remind him even further of the terrible tragedy.

"Are you okay?" she asked softly.

His shook his head, and said in a quiet voice no one else could hear, "I had not thought such tangible evidence would affect me."

Taylor Kinsolving stood ten feet away, panning the scene, and catching Alec and Bree in his viewfinder.

"There he is again," she said, "the cameraman from hell. What's he up to?"

"That's what I want to know," Alec said.

"Steady." Bree realized that Alec's muscles had tensed up.

"Kinsolving." Alec gestured him over.

Something seemed to click with Taylor, and he frowned, as if the sound of his own name meant trouble. He took a tentative step toward Alec, then stopped. "What can I do for you?"

"I'm tired of having you follow us around with that thing."

"No harm meant," Taylor said, backing away a step.

"If I see you taking one more picture of me, I'll break up that thing and feed it to the sharks."

"Hey, no sweat."

"Or I can break *you* in two and feed you to the sharks."

Bree noted with a sinking feeling that his words were caught by everyone on deck.

"Hey, usually people like to have their pictures taken," Taylor said, holding his palm up, as though in protest.

"I don't."

Robin, who had been hosing down the bell, now came stalking over, the hose still in her hand. "Take it easy, Alec—what the hell harm is he doing?"

"I don't like being followed around. Why isn't he putting in dive time working the site, like everybody else? I thought that's what he was hired for."

"He is," Robin said, with a defensive tone to her voice. "He's putting in the same work as you are."

"Bull. Every time I see the man he's got that one-eyed monster poking in my face."

"One-eyed monster?" Robin looked incredulous. "What are you, some primitive out of the jungle? Are you afraid your spirit is going to be captured on film?"

"That's right," Alec said. "I am. The camera is another newfangled invention meant to destroy man's privacy."

"Newfangled! The camera's been around since the *Alexis Moon* went to sea."

"Ye went to those cameras," Alec said. "They didn't follow you around."

Robin threw up her hands. "Ye gods, what's gotten into you, Alec? Sometimes you talk like you just got off a pirate ship. This is the modern world! Wake up!"

"I don't much admire a world where a man is always under surveillance," he said.

Bree stared at him in surprise. Did he realize he had all but told Robin he was a time traveler?

"Talk to him, Bree," Robin said. "Sometimes I can't make heads or tails out of the man. And when's your next dive scheduled?"

"Three." Bree went over to the ladder. "I've still got some work to do in the lab."

"Bringing up specimens today?"

"Expect to," Bree said. But her mind was still on Robin's offhand remark about talking to Alec. How many of the crew believed she and Alec were more than a diving team?

Ten minutes later, while Bree was preparing her tanks for the samples she would bring up, someone knocked on her open door. She turned to find Taylor there with his camcorder.

"Don't bother with me," he said to Bree, stepping into the lab. "Just keep doing what you're doing."

"Taylor, would you mind? I don't like playing the lead in this movie you seem to be making. I'm beginning to feel as if I ought to join the Screen Actors' Guild."

Taylor laughed and put his camcorder down. "Listen, if I were making a movie, I'd be armed with a bunch of releases you guys would have to sign. What's the matter with Alec, anyway? He turns purple every time he sees me."

A signal went off in her brain. As far as the crew knew, she and Alec were diving buddies, that was all. "You'll have to ask him," she said. "I'm not his keeper." She turned back to her work. "As a matter of fact, you might ask *my* permission next time. However, I don't intend to feed you to the sharks if you don't."

"I'm asking your permission."

"No. Now scat, I've got work to do."

"Oh, you're a hard lady, Bree."

Something in his tone made her think he wanted to add one more remark about her and Alec, but he went silently out when she did not answer him. He was after something, she would have bet her bottom dollar on it. She knew, as well, that Robin was in it with him—not a difficult conclusion to reach. Robin ran a tight ship, but Taylor was certainly a loose cannon. Alec was not the only one of the crew to grumble about him, but he was the only one to have threatened the man.

With a single knock at her door, Alec came up behind Bree and wrapped his arms around her. "You knew," he said.

She turned and put her arms around him. A lump had formed in her throat, and all she could do was shake her head. They were scheduled for their dive in twenty minutes, but she longed to kick the door shut, lock it, and lead him into her cabin. Her lips found his in a long kiss that banished her fears.

When he released her, she said, "We can't delay finding the gold tablet. If Zack finds it, or one of the crew does, it's going to take us by surprise."

He ignored her remark. "Get Taylor to go down with you on this dive. Give him any kind of excuse, but make certain he doesn't take his camcorder."

She groaned. "Alec, just because he's taken a couple of pictures? You're not going to destroy it, are you? Anyway, he never lets that camcorder out of his sight."

"Manage it," he said.

"I don't like him, but I don't think destroying his camcorder is a way to keep him out of your hair."

"Bree, if I want to ruin the man, I will not take you into my confidence, you can depend on it. I'm going to run his tapes and see just what the devil the man is up to."

Taylor, too, had a cabin to himself—another reason she knew he wasn't just a salvor with a passion for film. "You're going into his cabin, and you're going to steal his tapes," she said disapprovingly.

"Steal?" He shook his head. "What Zachary Martineaux did was steal."

"Two wrongs don't make a right."

"I may well prove they can, Bree."

She tried another tack. "Vic Cramer will see what you're doing."

"I can think of a dozen of the crew who would do the same thing if they had the opportunity. Vic Cramer is one of them."

Bree sighed. She had thought Alec was lost to her, and now she was dickering over Taylor Kinsolving's camcorder. She had to get her priorities straight. Theft of a camera was not a priority in her life. Having Alec with her forever *was*.

"Aye aye, *mon capitaine*," she said, saluting him.

She found Taylor on deck suited up for his dive. His camcorder lay at his feet. "Lucky you're coming along," she said. "You've got to do me a very large favor. Hold this." She thrust her own camcorder at him. "You've got to be my diving buddy," she said. "You're scheduled for this dive."

Taylor frowned. "What about Alec?"

"He's been having a problem with his right ear."

Taylor glanced nervously around, as though hoping to find an excuse to refuse. "Zack know you're asking me?"

"Taylor, the whole world knows. Come on, we're wasting time."

He didn't look happy about it, casting an eye on his camcorder. "Wait until I take this back to my cabin."

"Taylor, nobody is going to run off with it." She wanted to bite her tongue—it sounded like an obvious setup to her. But Taylor didn't catch it.

"Okay. Wouldn't want you to get lost chasing after a rare specimen," Taylor said, trying to sound cavalier.

The camcorder was in the same spot when they were back on deck a half hour later. As soon as she had deposited her samples in the tanks she had prepared, she hurried on to the control room. She found Alec alone.

"Where's Vic?" she asked.

Taylor poked his head in the door. "Alec, how's the ear?"

Alec turned to him, his brow furrowed. "Ear?"

"Your ear."

Bree drew in a breath. Damn, she'd forgotten to tell Alec what excuse she'd used to entice Taylor to dive with her. "It's okay, Alec," she put in hastily, "I told him about the problem with your ear." Bree smiled over at Taylor. "He doesn't want Robin to know. She'll absolutely forbid him to dive."

Taylor smiled. "It isn't a good idea, Alec."

Good Lord, Bree thought, a little white lie is turning into an event of epic proportions. She heard Alec's deep sigh of impatience. He had been dying to take a poke at Taylor all week.

"She's putty in my hands," he said with a smile.

Taylor withdrew with a wink at Bree, as though they shared a secret.

Alec blew out a sigh of relief. "Ear troubles. Next time devise an easier excuse."

"You think one up, then. Anyway, I'm through lying for you, Alec. Taylor hung around me like a lamprey on an eel."

Alec pushed his chair back and got to his feet. "I'll kill the son of a bitch."

"For heaven's sake, take it easy. It's just an expression." She hooked her camcorder up to the viewer and sat down to check the footage taken. "Where's Vic, anyway?"

"Some trouble with one of the cameras. He went below."

Bree looked at the bank of screens and realized that one of the cameras was out of commission. "So he wasn't around when you viewed the tape."

"Luckily."

She glanced sharply at him. "You mean you found something."

"I found a man very interested in what you and I are up to."

Bree's stomach seemed to flip over. "Are you telling me he's a voyeur?"

"No, he's interested in why *we're* so interested in everything but marine biology."

"But I *am* interested in marine biology. What does he think I do in my lab?"

"Daydream about me."

"Of course, while you're out doing man's work."

"That's the way of the world, yours or mine." He put a finger on her lips. "Bree, Kinsolving is very diligent. He knows that if he catches everything he can on camera, he will eventually capture the most important thing of all. He has managed to film me at the stern, and I'm afraid I don't look as if I'm after marine specimens."

"You mean he suspects you're looking for the tablet?"

Alec nodded.

"But why would he be interested in it? He's a salvor, and should be more curious about the gold bullion."

"I found something else in his cabin, Bree."

"You went snooping. Alec, you were just going after the tapes. He's a salvor and a photographer, not a criminal."

"No, not a criminal." He pulled open a drawer in the console desk. He withdrew a snub-nosed gun that Bree, even with her limited knowledge of firearms, recognized as a semiautomatic. "A make of pistol," he said, "but I am uncertain of its mechanics."

"Then you're the only one in the entire universe who isn't. Don't even try to work out the mechanics," she said, recoiling in horror as he turned it over in his hands. "You'll have to put it back, Alec. He'll know you and I are in collusion."

"I doubt the man will admit to owning this."

"It's called a semiautomatic, Alec. You put a clip of bullets in, and that makes it a lot easier and faster to kill your opponent. Are you telling me that you have never seen one before?"

"I am a man of peace," he said simply.

"You amaze me," Bree said. "I've never met a man before who would admit to such a thing. Now I know you're the real article, if I hadn't before." She bent over and kissed him and then delicately took the weapon out of his hand. "Suppose I remove the clip. Despite the fact that Taylor would be a fool to complain about his gun being stolen, I still don't want him on our trail any more than he is. However," she added, pocketing the clip and handing the gun back, "this is a lot safer with me."

"Bree." He caught her wrist. "If the man travels with one of those, he might have even more interesting things to hide. I did not so thoroughly search his cabin that I would know if this were true. I am certain of one thing. There's danger on board this vessel. I have no fear for myself, but I fear for you."

Chapter Fourteen

A few days after the discovery of the ship's bell, the sand dredges uncovered its cannon. Then a copper caldron was found, identified by Alec as dating from the eighteenth century. Speculation began that the top deck had disintegrated and what remains there were had slipped away in the current.

They were, in fact, dredging the upper deck, where the gold bars might be stored. The thrill of discovery filled the air, and the pique that had marked the beginning of the exploration eased off. And although Alec was consulted for his expertise on eighteenth- and nineteenth-century ships, he did not offer any advice about the safe that had held the gold. He and Bree needed all the time they could get.

It was Bree who suggested they try a night dive when no one was about. Alec concurred. At a depth of one hundred feet, with enough rest time in between, he figured they could manage three dives. And they could use the one instrument they had not been able to before, a metal detector. All along Zack had had the advantage of the sand vacuums, magnetometers and metal detectors.

On the night they planned their first dive, Vic Cramer found Bree in the mess, lingering over coffee with Alec and a couple of the salvors. She had a call on the ship-to-shore phone.

Bree frowned. "It wouldn't be James Harrison Seldon, would it?"

"Sounds like him. This older guy, right?"

"That's J.H. Be right there, Vic," she said, trying to contain her annoyance. J.H. had already called her twice during the week to check on her progress. She had explained each time that if she found the tablet, she'd let him know at once. If Zack or one of the crew found the tablet, the media would be alerted. And she'd let J.H. know at once.

She downed the last of her coffee. "I don't know what he thinks he can gain with these calls," she said to Alec in a low voice.

"He's nervous."

"Yes, I suppose you're right. One letter-size sheet of gold that's more valuable for what's on it than for what it is, I guess I don't blame him for worrying." She reluctantly got to her feet and headed for the door.

Vic Cramer was back in the control room when she got there. He nodded silently at the ship-to-shore phone when she came in, but made no effort to leave, and Bree couldn't very well ask him to. She had no way of signaling J.H. to talk in generalized terms.

A week away from the president of the Devane Institute hadn't changed her reaction to him whenever she picked up the phone and found him on the other end. A tight little knot always formed in the pit of her stomach. He did not disappoint her this time, either.

"Hello, J.H. How are you?"

"I'm scheduling a month's vacation in August. How about giving me some good news?" He never stood on ceremony, and his style was as abrasive as ever.

She glanced over at Vic, who seemed to be engrossed in his book. "August is a whole month away," she said, in as cheerful a tone as she could muster.

"And you guarantee I'll have a peaceful, quiet, unworried vacation?"

J.H. did not know that she and Alec planned to begin diving that night, and she couldn't tell him with Vic hanging around. "We're working as fast as we can, J.H. We really are."

"We?"

The word hung in the air. Bree's stomach turned to sponge as she realized the implication of his question. She had all but told him she had a confidant who was helping her in the search. "We," she said hastily, "all of us, J.H. That's what we're all doing, working on a puzzle on the seafloor, but the problem is we have to find the pieces first. I promise I'll call you."

"Just keep me informed," he said, and abruptly hung up.

Damn, she thought, that's all I need, J.H. thinking he can't trust me to do my work and keep my mouth shut. She turned to Vic. "He keeps hoping that if the gold tablet shows up, it won't have Alexander Devane's signature on it."

Vic nodded at her, marking his place in the book with his finger. He gave her remark some thought. "Oh, I see what you mean," he said. "That legend stuff." Then he smiled at Bree. "Zack would have a fit, wouldn't he?"

"Right," she said. "Zack would have a fit."

She found Alec in the divers' room, in a card game with Zack, Mortimer, and a couple of the other salvors. She hung around until she caught Alec's eye, and with a nod let him know that she had something to tell him.

Some of the other salvors were watching a video that didn't interest her.

She had noted before that in a week's time some of the divers had begun to pair off. They'd be scattered around the ship, looking for privacy, or sitting on the top deck, talking in soft voices. The cook could be found at the stern, fishing. If Bree wanted to talk to Alec, it would have to be either in her cabin or on deck, open and casual. She figured he'd look for her there, first, while hoping she'd be in her cabin waiting for him. But diving without anyone on board knowing about it was chancy enough. They had to keep their wits about them. She knew just what would happen if they were alone together in her cabin. The night dive would be postponed, and they couldn't afford to wait. Zack had all the implementation on his side. Alec had only a general notion, and one lone metal detector.

Alec found her topside ten minutes later, standing at the railing, waiting impatiently for him. "Who won?" she asked, referring to the poker game.

He leaned against the railing, arms folded on his chest. "I figured the best way to leave the game was to lose it."

A couple, arms around each other, stood farther down the railing, talking quietly. She saw a ring around the moon, which meant rain the next day. The night was cool and calm. Bree wore a sweater over her shoulders and thought lazily about slipping into it, but couldn't make up her mind.

"You look worried," Alec said. "Having second thoughts about the dive?"

"No. It's J.H. It's not something to worry about, but I'm worried anyway." She described her conversation with J.H., and his reaction.

"I don't see the problem," Alec said. "You didn't tell him about me."

"J.H. trusted me with handling the tablet, trusted me not to involve him, and certainly trusted me not to talk to anyone about it. And, unfortunately, I can't explain you."

"Bree, you'll more than earn his gratitude before this is over."

She had never cared about earning J.H.'s gratitude. Gazing at Alec, however, wanting to put her arms around him, she realized how indebted she was to the head of the Devane Institute. She resolved never to be impatient again when he called.

"Anybody see Kinsolving?" Robin came up the ladder and glanced around the deck.

"No," Alec said. "What's the problem?"

"He missed his dives today, both of them, never showed up for meals, and he's not in his cabin." Robin's expression was less one of worry than of annoyance.

"You're right," Bree said. "I haven't seen him. That's funny, when he's around you want to throttle him, and when he isn't, you don't even notice he's not there."

"The ship isn't that big. When did you see him last?" Robin asked.

"He was around last night," Alec said. "I commented on his not having that damn instrument in hand."

"Was that at dinner?"

"He sat down next to me," Bree said, "without the camcorder. I remember wondering just how many feet of film he had already taken of us eating."

"Photographers take a lot of film and edit it," Robin snapped.

"I know. I still thought he overdid it." Robin's brusqueness puzzled Bree. Maybe there was something going on between them, too.

"There are only three ways off this ship," Alec remarked. "Over the side, in the launch, or in the lifeboat. Does he drink? Maybe he's down in the hold, sleeping off a drunk."

"He doesn't drink. Let me check the lifeboat." Robin went around the bridge and came back seconds later. "Lifeboat's missing. I wonder how long it's been gone."

For the first time, Bree began to worry. "Did he have a dive scheduled late in the day? Maybe he didn't come up." She knew it was a dumb thing to say, and was doubly sorry she'd spoken when she caught the stricken look on Robin's face.

"He didn't dive late in the day, and you claim you saw him in the mess at dinner last night. That being the case, we're going to talk to everyone on board and try to trace his movements." Robin headed for the ladder. "Come on, I need your help."

Alec stopped Bree for a moment. "You stay with her. I'm going to search the ship from top to bottom."

Robin stopped first in the control room. Vic Cramer was there, with Billy O'Brian and the redhead, playing a hand of cards.

"Anybody call Taylor in the past day or two?" she asked Vic. He checked the log, and shook his head.

"Did he call out?"

"He asked to use the ship-to-shore phone and said he'd be back after dinner last night. Never showed, though."

Robin proceeded to quiz O'Brian and the redhead about when they'd last seen him.

Neither could give her any information, although O'Brian said, "Maybe he took himself off for a jaunt. Or maybe, if he was crazy enough, he decided to go back to Portland for some equipment or other.''

"Dumb," Robin said. "The launch goes back to Portland on a regular schedule. Sooner, in emergencies. Taylor may be a little absentminded, but he's not stupid enough to let the lifeboat down and then row through these waters all the way to Casco Bay and on into Portland Harbor.''

She hurried off, Bree in her wake, to ask the same questions of the salvors scattered about the cutter. She caught up with the cook last, cleaning a sizable cod he had landed.

At the end of a half hour, she returned with Bree to the control room. They had come up empty, with all the salvors accounted for except Kinsolving. When Alec returned, he had nothing new to report, either.

Robin was galvanized into action. "First we check the cabins, Taylor's included. Don't anybody panic. Maybe he took the lifeboat out to get some shots of the *Doubloon*, at sunrise or something."

"And the tide pushed him in to shore, or he ended up mincemeat at Marauders Point," Zack said.

Robin shivered visibly. "That's it. I'm searching his cabin first. Bree, you come with me. Alec, maybe you and Zack had better search the rest."

Alec, standing with Bree at the entrance to the control room, raised his eyebrows. He had already gone through Kinsolving's cabin and found the gun. Bree began to wonder if Kinsolving had deliberately come on board an empty slate. Except for the gun.

Simon Mortimer, who had the cabin next to Kinsolving's, said, "What's the possibility he found the gold, managed to bring it up without anyone noticing—"

"And decided to abscond with it, in the lifeboat?" Alec finished. "He'd have hidden it somewhere on the ship, sooner than use the lifeboat in these waters."

"Bree, come on. If we can't find him, I'm calling the Coast Guard." Robin hustled her down to Kinsolving's cabin on the third deck. "Oh, hell," she said, "if something happened to him... I got him into this." She broke off.

"Got him into what?" Bree asked. "He's a professional diver. He takes his chances like everyone else."

"Forget it," Robin said.

Alec had not yet returned Kinsolving's gun. Watching Robin go doggedly through his effects, Bree worried that she knew about the gun and was looking for it. The only thing Bree was asked to do was examine the shelf in the closet. Bree discovered a couple of pairs of shoes, and a pair of water goggles. In the end, Robin admitted defeat.

"Camcorder's missing, and also all the footage he took. What do you think of that?"

"That he foolishly lowered the lifeboat and went off to take some more footage." From the way she read Robin's mood, the simplest idea seemed the best.

"Otherwise, nothing looks suspicious." Robin carefully locked the cabin door when they left. "Well," she added, hurrying toward the ladder, "our next step is the Coast Guard."

When they went topside to await the arrival of the Coast Guard cutter, the general consensus was that he had taken the lifeboat to do some distant shots of the *Doubloon.*

"Do you agree?" Bree asked Alec.

"I'd say he either took the lifeboat to get out of someone's way, or he was let down in the boat, already dead."

Bree shivered. Until that moment, she'd believed Kinsolving was alive, just someplace else.

"Hey, Devon, if they find Kinsolving dead, they're going to be asking a lot of questions." O'Brian came up to them, wearing a cocky smile. "Last time I saw you, you were threatening to kill him."

"As I recall I threatened to kill him *every* time I saw him."

"Great," Bree said as O'Brian sauntered away. "If Kinsolving is dead, you're high on the list of suspects."

"My dear Bree, when I announced my intention to kill Taylor Kinsolving, I gave someone permission to murder him."

"My dear Alec, tell that to the prosecutor." She went on to talk about the dogged, methodical way Robin had searched Kinsolving's room. "I thought she was looking for the gun. She's bound to say something. You're going to have to put it back."

A loud, piercing horn sounded over the water as the Coast Guard cutter approached. "They made pretty good time," Robin said hurrying up to them. "They were on the way here even before I called. I wonder what that's about."

"I'd say Taylor Kinsolving," Alec remarked.

Robin blanched. "We don't know that."

The entire crew was on deck when the *Doubloon* was boarded by two officers of U.S. Coast Guard Cutter #61. "Oh, hell," Robin said to Alec. "I've known the first officer, Caleb Dempsey, since he was a pup. And I don't like the look on his face."

Both officers shook her hand. Caleb Dempsey was young, blue-eyed, with a faint flush to his skin that revealed how uncomfortable he was with Robin. "Captain

Krashaw, you reported that one of your divers is missing, Taylor Kinsolving?"

"Quit the formality, Caleb. Did you find him?"

"I'm sorry," he said, "but we found his body today, washed up at Marauders Point."

"Damn." Robin paled visibly, took a step away, hugging her arms tight, as though a freeze had just come down from the north. "Are you sure?"

"We found his papers. We've already notified his family. They said he was out with the *Doubloon*."

Bree sensed the apprehension that came over the entire crew, rolling relentlessly from one person to the other. Even Zack seemed to want to fade quietly into the background. She caught Billy O'Brian's eye, and her blood ran cold. Given the chance, he would offer up Alec's head on a plate.

Robin let out a deep breath. "Okay, Caleb, you might as well let us know. How did he die?"

"For the moment, pending autopsy, we're treating it as an accidental drowning."

"Well, it's almost certain he took the lifeboat. We speculated about that."

"How come you didn't report him missing sooner?" Caleb asked.

"Wait a minute." Robin puffed with indignation. "I'm not, I *wasn't* his keeper. Our lifeboat's missing," Robin said, "and nobody realized it. We don't go around checking up on who's what and where, unless he's diving. Ditto for lifeboats."

"Is there somewhere we can talk?" Caleb said, looking around at the salvors surrounding them.

"Sure, my office." Robin led them down to the cubbyhole she had taken over as her office, leaving the salvors on deck to murmur among themselves. Fifteen minutes later, they were back with instructions not to touch anything in Kinsolving's cabin. They asked for assurances that the divers were going to stay aboard the *Doubloon*, at least until the coroner's report came in.

When the cutter left, and the subject was generally exhausted, it was nearly ten o'clock at night. The dive roster was posted as usual in the divers' room, and as usual Bree and Alec were scheduled for midmorning. The problem was, Bree said to Alec, nobody was going to sleep easily that night. "We can't possibly make that night dive," she said, as they made their way topside, where they could speak more openly.

"No. It looks as if the poor man's death was inconvenient all around."

"Alec, you didn't . . ."

For a moment, he stared at her, his gaze hardening. "Would you have me a murderer?"

"I—I didn't mean it that way," she stammered. "I meant, did you sort of *encourage* him to go back to Portland?"

"Bree, I didn't care for the man, but I like even less your assumption that I would see him set adrift in these waters."

She had done it, put her foot in it twice that day, with J.H., and now with the man she trusted more than anyone in the world. She needed to touch him, to reassure herself that nothing had changed, that he realized the strain she was under, that they were all under.

"He's a troublemaker," Alec said.

"Who?"

"O'Brian. I don't know what he's up to, but he carries as mean a grudge as any man I've ever known."

"Do you mean this is all over his losing to you at poker?"

"I lost to Zachary Martineaux and knew that our friendship was at an end."

"But you had good reason to be angry."

He shook his head. "I was angry enough with the man, because of what he was, but if I had won, I'd have forgiven him much."

"Where's the gun?" Bree asked.

"Why do you want to know?" he said, looking at her in surprise.

"You have to put it back."

"Afraid I'll use it on O'Brian?"

"No, Alec, I have the bullets. Robin is bound to say something, that's all."

"If she knows about the gun."

"She knows something."

"Okay, my sweet Bree, I'll let myself into the cabin, now that Robin has methodically searched it, and place the gun back where I found it."

"No, I've been thinking about that. The cabin has a small closet with a shelf. Just push it way to the back of the shelf. Robin is small—she asked me to check the shelf. I told her there was nothing there but some shoes and a pair of goggles."

"The key to Kinsolving's cabin should be in Robin's office," Alec said, digging into his pocket and producing a key chain, "and as second in command, I have the key to Robin's office."

"And since she goes to bed early," Bree said, "we can get the key now."

At that late hour, the upper deck was quiet, pierced by the occasional sound of a door being shut, and of water running. The pale blue light of the television screen shone into the passageway from the open door of the divers' room, which meant someone was still up. They entered

Robin's office through the darkened control room, closed the door and turned on the light. Alec went immediately over to her desk, opened the center drawer and drew out a circlet of keys. "Very obliging of the captain to put her trust in me. Let's go," he said.

"We're going to have to put off our dive," Bree said. "I suspect that the natives, even if they are bunking down, might be too restless to sleep." Just as Alec reached for the light switch, Bree put a hand on his arm. "The roster," she said. "Robin keeps a record of every dive, doesn't she?"

Alec immediately got her point. The roster, kept in a three-ring binder was on the desk. "According to Robin, he did not make his first dive today. Suppose he did, and someone is lying."

Bree opened the book, found the day's roster, and stopped. "Robin, Zack, O'Brian, Mortimer and Kinsolving. The question is, was he there or not?"

Alec came over and turned to the previous day's roster. "The last dive before that, Robin, Zack, O'Brian, Mortimer and Kinsolving. If he managed to catch one of them in his camera doing something they shouldn't have been doing..."

"Such as discovering a cache of gold bullion."

He closed the book. "The bullion was stowed below the quarterdeck, in an iron safe, but there's no saying how it ended up on the seafloor."

"Right," Bree said. "Let's get out of here."

They let themselves out of the control room without encountering anyone, and headed for the third deck. Bree asked Alec how he intended to get the gun without awakening his bunkmates.

He put his finger to his lips, and only when they got to her cabin did he explain. "The gun is here."

"What?"

"When Zack and I did our search for Kinsolving earlier, I decided to move the gun from my bunk to yours."

"Well, thanks. And if the Coast Guard did a search, I could take the fall."

He opened the door to the microwave in her lab and produced the gun. "You, my dear Bree, did not threaten to kill Kinsolving."

"That's because I'm going to kill you, instead."

Kinsolving's cabin was three doors down from hers. Before they left her cabin, Bree remembered to tell Alec that they had to be careful about leaving fingerprints.

"I haven't been careful before," he said.

Bree began to laugh. "Right. Your fingerprints aren't on file. If it turns out to be murder, they'll fingerprint us all. But since I've been in Kinsolving's cabin, I won't have any problems."

Inside the cabin, while Alec wiped his fingerprints from the gun and carefully put it at the back of the closet shelf, Bree looked over the papers on Kinsolving's desk. "Whatever Robin was looking for," she said, "she wasn't much interested in anything here. Receipts, work orders, personal letters. She didn't open any of them. She only mentioned the missing camcorder and cassettes. There's no film, nothing at all. Odd. Well, he liked poetry, anyway." A book lay at the back of the desk. She reached for it and turned it over. "Walt Whitman." The book lay on a piece of torn paper that struck Bree as being of interest, only because it was so well hidden.

"Alec," she said, "take a look at this."

Alec looked over her shoulder, and read, "'time enough. We had a deal and I expect you to honor it. If you give me any trouble.' It's Robin's handwriting. And there's the florid *R* she signs her messages with. Well, this will be a good one for the Coast Guard. It's incomplete, though."

"That's what she was looking for," Bree said.

He replaced the note under the book of poetry. "Let's hope her friend, Lieutenant Dempsey, doesn't read Walt Whitman."

He opened the outside door, peered out and closed it. "I'll be damned, Zachary with his little friend from the Marauders Point Diving Club."

Bree's eyes grew wide. "Really? Well, good for him."

"Enclosed in each other's arms, and kissing their way up the ladder."

"Wow. Where do you suppose they're going?"

"I don't know, but I suspect they'll be a long time getting there." He held up the circlet of rings. "Suppose we do a little research in his cabin?"

"For a brand-new gold tablet?"

"I couldn't persuade you to go after Zack and his friend and keep an eye on them, could I?"

"Not on your life, Alec. Besides, I'm not a voyeur."

There was no need of a key to enter Zack's cabin, as he had left it unlocked. "Is breaking and entering the same crime on land and sea?" Bree asked when they had closed the door behind them.

"'Tis no crime to find a murderer," Alec said.

"We don't know for certain there was a murder. Or if Zack is guilty. After all, Robin wrote that odd note to Taylor."

"I'll take no chances, Bree. Now, quickly, look about."

Bree was surprised to discover how neat the cabin was, but for the bunk, where the sheets and blanket showed signs of vigorous use. His small metal desk held only a leather-covered journal. She did not hesitate to open it, to discover that Zack was obviously planning to write a book. Just like him. She considered telling him that he'd need editing help.

She was about to put the book back when something slipped out and fell to the desk. She drew in an audible breath. She picked it up. "My God, Alec, come here."

She held up the ace of spades. "My playing cards. He's been in my apartment, not once but twice. Somehow he knew that's where I'd bring them."

Alec scowled. "It looks as if Mr. Martineaux is ten steps ahead of us." He took the card from her, felt its edge. "Where..."

"Here." She flipped through the pages of the diary and dislodged the deuce. "Alec, I'm scared. If he meant to get rid of the cards, why are they here? And the door unlocked?"

Alec put his finger to his lips, signaling that there was someone outside. Bree slipped the cards back into the diary. Alec motioned her over to the closet, which was stuffed with clothes and diving gear. They squeezed inside just as the door to the cabin was opened. Someone came in and headed straight for the closet.

Alec cursed softly under his breath. The interior of the closet had a small utility handle. He grabbed it and held on tight. Whoever was on the other side tried turning it, but after a few attempts gave up. If the intruder was Zack, he caved in too easily.

He moved away and began a systematic search of the room, drawers opened and, after a while, closed, one by one. Alec's arms tightened about her, and in the darkness of the small space, Bree felt his nearness like a cloak. Even with the scent of danger all around them, of discovery, she felt a longing for him that shocked her.

His body touched hers at every juncture, and the sounds outside, not more than a few feet away, ceased to reach her ears. She wanted Alec, and could almost feel the surge of desire pass through his body. His mouth came down on hers before she could draw in a breath. His arms tensed around her, and she gave in to blind lust, knowing that she was more brazen than common sense should allow, more wanton than the loosest woman. He had changed something fundamental in her, and she would never be the same again.

"Bree, we can continue this in your cabin," he said, his mouth close to her ears.

She stirred in his arms and reluctantly listened for sounds from beyond the closed door.

"I think our friend has left. Save all that heat for later, my girl." He kissed her open, hungry lips.

When they opened the door, nothing about Zack's cabin had been disturbed. "I wonder what the intruder was looking for," Bree said.

"Just what we're looking for. The facsimile of a gold tablet."

"He may have found it, Alec."

Alec turned back to the closet and quickly began to search it. "Nothing," he said.

"Maybe we're barking up the wrong tree," Bree said. "Look how orderly Zack is. This is the space of a man, for all his scruffiness, who doesn't want to mess up his life with something that might get him into a lot of trouble."

"There is a way to find out. If Zack had a copy made in Portland, we may be able to locate the goldsmith," Alec said.

"If he ordered it in Portland."

"Zack was complaining in the mess that he hasn't been away from the Portland area since he discovered the wreck, two years ago."

"Did you ever hear of mail order, Alec?"

When he creased his brow, she said, "I won't go into the details, but he could order the tablet from across the country, without ever leaving his living room."

"The man likes to be in control." Alec waved his hand to encompass the room. "This room is certainly in control."

"You sound like a twentieth-century psychologist."

"That thought is as old as Methuselah. Where are the playing cards, Bree?"

"I put them back."

"You didn't want Zack to know his room had been searched, but there is no need. Perhaps that's what our mysterious visitor was looking for."

Bree went quickly over to the diary and retrieved the cards. "Maybe it's much ado about nothing, but these are my nothing." She pocketed them. "Now, when will we go to Portland?"

Alec went to the cabin door and opened it. "As soon as possible."

"And what will Robin say?"

He hurried her down the passageway. "There's a storm coming, and if the seas are heavy enough, we can set off tomorrow morning."

"I have to call my neighbor," Bree said, "to see if she noticed that my apartment was broken into again. If the lock needs fixing, I'd better have that done."

"We'll stop by tomorrow, Bree. I'd suggest we tell no one about the break-in, for the time being."

Alec turned her around and pointed down the passageway to her cabin. "We'll stop at your apartment tomorrow. At the moment, my dear Bree, we have some unfinished business between us."

Chapter Fifteen

Alec had been right. Deep currents and choppy seas under a leaden sky kept the divers from work the next day.
The time was right for a trip to Portland. When the
launch left early in the morning, Bree and Alec were
aboard, along with several salvors and the cook. Careful that they not seem to be traveling together, Bree spent
the trip talking exotic dives with a couple of the salvors.
Alec played his part by flirting outrageously with
O'Brian's redheaded poker partner. The trip through
heavy seas wasn't the most comfortable Bree had ever
taken, and she was happy when the skyline of Portland
could be seen in the distance.

At the dock, they seemed to go their separate ways.
Bree walked up Pearl Street to the Chamber of Commerce building, on Middle Street in the old port. Alec,
who had taken Market Street to arrive at the same desti-
nation, was already at the information counter when she
arrived.

The first thing Bree did was call her neighbor about the
state of her apartment, and she was assured that nothing
seemed out of order. She thought of Zack and his surprising neatness. If that included breaking and entering,

and tidying up afterward, she was at least grateful. They decided to put going to her apartment off until last.

When they left the Chamber of Commerce building, they had a map of Greater Portland, and an impressive list of local goldsmiths. Because of the renaissance of the old port and the number of craft shops doing business there, the list numbered more than a dozen.

"I love this section of town," Bree said of the charming shops and restaurants that lined the cobblestone streets of the old port. "It's commercial, overcrowded, and should be corny, but it isn't."

"And I scarce see a familiar sight," Alec said, "but for the cobblestone roads."

"The fire of 1866 pretty much leveled this section of town. The cobblestones are the same," she added cheerfully.

Because Portland was a busy tourist center in July and August, they had to push their way down busy streets, past jeans-clad couples wheeling baby carriages, tourists walking backward with cameras and camcorders, and teens taking up the entire width of streets.

They found the jewelry stores crowded, although Alec had no trouble being waited on. They were able to cover all the shops in a little more than a half hour. None had been approached with an order for an engraved sheet of gold, but since they specialized in crafting jewelry, Zack would probably not have approached them.

"It makes sense to check everybody out," Bree said as they walked the short distance to Congress, "then we'll know for sure."

"We won't know," Alec said. "We will only know that he did not have a tablet produced in Portland." The odds began to work in Zack's favor when they checked out the two shops off Congress. Neither had received inquiries about making up the gold tablet.

"Onward," Bree said. They hired a taxi to help them cover the outer areas, up through North Deering, then down through South Portland.

"The streets are a jumble," Alec muttered as the taxi took off over ancient cobblestones. "How do people manage to get about?"

The driver, a bearded young man with the look of a poet, took the question as directed at him. "This is nothing," he said. "You should see it at rush hour. Or in a snowstorm."

"I remember it well in the winter," Alec said. "Horses with sleighs, silence but for the bells." He put his arm around Bree and hugged her close.

The driver looked at Alec in his rearview mirror. "What century are you from, anyway? Horses with sleighs? Silence? In the middle of Portland? Jeeps is more like it, four-wheel drive, trucks like tanks."

The trip to the outermost reaches of Greater Portland produced nothing. Two hours later, in South Portland, their list had dwindled to four.

"We're running out of luck," Alec said.

"No, we're not. The last one is always the one you're looking for."

He thrust the list at her, grinning. "Okay, which is the last one? We'll go there first."

Bree pointed to a name. "Hammer and Sons on Sawyer."

The proprietor of Hammer and Sons shook his head at their question. "No," he said. "No. I wouldn't forget an order like that."

"And no one asked for a quotation."

"No, definitely not, no. I'm sorry," he said, still shaking his head. "No. Mind you, I could've used the business, but no. Listen, try the Elmore Company. Turn right to Hillside, continue on to Everett. Down the middle of the street. They're a jewelry supply house. They'll know if an order came in wanting a gold sheet that size."

Bree exchanged a glance with Alec. The one name they had not been given was that of a jewelry supply house.

The manager of the Elmore Company, a harried-looking woman who appeared from behind a huge crate when they stepped into the warehouse, scowled as if she wished they hadn't come.

"Allow me," Alec said.

Bree smiled. "Be my guest."

It took him minutes to discover that a jeweler called Pandars in the East End had ordered a gold sheet for engraving a month before. Bree felt an extraordinary thrill at the discovery. They weren't wrong. Zack had been foolish enough to use a local goldsmith to copy the gold tablet.

"I'm really excited," Bree said, once they had left Elmore's. "At least we know what to expect. If Zack does find the tablet, we can always question its authenticity."

"My dear Bree, don't cry herrings till they are in the net."

"That's quaint," she said. "We'd say, 'Don't count your chickens before they're hatched.' And you're still not going to dampen my enthusiasm."

He bent to kiss the tip of her nose. "We also said, 'Don't prophesy unless you know.' Come on." He took her arm in his. "I won't dampen your enthusiasm, but perhaps the sky will."

The sky had darkened sufficiently for them to hail a taxi north. "That's my territory," Bree said, "the East End. My apartment's near the promenade."

"Pandars Jewelry is on Monument. Is the name familiar?"

"I know the neighborhood, but the truth is, I'm not much of a shopper."

Pandars Jewelry was a modest shop whose interior looked as if it hadn't been painted in years. Mr. Pandars was alone when they came in, a short, squat man with a long tongue of hair swept forward in an ineffectual attempt to cover a bald spot.

From the jumble of gold and silver goods on display, it seemed the principal part of his business was engraving. There were gold watches, silver plaques given employees upon retirement, gold cups awarded for human effort beyond measure. Bree gave Alec's hand a hopeful squeeze. This was it.

"May I help you?" Pandars regarded them with a rheumy eye, as if they had wandered in off the street to get out of the rain.

"Yes," Bree began. "We're looking for—"

He gave a sorrowful sigh. "Someone is always looking for something."

"In this case, it's an order for a gold tablet," Alec said. "We're trying to chase such a tablet down."

"Maybe you've come to the right place," Pandars said. He waited, clearly a man of few words.

"This one was in the form of a document, and is letter-size on thin gold."

Pandars leaned on the counter and thought. "I see. What is your business, may I ask?"

Bree's heart sank. They should have realized that anyone ordering the tablet would have sworn the engraver to secrecy.

"We have reason to believe the tablet is being used in a swindle," Alec said, "concerning an elderly gentleman."

Bree took in a deep breath to stop her smile. Elderly gentleman, indeed.

Without looking perturbed, Pandars nodded. His gaze flew from Alec to Bree and back to Alec. "The police."

"The document in question was an official deed. That is, if the elderly gentleman signed it, he would be giving away his worldly goods."

"The important question," Pandars said, "is who ordered the tablet and when did I deliver it. I did neither."

Alec, who by then had caught Pandars's laconic manner, waited.

"A gentleman called me on the phone, told me to expect the order in the mail, along with the engraving information. I was to make an exact copy. He told me he was in a rush and would pay me well." Pandars paused and gave them a small smile. "I seldom have interesting orders of that kind. The next day, an envelope was delivered to me. When he next called, I gave him a quotation. Within a day, I received the money to cover every contingency. I never saw the gentleman. I don't know where he resides. He enclosed a return envelope to a postal number."

"No name on the post office box?" Bree said.

"Voyager. That was the name."

"Did he pay by check or credit card?"

"Neither. Money order. Since he had overpaid me, I asked him to drop by, and I would give him a check to cover it."

"And did he come by?" Bree asked.

"No."

"May I ask why you didn't mail him the difference?"

Pandars brushed his hair, then took off his glasses and put them back on. "I wanted to meet him. Perhaps learn if I would get more such orders."

"From the sound of his voice," Alec said, "could you tell us anything about him?"

Pandars thought for a while, then shook his head.

"And can you tell us anything about the document itself?"

"I merely executed an order. That's all I did, sir."

"We understand that, Mr. Pandars."

The shopkeeper lifted his shoulders in a shrug and, after a moment's thought went wearily over to his desk. He returned to the counter, bearing a heavy ledger. "The order came in a month ago." He began turning pages. "Here we go." He turned the ledger around so that they could read the entry, written in a clear, open hand.

They saw at once that they had hit pay dirt. "Voyager, indeed," Bree said. Zack had ordered a gold tablet, and at great expense. He knew just what he wanted to do, and that was to make certain the tablet was found. Everything revolved around it. Enough time to explore the wreck and then to hide the false tablet. If the real one was found, he would still come out on top.

"I suppose you want to see the photocopy," Pandars said.

Alec exchanged a glance with Bree. "If you don't mind," she said politely, trying to hide her excitement. She felt once again the thrill of discovery, and without Pandars noticing, she put her hand on Alec's arm and squeezed it. They were going to nail Zack. She could all but taste victory. Let him share in the rewards of the wreck itself, but the Devane Institute and all it stood for could never be his.

Pandars went to a filing cabinet, pulled out a yellow clasp envelope and presented it to them. Inside were several sheets of paper. The one on top was a clear copy of the original document belonging to Martineaux's family, torn at the edges, with the marks of foxing.

"Blast the man," Alec said under his breath. "He has left no stone unturned."

"They have a copy of this at the Devane Institute, you know," Bree told him.

Someone came into the shop, and Pandars excused himself to wait on her, which gave both Alec and Bree some breathing space. "Is it the same?" Bree asked.

"The same, my dear. The same seal." He pointed to a beautifully rendered etching of the *Alexis Moon*. "The same calligraphic style. I remember every word, the crossing of every *t*."

Alec read the document over Bree's shoulder, his hand at her waist. She could feel the soft warmth of his breath against her neck. His voice hushed, devoid of rage, the voice of a man who understood what his enemy had done, but placed the blame for the doing on himself.

"I herewith on this date bequeath my entire estate and fortune to Zachary Martineaux, said fortune consisting of the following..."

The entire holdings of the Devane family followed, including Devane House and the other estates, and the *Alexis Moon*. At the bottom of the tablet, a horizontal line had been incised for Alexander Devane's signature and the date.

"The question is," Bree said, "did he ask Mr. Pandars to affix your signature?"

"Since he ordered a replica of the original document, and a copy exists at Devane House, perhaps he did not want to arouse suspicion, even with the goldsmith."

"And he had to find a copy of your signature and write it in himself. It wouldn't have made sense to ask Pandars to sign it with a too-careful hand."

Pandars returned after wrapping a small gold charm for his customer. "Have I shown you what you were looking for?"

"Yes," Alec said. "But I would like to see a copy of the engraving you made, if you have it."

Pandars flipped quickly through the sheaf of papers taken from the envelope and produced a copy of the gold tablet.

"It could not be more exact," Alec said after a moment.

Pandars shook his head sadly. "This swindler has gone to a great expense to ply his trade, hasn't he?" He was clearly ignorant of the legend of the *Alexis Moon.*

"Some men," Alec said, "spend a lifetime preparing for such a thing."

Bree asked if they could copy both the order from Voyager, and a copy of the tablet that Pandars had made. Pandars agreed, saying that he had a copier in his workroom.

They waited for his return, not daring to touch, to say what was in their hearts. They had chased down a hunch and proved it all too true.

"Zack has to be stopped now," Bree said. "We have the proof."

"We only have proof that a document was reproduced by someone who travels under the name of Voyager."

Pandars returned with the copies. They thanked him profusely, and Bree vowed that she would return to buy a piece of jewelry from him.

When they stepped outside, Bree explained that her apartment was close by, and that she had to face the fact that someone had gone back to her apartment to steal the cards.

"Odd," Alec said, "I thought this street looked familiar. Down two or three streets, one comes to the promenade. I had a small house, a private place no one knew about." He took Bree's arm. "I wonder if it still exists."

"It could," Bree said. "The area still has some fine old homes. You weren't, I mean . . ." She hesitated finishing the sentence.

Alec stopped and shook his head, smiling. He kissed her cheek. "No, my dear one, I did not keep a mistress there. Both my mother and Franklin felt that when I returned to Portland I was theirs to do with as they wished. My brother shadowed my every move, and Mother made it her duty to introduce me to modest maids who would make good wives. My only hope was escape when I saw that gleam in her eye."

"And I suppose Beatrice Martineaux was one of the modest maidens."

"Beatrice was anything but modest."

The street they entered angled crookedly and was an enclave of eighteenth- and nineteenth-century homes. It ended on a cul-de-sac that held three houses in the midst of a grove of leafy trees. "Which one?" Bree asked, taking his hand in hers, and holding it tightly.

He pointed silently to the center one, a Federal-style redbrick house with black shutters. A child's red wagon stood in the front, and on the center door was a wreath made of dried flowers. Through an open window they discerned the figure of a woman holding a baby in the air. The sound of laughter drifted out.

Alec put his arm around Bree. "I did not know what it was to love," he said, "until now. Perhaps until this moment, I did not know that love means continuity and unselfishness."

They walked the small distance to Bree's apartment, arms tight around each other. "I dread going back," Bree said. "I feel as if I've been mugged. And by Zack Martineaux. I never liked the man, but we *have* known each other a long time. And why is he holding on to the cards?"

"That, my love, is something I may have to wring out of him when we return."

The deadbolt lock on Bree's door was operative, but Alec assured her that a very clever thief could have forced it.

"And locked it on the way out?"

"Your neighbor undoubtedly thought she had left it unlocked by mistake."

Bree had slipped the playing cards into a cookbook, but the bookshelf looked untouched.

"Zack didn't even raise a dust mote," she said glancing around her living room. "In fact, I'm surprised he didn't dust for me, while he was at it." To find the cards, he would have had to go through a large collection of books. "Well—" she sighed "—he had all the time in the world."

Alec, who had gone into the kitchen, came back to the door. "No, he didn't. As far as I can remember, Zack has not left the *Doubloon*."

"Then he has an accomplice. Someone who did come ashore."

"That will take some thinking," he said.

Bree picked up her mail and began to go through it, but her mind was on Zack. She had the cards back, and now Zack would be on his guard. She wondered who his accomplice was. Taylor Kinsolving came to mind.

"Are ye finished with the office work?" Alec called. He had gone back into her kitchen, where he found a bottle of Scotch and poured himself a glass.

"Finished." She came to the door of the kitchen. "I'm afraid the pantry is pretty empty. Are you hungry?"

"Aye." He put his glass down and came over to her, wrapping his arms about her. "As hungry as man can ever be."

With a great swoop, he picked her up and carried her to the bedroom. In a moment, he had removed her clothes and stood gazing at her nude body with a reverence that made her tremble with expectation. She thought of the miracle that had brought him to her, and did not dare question how it had come about, and what she might lose in the future.

He stripped his clothes and led her to the bed, pressing his body to hers, cradling her and whispering her name in a chant. He caressed her with infinite tenderness, holding back his own lust until he showed her how precious she was to him.

What he could do to her was magical. He could set off a passion in her that was unlike anything she had ever known. Spigots of flame were ignited under her skin at his touch, and when he used his tongue to bring her to the pitch of desire, she knew she could no more resist him than the earth could stop revolving.

She felt weak and out of control, then hot and powerful, every inch of her wanting more and more. When he finally came to her, she surrendered with an exotic shudder that racked her body and shook her soul. And it was only when his labored breathing quieted that her own body rested. She closed her eyes on a deep sigh.

THEY TOOK separate taxis back to the wharf, with minutes to spare. And as soon as Bree stepped on board the launch, she found an additional passenger sitting there—James Harrison Selden. And from his expression, she thought, J.H. wasn't too happy to see her.

"Well, this is a surprise," she said awkwardly. "Is this a day jaunt, or are you spending the night?"

"I'll take the launch back tomorrow morning," J.H. said, in his usual pithy style. Robin had a V.I.P. cabin set aside for the backers of the expedition.

Bree knew that the launch made the journey every two or three days, and wondered whether Robin would make an exception for J.H. But then, that wasn't Bree's problem. Bree's problem was getting him aside to tell him about Zack and the facsimile tablet.

"I was going to call you," she said, "but ran out of time." Alec and she had lingered too long in bed, in a comfortable afterglow. Everything, including calling J.H., had been forgotten.

Seconds later, Alec came on board. She nodded a distant greeting and introduced him to J.H.

J.H. had time for a quick handshake before turning to Bree. "Taylor Kinsolving. The newspapers call him a documentary filmmaker. How in hell can a documentary filmmaker take such risks?"

Bree stared at him aghast. "Do you mean about the lifeboat? We really don't know what went on. Kinsolving was a salvor, that's all." She exchanged a fleeting glance with Alec.

"Suit yourself," J.H. said. "I'd like to know what's going on, that's all. If there's some problem on board the *Doubloon,* tell me."

"The Coast Guard believes that Kinsolving accidentally drowned," Bree said. "That's all I can tell you."

She was thankful for the noise of the engine, which made conversation tedious. She sat back. Alec, she noticed, studied J.H. with a coolness she found unnerving. It was only when the *Doubloon* came in view that Bree saw the Coast Guard cutter on the starboard side.

"Company," J.H. said dryly.

As they drew near, she saw Robin waiting for the launch. The look on Robin's face told her everything.

Chapter Sixteen

It was four-thirty when they stepped aboard the *Doubloon*, with Bree as worried as she had ever been. J.H., as usual, gave the impression that he had arrived on a yacht about to cruise the Mediterranean.

However, Lieutenant Caleb Dempsey of the U.S. Coast Guard was not impressed. In fact, J.H. couldn't have boarded the *Doubloon* at a worse time. With Dempsey was a slender, handsome man with a cherubic smile on his face. He turned out to be with the Portland police department, and he had come to investigate the murder of Taylor Kinsolving.

"Murder?" The indignant expression on J.H.'s face was that of a man who would, in seconds, take charge. "I thought the case was closed, that the man drowned."

The newcomers were told that Taylor Kinsolving had been asphyxiated, then presumably placed in the lifeboat and set adrift. Because of the high winds and heavy seas, the boat, with its occupant, had smashed up against the cliffs at Marauders Point.

The presumption that the murder had occurred aboard the *Doubloon* made the entire crew suspect. Alec was immediately taken for questioning into the divers' room.

Bree only had to look at O'Brian, lounging on the deck, to know why. She wanted to throttle him.

But there was more to worry about. Alec's short fuse was well-known. Zack certainly held a grudge against him. But more than that, Alec had, as often as not, returned to his bunk at sunrise after being with her. She would have to provide an alibi for him.

She had an uncomfortable hunch that their plans to find and destroy the gold tablet were being cracked into little pieces. And if he was arrested, what would happen to him? She shuddered. For Alec, that meant a lot more than a court trial. She could not bear to think of the consequences.

Robin, who appeared pale and distraught, wanted to talk to Bree alone, but J.H. had to be taken care of first. Bree escaped to her lab as soon as she could, then found she was unable to concentrate on her work as long as Alec was being questioned.

Robin stopped by after settling J.H. in. "He's having a fit, as if somehow we're conspiring to ruin his life," she said.

"How come he's here, anyway?"

"He called and asked. I don't mind, as long as he doesn't get in the way. I know how much he has at stake. Truth to tell, I have the oddest feeling that Zack is going to pull some kind of stunt. Having J.H. on the scene might stop him, at least until this Taylor business is cleared up."

Bree drew in a breath. "Is this something new—about Zack, I mean?" She wanted desperately to confide in Robin about the facsimile, but knew the time wasn't right. There was something about Robin and Kinsolving that also needed airing.

"I don't know. He's been acting a little light-headed. Silly."

"Maybe he's in love," Bree said.

"Love? Zack? Who would fall in love with Zack?" Robin made a quick tour of Bree's lab, stopping to examine some of the specimen jars. "God, those anemones are huge," she said. She shivered, then came over to Bree. "Listen, do you think Taylor had something on Alec?" She grabbed a chair and pulled it up close to Bree. "Alec was a fool to threaten him, you know that."

Bree, who was already anxious, didn't like the earnest look on Robin's face. "Alec had nothing to do with Kinsolving's death," she said impatiently.

Robin stared at her, as if seeing Bree for the first time. Then she leaned back, and Bree's heart began to beat unnaturally. She expected the worst. Sometimes it seemed the whole ship could see how she felt about Alec, written all over her, imprinted in her body language.

"You're right," Robin said. "I hired the guy on instinct, pure gut instinct. I like to think it was the recommendation he brought along with him, but it wasn't. He was a tower of strength, I saw that right away. And a tower of strength is what you need, when so much is at stake. He may have thought Taylor Kinsolving a royal pain, but he wouldn't kill him. I thought the same thing."

"Kinsolving was a diver, not a salvor, wasn't he?" Bree said. "He certainly didn't seem to know too much about salvaging old wrecks. How come you invited him along?"

Robin got to her feet. "It hardly matters now, except what happened to the camcorder and film. The murderer probably tossed them over the side."

"Maybe," Bree said, "but he couldn't have tossed them very far. Maybe they're straight down on the seafloor."

For a long moment, Robin's eyes lit up. "Possible," she said, "but think of what the salt water will do to them."

"That's what the killer hoped."

"Well, it's a damn pity. He put a lot of work into those films."

Bree raised her eyebrows. "Work? I thought it was his hobby."

"Right," Robin said, stepping through the door. "When is a hobby work? Poor guy."

Robin went back on deck to deal with the Coast Guard. Bree, alone in her lab, concluded that Kinsolving had taped something he should not have, and that Robin knew what it was. She was looking for the camcorder and film, possibly because of the film still in the camcorder.

But what? Who? He'd been all over the place with that damned thing. After a while, she gave up and applied herself to her work. It seemed the best way to ease off worrying about Alec.

And in the back of her mind was a knot of worry about the dive she and Alec had decided to make after midnight, if Alec emerged from the detective's questioning unscathed. They would be alone on the seafloor, in the intense dark, with only their dive lights to illuminate the wreck. They'd be working at a remove from the anchor line and the decompression line. They'd be in an inky-black world inhabited by creatures both dangerous and powerful. She managed to find a little consolation in the fact that humans were still the most dangerous creatures of all, and there wouldn't be any down there at that time of night.

A half hour later, Bree was asked into the control room, where the detective flashed his cherubic smile at her, and made her feel comfortable immediately. She told him what she could, and fudged her answers when possible. She obviously made a poor witness, and was probably not a suspect.

But then, neither, it turned out, was Alec. She found him with Robin in the chart room, ostensibly planning the next day's dive roster.

"Hi," she said blithely to him, trying unsuccessfuly to stop a tear welling up in the corner of her eye. "They let you go." She had not realized until that moment just how fearful she had been.

"Let me go?" Alec shook his head. "They never had me. Simon Mortimer set himself up as informant. And O'Brian came in for his share of trouble."

"Simon Mortimer? That doesn't sound like him," Bree said.

"You can thank him," Robin said. "He muddied the waters sufficiently. The good detective is going over Taylor's cabin now."

Bree's pulse quickened. The gun was in Kinsolving's cabin, and the magazine was still in hers.

She excused herself. She was going to have to do something about the magazine. She glanced at Alec and saw the expression in his eyes. He had thought of it, too.

"By the way, J.H. is looking for you," Robin said. "I saw him heading for the ladder. You'll probably find him on the top deck."

The magazine, with its thirty-six rounds, would have to wait. Bree wanted J.H. to know about the facsimile. It was somewhere on the *Doubloon,* she imagined. Unless Taylor Kinsolving's death had something to do with the tablet, Zack wouldn't be in a hurry to show his hand. She was still contemplating whether or not she should tell him about Alec when the dinner gong sounded. Well, they would meet in the mess. She'd save talking about the facsimile until tomorrow. Or maybe after dinner.

At dinner, J.H. was subdued. He was clearly shaken by Kinsolving's death, although he had not known the man. Perhaps for the first time he understood that not only was Bree searching for a needle in a haystack, but that the haystack harbored some dangerous creatures, human and otherwise.

After dinner he began a game of chess with Alec that lasted until the last salvor made his way to bed. Bree watched a movie on the VCR with Simon Mortimer, but at last gave up and returned to her cabin. She found the magazine, opened the porthole and dropped it over the side.

She showered and crawled into bed. Until she met one Alec Devon, her life had been interesting enough, but it had lacked not only passion, but the dark edge of danger. What a trade-off, she thought as she drifted into sleep.

She trusted Alec to wake her up in time. He climbed into the bunk somewhere around eleven, and warmed her shivering body until it was time for their dive.

THE FISHERMEN'S NETS that had come loose from their moorings floated freely through the depths, attaching themselves to the wrecks or reefs, or floating adrift, capturing everything in their lethal paths.

Bree thought she worried more about nets in those depths than sharks. Nets could not be seen more than a couple of feet away, their ghostly shapes waving and beckoning in the bottom currents. The *Alexis Moon* had its share of these nets, most of them cut away and hauled up in the lift bag. However, there were always others, gliding through the wreck like holiday sightseers, that might reattach to a wooden beam or grid.

They had topped their tanks earlier that evening, checked their gauges in Bree's lab, and suited up on deck in the dark. They went into the water making the least amount of sound they could, and followed the lead line down to the central grid. From there, they splayed out a line from the central grid to the keel.

So far, so good, Bree thought. She had made night dives before, but they had been in the Caribbean, where the richness of the flora and fauna were even more compelling than in the day.

In the cold black depths, timing was everything. A couple of minutes to find the keel, so much time to clear away sand, so much time to find their way back to the line, so much time for degassing. Then, back to the diving platform and up on deck, without a soul knowing about it.

Five minutes into their undersea work, Bree hit a smooth, round shape, deeply embedded in the sand. She looked across at Alec, but his eye was on the seafloor and his metal detector. She went back to work, carefully brushing sand away. When the deep sockets appeared, she stopped.

A skull. Zachary Martineaux's? Alec said Zachary had held the tablet in his hands, and then it had dropped and skittered away. She began to remove more sand, until she felt a touch on her arm. Alec. He held up his wrist. Time to surface. Alec reached past her to examine the skull, then, in another moment took her arm. They had no more time to waste.

THE NEXT AFTERNOON, Bree discovered a depression in the seabed that she had not noted on the chart. At the bottom, twelve feet down, she discovered a miniature hillock made of unidentifiable pieces of iron—pilasters, she thought. A colony of barnacles and anemones had taken hold, along with the usual marine growth found on the floor at that depth. She collected samples, made a film of the site and was back at the main grid ahead of Alec, because she had used up additional oxygen.

When they met on the surface, Alec signaled that his work was progressing. She reported her discovery of the depression to Zack, who duly made a note of it on his chart.

"Did Alec manage any new discoveries?" he asked.

"Oh, you might mark this one down as a joint discovery," she said.

He gave her a long look, but then, she had already caught members of the crew not only discussing Kinsolving, but giving one another speculative looks. A slow, subtle malignancy seemed to have planted itself aboard the *Doubloon*.

"What's this about discovering a twelve-foot depression?" J.H. asked at dinner. The question was meant to tell her to stop discovering anything that did not have to do with the gold tablet. She wished J.H. would leave, but Robin had told her that he planned to stay another day or two.

She couldn't explain to J.H. that such discoveries as the depression kept their real work hidden, and decided that she would try to get him alone, perhaps even tell him the truth about Alec.

But now Simon Mortimer and J.H. had found they had a mutual affinity for chess. Bree had begun to think she wouldn't tell him about Zack and the facsimile after all. J.H. didn't have to know everything.

Alec checked the chart to find out where her discovery lay in relation to the keel. That night they worked at the keel, the lone skull keeping them terrible company. When they surfaced, Alec said the next morning he was going to investigate the depression Bree had found.

"Looking over the chart, it strikes me as a possibility."

"You mean the tablet might have ended up there?"

"We'll see."

"It's twelve feet lower than we've been working," Bree pointed out. "We'll be using up more oxygen, and increasing our degassing time."

"I know, but I have what Robin refers to as a gut feeling."

A heavy chain, corroded and thick with algae, lay the length of the depression. Alec signaled an okay to her. He apparently recognized it. They might be in the right spot, after all. They divided the work, Bree taking the south portion, Alec the north. The work was slow and exhausting, and when the time was up, Bree was ready.

She had been so intent upon clearing away the sand that she had not looked up. His dive light was off. A quick explosion of fear roared through her. But she couldn't afford to exhibit any kind of fear. Stay calm, she told herself. A million possibilities passed through her mind, like ticker tape. She grabbed the lead line, and holding on to it, slowly flashed her light around, aware of every breath she took.

Then she saw him, wrapped in the octopus arms of a heavy fishnet, his knife in his hand.

She realized he had probably dropped his dive light. A check of her wrist computer told her that they had no choice about freeing him there. They had to get to the degassing line.

She swam to him, signaled that they had to rise together. Using the lead line, they managed to reach the decompression line that was anchored to the ship. Together they rose through the murky world around them, Alec still in the grip of the heavy net, Bree leading him. She knew they had to stay calm, and she could see in his movements that he held himself back from fighting the thick hemp.

When they landed at the degassing line, fifteen feet below the surface, they had scarcely enough oxygen for the five minutes they would need. When they surfaced, Bree used her knife to free him, working silently and quickly. They had no choice but to let the net fall back, hoping the current would carry it away.

When they fell into bed, they curved into each other's arms, exhausted. "Ohhh," she groaned, "I ache all over. Can't we just forget the damn tablet, run away to the ends of the earth? Beat the devil at his own game?"

Alec buried his head against her breasts. "But I am not fighting the devil," he said. "I am trying to save my soul."

The next day, the aches turned into a cold. Bree knew she could not go down. Alec said he would have to work at the main site. Bree didn't feel well enough to go down on the second dive, either. She asked Alec to bring her up some samples from the twelve-foot depression.

She sat on the deck in the sun, and J.H. found her there after lunch and sat down on a deck chair next to her. "I'm heading back tomorrow morning," he told her. "What's the good word I can take back with me?"

She took a deep breath, and told him about Pandars Jewelry and the facsimile. "That was very careless of him," he said when she finished.

"I think they call it arrogance," Bree said.

"We can institute a lawsuit the minute he surfaces with the tablet. That is, if it's signed."

"He's going to make sure of it."

"And you have a copy of the facsimile this goldsmith made."

She smiled. "We'll nail him, J.H."

He patted her hand absentmindedly and stood up. "As I recall, he wasn't much of a student, either." He walked off, hands dug into his pockets, contemplating the costs of a lawsuit, Bree guessed.

As the salvors began to surface, Robin ticked them off, until only Alec was left below with O'Brian. "They should be up by now," she said.

"Where's Zack?" Bree said.

"He's at the anchor line. The lift bag got tangled in some fishing net about twenty-five feet down, and he's out there cutting it free. O'Brian said he caught himself a big gold fish and it's in the lift bag." Her eyes shone at the prospect of a piece of the *Alexis Moon*'s treasure appearing without their even asking for it. "Sometimes those gold bars wash free, like crabs crawling out of the sand."

"Where did he find it?" Bree asked.

"Working on the grids that had toppled over in the current. That's the news I got."

"Pretty lucky find," Bree said. "Does Zack know?"

"He was at the monitor when O'Brian flashed the tablet up."

"Amazing," Bree said. How carefully everything seemed to be working out.

"Then one of the guys found the lift bag had tangled in netting, so Zack said he'd set it loose."

"He's all heart, Zack is. I'm going in," Bree said.

"No, you're not," Robin said. "I thought you had a cold."

"I just lost it."

"Alec is on his way up with O'Brian. That's it. No more diving today. Now cool it, Bree."

Bree threw up her hands. "Okay Robin. When you're right you're right."

"Both Alec and O'Brian will be on decompression soon. What did you expect to accomplish?"

"I thought I'd help escort the tablet up, Robin. I can't wait to see it. Well, I ought to get back to the lab. Did Alec say he had some samples for me?"

"That's what he said."

"Good."

She left Robin and went around the bridge. In ten minutes, Alec would be at the fifteen-foot decompression line. She had no doubt Zack would be waiting for him, but then, so would she. Whatever tablet might be in the lift bag, she didn't trust Zack not to try something with Alec.

She checked her gauges and her tank, then suited up. The activity on deck had increased as the last of the divers came back on board. Bree went aft, tied a line to the rail and slipped over the side. She discovered at once that the current was a lot stronger than she'd counted on, and the sea a lot choppier. She was doing what every sane diver knew not to do, diving without a buddy, without letting anyone know, and into a treacherous current. But she would go no farther than fifteen or twenty feet down along the anchor line.

She'd find Zack there, and whether he liked it or not, he'd be her buddy for the time being. The rope she clung to was long and had enough play to get her to the anchor line, or so she hoped. Afraid of being battered against the ship in her attempt to grab the anchor line, Bree forced herself to proceed slowly.

"Hey."

She reached the anchor line and looked up.

Robin's voice came clearly over the water, and Bree could hear her even through her neoprene hood. "What the hell do you think you're doing?"

"Making a fool of myself," Bree muttered. She cocked her free hand to her ear to show that she couldn't hear a word Robin said.

"You'll kill yourself."

Bree began the slow descent along the anchor line. Something large and black bumped against her. She recoiled, and then saw in her dive lamp that it was a species of cod, moving haughtily away, like a dowager along Fifth Avenue.

Where the devil were Alec and Zack? Or O'Brian, for that matter? Zack might still be trying to free the lift bag from a stray fisherman's net. She shone her lamp in an arc in a systematic search over the area, holding on to the swaying anchor line with her free hand. In the fast-moving current, she could find herself off the coast of England, if she wasn't careful.

Then she saw them moving into the light cast by her lamp. Oh, hell, Alec and O'Brian going at it. One broke free, O'Brian, moving too quickly to the surface. He had the lift bag with him. If he was suffering from nitrogen narcosis, he was in for a lot of trouble. She signaled frantically to him, but he ignored her. She hoped he knew what he was doing, but it was too late to stop him now.

Then, when she tried to signal to Alec to get a move on, someone new came out of the shadows and headed straight for Alec. The black-and-yellow wet suit identified the man swimming intently toward Alec. Zack Martineaux.

Chapter Seventeen

It happened suddenly. Zack lunged at Alec when Alec was off guard. Alec turned, clearly taken by surprise, and smashed his elbow into Zack's chest. Bree froze. For a moment, she felt that there, in the murky gray fifteen feet below the surface of the water, Alexander Devane and Zachary Martineaux were locked in a deadly battle over the *Alexis Moon*.

A shiny object was caught in the glare of her dive light. It took but a second to realize that Zack had pulled out his knife. He grabbed Alec's air hose, and was about to slice it in two when Alec twisted away and lunged for the knife. As the two men battled, Bree fought through the heavy currents, trying to reach them. They were using up oxygen fast, and they had to surface. Both their lives were at stake.

Alec grabbed Zack's wrist. In a moment, he forced Zack's arm behind him, twisting it so that Zack had no choice but to release the knife. It floated down into the depths. Bree then realized that Alec was holding his own knife up, and that in his rage, he might easily sever Zack's air hose.

Bree signaled wildly to him. When he saw her, he held the knife up, then seemed to realize what he was doing.

He let Zack go and sheathed the knife. Zack backed away and quickly rose to the surface.

Alec signaled that he was okay. Then he showed her the mesh bag tucked into his belt. In it she saw a flat metal piece that was unmistakably gold. He took her hand and drew her up.

When they surfaced close to the dive platform and removed their mouthpieces, Bree felt like knocking his teeth out. "What in hell got into you down there? You were going to kill him."

"Was I?"

"You know damn well you were."

"No, I don't. He came at me suddenly, and the next thing I knew he tried to cut my air hose."

"Alec, you're above Zack's motives. We both know that."

Alec beckoned her over to the hull, where they couldn't be observed from the deck. "Bree, leave it be. Perhaps I did want to kill him, Alexander Devane settling an ancient score with Zachary Martineaux. I believe Zack saw that O'Brian had the tablet, and he figured I'd try to stop him from bringing it up."

"But you have the tablet."

He bent forward and kissed her wet cheek. "Today's a fine day, my Bree. We have managed to find two tablets. But I have the real one. I was going to dig it so deep, it could only surface in China. Then O'Brian showed up and beckoned me to get moving. What we have to do is figure out a way to smuggle it on board."

"You're sure it's *the* tablet," she said.

"We have no time to examine it now."

"Oh, God, it's wonderful." But she knew they did not have the time to savor his accomplishment. "Do you know what this means?"

He turned to her and cupped her chin. "I'll only know when we consign this thing to the devil."

Bree pointed to the rope from which she had let herself down. "Tie the mesh bag there, for the time being. We'll lift it up when it gets dark. Now I know how to pillage a wreck, with no one the wiser."

"We're not pillaging, we're setting to rest."

When they came back on board, they found the crew crowded around Zack, Robin and O'Brian.

"What the hell? It's not signed!" Zack, still in his wet suit, stood on deck with a gold tablet in his hand, his face red with anger. "A fake. I should have figured somebody would try something. What do you think, Mortimer?" Zack frowned, as if the possibility of the tablet not being signed by Alexander Devane had never been a consideration before.

Simon Mortimer looked over his shoulder at the tablet. "I suppose we could have it tested."

"You're no help," Zack said. "Gold is old, even when it's new. What kind of test is it supposed to go through to determine its age? Are you an idiot? I can't believe I allowed you to back this expedition."

"He's a backer?" Robin shouted. "Well, I'll be damned! Is anybody else in on this little secret?"

Simon Mortimer blushed a deep red. "I've backed this personally, but Leighs of London will certainly demand its share."

"Nice," Robin said. "This is turning out to be some underwater team. If trust is the name of the game, you won't find it anywhere aboard the *Doubloon*."

Alec came over to her and put an arm around her. "We could use a little of Mother Krashaw's trust, too. How about telling us the truth about Kinsolving?"

"His murder?" She stretched around and gazed at him. "I don't know who killed the poor beggar."

"What was he doing for you with the camcorder, Robin?"

"Oh, for God's sake, Alec," she exploded. "Making a documentary. We'd have told you in time. It was his modus operandi, you know, hoping everyone would ignore him after a while."

"This isn't getting us anywhere," Zack said. "Somebody planted this. Where'd you find it?" he asked, handing the tablet to O'Brian, who stared at it, stupefied.

"I found it at the outfall," he said, referring to the residue spilled by the sand vacuums. "It's soft enough. See, it's bent. It was sucked in by the vacuums."

Zack exploded. "It's a fake, man! Are you blind? A *fake*."

"Give me that," Robin said, but before she had a chance to grab it, Zack looked at Alec through narrowed eyes.

"Oh, I get it now. You're the one," he said, rushing Alec. "You figured on settling things once and for all, didn't you? You came here all the way from Australia to make sure you got your share. I should've figured you had something up your sleeve."

Alec shrugged his remark away. "Zack, my friend, I'm going to have to do something about you soon."

Zack roared and threw a punch at him, missed, and in another moment found himself in a throw hold on the deck. O'Brian and a couple of the other salvors were about to move in when Robin put up her hand.

"Hey, knock it off, you two. We got a problem here."

"Right," Alec said, getting to his feet and dusting his hands. "And what do you propose we do about him?"

He hauled Zack to his feet, twisting his arms behind his back.

"Let him go," Robin said.

"Sure. The man's harmless enough, without his knife."

"You S.O.B.!" Zack bellowed, as soon as Alec released him. He lunged once more, but at that moment J.H. came up on deck. "What's going on here? It sounds like the fight of the century." He stopped, saw Robin with the gold tablet, and paled considerably. "Where did you get that?"

Alec looked curiously over at J.H. "An authentic document, dating back to 1842," he said.

"The gold tablet?" J.H. took the tablet from Robin and stared at it. A series of reactions seemed to break over his face, from anger through incredulity to a tentative smile. "It's not signed."

"That's what I said." Zack glared at Alec. "Something you and Bree cooked up, isn't it? Marine specimens, my foot."

"Unsigned." J.H. turned it over in his hands, as though the possibility might exist of an authentic signature on the reverse side. "Well," he said, a triumphant smile now wrinkling his cheeks, "Mr. Martineaux, I'm afraid your ancestor Beatrice concocted about as tall a story as I've ever heard. I think we can safely lay to rest the legend of the *Alexis Moon*. What do you say, Bree?"

She smiled, hoping her real feelings would not show. They were not quite out of the woods yet. "Oh," she said, "I think I'm going to miss that legend."

"We'll find you another," J.H. said. "The sea's full of them. As for Alexander Devane, we owe the memory of the man an apology. I might even have some sort of celebration at the institute for him. Use the event as a fund-raiser."

He came over to Bree and put an arm around her shoulder. "Well, I'd say this is cause for celebration, wouldn't you?"

His grip was so tight, she knew there was not an ounce of self-congratulation in it. He was telling her to keep quiet about the tablet. Zack had been shot down, because he couldn't say anything, either.

"I'd say so, J.H.," she said, continuing to smile, although she was certain it would soon crack her face in two. She looked over to find Alec scowling at J.H., not even trying to hide his evident annoyance. She slipped out from under J.H.'s grasp and put her hand out for the tablet. She longed to take it back to her cabin to compare it with the copy Pandars had given them.

It certainly looked authentic. The piece might have lain under the sand for a century and a half, just like the one Alec had found, with its faint discoloration and scratches.

She handed it back to J.H., and saw him looking at her with a fixed smile. Damn, she thought, she never should have told him about Pandars. He was worried the jeweler might talk.

Then a fresh thought struck her, just as Alec began to move away. She caught his eye. He nodded toward the stern. He was telling her to follow him.

She found Alec leaning on the rail, looking out to sea. She ran her hand along his back, felt him arch at her touch, and thought that now they could have a full-blown affair aboard the *Doubloon*, just like everyone else. Robin be damned.

"Zack did not order the gold tablet," Alec said quietly.

"I figured that out, too. He might have ordered one, but not that one."

"I've changed my mind about him, Bree. He's a bully, but he's too sure of what's down there to bother complicating matters. The one thing the poor man will never know is that the tablet existed, has been found and destroyed."

"He tried to kill you, Alec. He wanted to cut your air hose, I saw it."

"Fifteen feet from the surface?" He shook his head. "He thinks he knows who I am, and what my purpose for being here is, that's all."

"If he didn't order the tablet, then who did?"

He took her hand up and pressed it to his lips. "We may never know."

"If it's tied into the death of Kinsolving, the police may find out."

"Pandars might tell the police or the press what he knows, too," Alec said. "We can't speculate on what is going to happen. We have the original, and that's all that matters."

"We'd better bring it up tonight."

Alec looked at her. "Why not now?"

The deck was quiet, everyone apparently having gone below. To make certain, Alec checked the forward deck and the bridge. He came back. "They're below, celebrating. Let's see what we have."

The mesh bag was pulled up, oozing water, the rope holding it quickly undone, coiled and put away. "I suppose you mean to hide this in the lab," Bree said.

"You're right. Let's go." He removed the tablet from the mesh bag, and was about to shove it under his shirt when Bree said, "Wait a minute. Let me take a look."

Gold, a noble metal, would need minimum care to revive its luster. The tablet was of a soft, delicate gold that had been broken at the four corners and at the bottom. Alec carefully brushed away the sand, and the shells of long-dead barnacles. And then they discovered that the tablet, with its cursive calligraphic style and Devane seal, was ragged at its base.

"There's no signature," Bree said in a breathless voice. "Alec, there's no signature. It broke away. We needn't bury it after all. There's not a smidgen of a signature left."

He took the tablet and gazed at it, a thoughtful smile on his lips. "Time worked what I could not."

The cursive calligraphic style was still clear as the day it was written. The Devane seal of the clipper ship showed all the art of the engraving. "Zachary thought of everything," he said, pointing to a small star. "I had that star made up to add to documents separately. Franklin could then deem my signature as authentic."

"I don't think it's on the copy," Bree said.

"It won't matter, Bree. It won't matter at all." He slipped the tablet under his shirt. "They'll be spilling out into the passageway. We'll have to run the gauntlet, and we might as well act as if we have a lot to celebrate. I'll meet you in your lab in twenty minutes."

"Just watch that tablet. I wouldn't try hugging any of the salvors, if I were you."

But the gauntlet turned out to be an easy one for Bree to get through. A drink with J.H., and another with Robin, who refrained from asking her why she had made the dive in the first place, and she was on her way.

In her cabin, Bree pulled out the copy given her by Pandars. Kinsolving was dead, someone had ordered a gold tablet with room for a signature that had never happened, and only one person—or rather one college, in the form of James Harrison Selden—benefited from the switch.

Therefore, whoever benefited had killed Kinsolving, who must have stuck his nose, or his camcorder, into something he should not have. And somewhere, perhaps deep in the ocean, lay a camcorder and several tapes.

And the only one on board who could not be considered a suspect was James Harrison Selden. She continued to stare at the copy. J.H. could have had easy access to the Devane seal at the Historical Society. A seal that did not have a star on it. A seal Zachary Martineaux had known about and used on the gold tablet after it was made, and that was not on the original sketch.

J.H.

Her reflection was broken by a knock at her cabin door. Alec, she thought with a sigh of relief. She needed to talk it over with him. She opened the door to J.H.'s smiling face, took a step back in surprise, and sounded a small "Oh."

"Well, may I come in?" He carried two glasses of wine, and did not wait for an answer, but walked past her and sat down on the only chair in the room.

She must keep her cool. She deliberately left the door open and came over to her bunk and sat down. From the deck above, she heard the sound of laughter. Celebrating over a phony tablet that would affect none of their lives. Funny, how concentrated her mind was. She felt the wash of water against the sides of the ship. Where was Alec? She glanced at the open door and willed him to come charging in, bringing all his strength and purpose.

J.H. followed her glance and smiled, as though he understood Bree did not want any of the crew to get the wrong idea about them.

"Well, we're in luck," she said, keeping her smile cheerful. "Imagine finding the engraving, just like that."

"Too bad you interviewed Mr. Pandars. Now he knows the tablet is of interest to someone other than the buyer."

She blanched. "Sorry," she said. "I thought I was being helpful. Actually, Pandars couldn't have been less interested in it. He didn't even know about Alexander Devane."

J.H. looked hurt. "I only asked one thing of you, Bree. You couldn't leave well enough alone, could you?"

"What are you talking about, J.H.?"

"Chasing after chimeras." He shifted in his chair, and focused his icy eyes on her. "All you had to do was find the tablet and bury it. I didn't think you'd be so foolish as to let the whole world in on what you were doing. From what I've observed over the last couple of days, you and Alec Devon are quite a team."

Her heart sank. Had they been that obvious? "J.H.," she began, not even certain what she wanted to say next.

He interrupted her. "Of course, I intended to muddy the waters with a second, unsigned tablet, if the first were discovered."

"But you didn't trust me with it, did you? It's someone else on board, isn't it? Someone who strangled Kinsolving, because he discovered your plan."

"Bree, I don't like to see you thinking that way." His words were soft, but the hard edge in his eyes belied them. "Kinsolving was a snoop. That's what caused his death. Close the door, Bree."

"Not a good idea, J.H. My lab door is always open during the day."

He gave her a level smile. "Go ahead, Bree. What we have to talk about is nobody else's business."

Yes, it might make sense. Go easily to the door and, in a flash, slip outside, slamming it behind her, then run screaming to the ladder. But when she reached the door, J.H. spoke again.

"Slowly. And don't try to run away."

She whipped around. A snub-nosed gun was leveled at her heart. She thought fleetingly of the gun they had put back in Kinsolving's room, and the magazine lying on the seafloor.

"Close the door, my dear."

But she had a sudden reprieve when Vic Cramer came by, earphones on, shaking to music she could not hear. "Hi," she called out.

He grinned and waved and was about to move on when she waved frantically at him to come over. He waved again, and she ran out into the corridor. J.H. couldn't let the gun go off.

"Hey, Bree, that's something, isn't it?" Vic said.

"You mean about the gold tablet?" She grabbed his arm and began to keep step with him down the passageway. "Say, Vic, listen, there's something I have to tell you."

Vic looked at her. He lifted one of the earphones. She could hear the music, tinny and unrecognizable. But it was too late. J.H. came up behind her and jabbed the gun into her back.

"Let's take a walk on deck," he said. "You promised me."

"What's for dinner?" she called out desperately to Vic as he hurried on. He still held his earphone up.

"Fish—can't you smell it?" He continued on his way.

"Let's go," J.H. said. "They say drowning is an easy death, especially in frigid waters."

Keep him talking, she told herself. Alec will be on deck. He'll know something is wrong. J.H. prodded her past a couple of the crew. Bree could see Zack and Robin talking in the chart room.

"Keep moving," J.H. said into her ear. They went up the ladder to the top deck. "The trouble is, when you begin asking questions, you want answers. You would have stumbled on them after a while, Bree."

He brought her aft, and sat down a few feet away from her, the gun steady. "I've been selling off some of the old pieces that belonged to the Devane estate. Petty cash, some might call it, but everybody wanted a piece of me, and I couldn't keep up with it. The school's an aging plant, and you know as well as I do how funds have been tapering off. The Devane legacy was never enough to keep up with expansion plans, the replacement of old equipment."

The sun was low on the horizon, fat and orange. She hadn't realized the time. The crew would be wandering into the mess soon. She was surprised to find no one on deck, except O'Brian, standing at portside. Alec must have removed the mesh bag safely. Where was everyone?

"Hey, O'Brian," she called, knowing that for the moment, even with the butt of a gun at her back, she was safe.

He turned, smiled and came toward them. "Bree, how ya doin', kid? J.H." He put a beefy hand out, which J.H. was obliged to step forward and shake. "Been admiring the sunset?"

"Going for a little walk around the deck before dinner," J.H. said.

Bree saw that he had pocketed his gun. "Maybe I'll take a rain check on that, J.H." Bree took a tentative step away, but O'Brian put a lock on her arm.

"I don't think so, Bree."

She looked sharply at him, her heart sinking. He was not Zack's man, he was J.H.'s. He was the one who had claimed he'd found the gold tablet and brought it to the surface. Keep talking, she told herself. Alec would be looking for her, first in her cabin, then her lab, then the mess, and then topside. Just keep talking. And the worst of it was that J.H. didn't need his gun at all. They had only to act in unison to toss her to the sharks.

"You killed Kinsolving, didn't you?" she said to O'Brian.

O'Brian merely looked at her, his expression pinched. Then his eyes slid to J.H., who shrugged. It didn't matter to them what Bree knew or didn't know. She was shark bait. All they were waiting for was the crew to sit down to dinner, and the noise in the mess to grow so loud, no one would hear a struggle above deck or a woman's scream.

"He taped the conversation we had on the ship-to-shore phone," O'Brian said, "when J.H. said you were working with someone, to find out who. Alec, isn't it?"

Bree blanched, but held her tongue.

O'Brian's smile told her she didn't have to say a word, that he'd take care of Alec in his own good time. "As for Kinsolving," O'Brian went on, "he was a nosy little bugger. I told him that camcorder would get him into trouble one day."

"That's enough," J.H. said. He turned to Bree. "What you know and what you don't know will matter little to you now.'' His gun was leveled at her, but the expression on his face was avuncular. It was quite a contrast, she thought.

How quiet everything was. The *Doubloon* had shifted so that the sun was setting directly across the stern. She thought how golden it was, how she would die in all that gold, how Alec would be lost to her forever.

Into that golden light stepped Alec, his eyes locking with hers. She understood him at once. She was not to move, not to show a single emotion. She closed her eyes, aware of how her life and her love for him roared in her veins.

''Taking a stroll in the evening air, gentlemen?''

J.H. whipped around, his gun held steady. ''Alec Devon?'' he asked politely.

''Let her go,'' Alec said.

J.H. shook his head slowly. ''I don't know what your game is, Devon, but I'm afraid the ocean is going to claim two victims.'' He raised his gun.

''No!'' Bree cried, pulling herself free of O'Brian's grip. She slashed out at J.H.'s arm and threw herself between him and Alec. A shot rang out, the bullet slamming into her shoulder. She felt Alec's arms go about her, heard his shout to J.H., and then another shot, and Alec's deep moan. His arms loosened about her, and the last thing she saw was O'Brian standing there, a look of rage and satisfaction upon his face.

She could not move. Her world went black. She heard a scream in her head that she knew must be her own.

THE LIGHT shining in her eyes was becoming unbearable. She raised her head, saw the morning sun streaming through the hospital window, and lay back. The room seemed to echo with her cry.

"Bree?"

She opened her eyes. Robin Krashaw stood at her bedside, an enormous bouquet of flowers in her hand, a smile bravely pasted on her face.

"Alec," Bree said, a coldness suddenly gripping her. "Is he—?" She stopped when she saw the smile cloud over. Robin busied herself putting the flowers in a vase. Then she crossed the room to fill the vase with water, came back and fussily placed the vase on the window sill.

Bree tried to lift herself, then fell back when the pain in her shoulder became too much to bear. "Robin, I want the truth, the simple truth, and now." How could she explain that the world had abruptly stopped for her, that Robin had already told her the truth without uttering a word? Yet she must hear everything.

Robin sighed. She pulled a chair close to the bed and sat down. She took Bree's hand. "I can't imagine what got into J.H.," she said. "He went berserk."

"I don't care what happened to him," Bree said. "Tell me about Alec, tell me he's all right."

Robin squeezed her hand. "I wish I could, Bree. I wish I could. I came up on deck when I heard a shot and saw O'Brian moving in on Alec. For a moment, I thought it was more of that bad blood between them. Then another shot rang out, and I realized that J.H. had a gun, and there you were on the deck. The shot went a little wild. I swear, it only grazed Alec's arm, that was all." She stopped when she caught the pained look on Bree's face. "Why don't we wait until you're feeling better?"

"Go on," Bree said.

"I screamed at O'Brian, but he only laughed. He slammed into Alec. The two of them were thrashing around when J.H. aimed his gun at O'Brian and shot. By now I think J.H. figured he'd pick all his witnesses off one by one, me included. Then the most incredible thing happened. The bulwark gave, and O'Brian and Alec disappeared into the ocean." She paused and put both her hands over Bree's. "I'm sorry, Bree. They found O'Brian's body, but not Alec's."

Bree felt her heart dissolve. She knew the heated puddle it left would not sustain her for long. He was gone. That was all she knew.

Portland, Maine—July 1842

THE HOUSE at the center of the cul-de-sac was dark, except for a lone lamp's yellow, shadowed light in the library. Alec Devon, for so he thought of himself, sat unmoving in a high-backed chair, his hand around a glass of port.

Beyond the sturdy brick walls of his house, he heard the sounds of 1842 Portland, a clatter of horse's hooves, the high-pitched laugh of a woman, the slam of a carriage door. He thought, as he listened for the wind, that he was a stranger in his own time, as he had been a hundred and fifty years hence.

The port was crowded with clipper ships, some just arrived and unloading, some ready to set sail. The *Alexis Moon* lay at the bottom of the sea, and he, through a twist of fate, was back in Portland, alone. He could let no man—or woman—know that the captain of the *Alexis Moon* was in their midst.

And he knew one terrible thing. His heart lay far ahead, in the mists of time, where he had loved a woman and she had loved him.

He picked up his glass, examined its ruby throat through the lamplight, and thought of ruby lips. He took in a deep, shattering breath, and in another moment leapt to his feet. He would go to Marauders Point. His life, or his death, awaited him there.

THE LONG JULY DUSK was incandescent, yellows on the horizon softly paling into a long twilight suffused with violet. Bree had no idea how long she had stood at Marauders Point. She had no idea how long she had cried his name into the wind. The same sweet wind that circled the earth, and circled it again, added years immemorial, until the wind that touched her skin might have been the wind that touched his.

"Alec." She cried the name again and let the tears fall. Tears or no, she admitted to herself that she was a pragmatist. A very real bullet had pierced his skin and killed him. He could not be made whole again, could not appear to her again, because she called his name on this godforsaken rock.

She turned and retraced her path toward Gull House, the sound of his name still ringing in her ears. She had come to Marauders Point on a fool's errand, but could not leave.

The inn was nearly full, the summer season in full swing. Guests had begun to gather in a convivial spirit for dinner, and were dawdling over drinks in the spacious lobby. Bree was alone and wanted to talk to no one. How could she explain what she was doing there? She thought of taking her car and driving to a roadside restaurant for dinner.

But it scarcely mattered where she was or what she did. Perhaps life would always be like this, with her waiting for the impossible to happen.

Perhaps she should just go up to bed, read awhile, then fall into what she hoped would be a dreamless sleep. She could not continue to dream of him, and to awake full of the pain of loss. And yet perhaps dreams were better than reality. She headed for the reception desk to retrieve her room key, idly noting the man signing in at the register. A canvas bag lay at his feet. Tall and broad-shouldered, he was dressed casually in chinos and a denim jacket. She stopped in her tracks, aware of a slight dizziness. Not possible. She was beginning to hallucinate. Although his hair was cut short, there was no mistaking its color, nor the shape of his head.

"Fine, Mr. Devon," the receptionist said, giving him a dazzling, interested smile.

Bree grabbed the back of a chair to steady herself. Alec. How could she have been such a fool as to believe he might be—? No, she dared not even think it. The receptionist handed him a key. "We have your room ready. It's 207. Just go up the stairs and turn left."

"Am I in time for dinner?"

"We start serving at seven. Any time after that, until ten o'clock."

He grabbed his bag, turned and saw Bree standing there. At first he narrowed his eyes in a faint show of curiosity. Then his face lit in a half smile.

She stood, her heart pounding, wanting to run into his arms, but something stopped her, some nagging little feeling that he did not quite know who she was.

He came quickly toward her, hand extended. "We've met, haven't we? Miss Kealy, right?"

She nodded, too dumbfounded to speak.

"I have a notion you might remember me. Alec Devon. We met briefly in Portland. Miss Krashaw introduced us. I believe we're going to be shipmates aboard the *Doubloon*."

She let him take her hand. "Yes," she said on a held breath, "we did meet. The ship is actually at the wreck now. I'm afraid I'm a little taken aback at seeing you here, Mr. Devon. I . . . I thought you weren't going to go after all.''

His brow furrowed for an instant, as though even he could not quite make out what had happened to him. ''I was delayed unexpectedly. What about you?''

Her hand went automatically to her shoulder. ''I'm afraid I've been delayed, as well, Mr. Devon.''

''Alec. I think you Americans excel at informality these days. Can I offer you a drink?''

''Dinner's in ten minutes,'' she said. ''And my name is Bree.'' How amazing, she thought. How wonderful the world suddenly was. Life would begin anew for them, with no memories, no anxieties. She already felt the memory of their past leaving her.

''Just let me drop this in my room.'' Alec gestured toward his canvas bag. ''I wonder if you would object to my joining you at dinner.'' He looked briefly around. ''That is, if . . .''

''Yes, please,'' she said, over the lump that had lodged in her throat.

He bowed slightly before leaving her, then headed up the stairs, two at a time.

She watched him disappear around the turn of stair, and knew that this time he would be back.

HARLEQUIN®

I N T R I G U E®

COMING NEXT MONTH

#297 EDGE OF ETERNITY by Jasmine Cresswell
Weddings, Inc.
Recluse David Powell got the unlikeliest guest at his isolated lighthouse
hideaway—his ex-wife, Eve. Hell-bent on a tell-all exposé, Eve probed
too deeply into David's hermitage, and now someone wanted her stopped.
Was it David, the man she'd never stopped loving?

#298 TALONS OF THE FALCON by Rebecca York
Peregrine Connection #1
She'd once been in his heart, now psychologist Eden Sommers
had to get into Lieutenant Colonel Mark Bradley's head. Helping
him recover his memory of a top secret mission might bring back
the lover she'd once known, but it might cost him his life....

#299 PRIVATE EYES by Madeline St. Claire
Woman of Mystery
P.I. Lauren Pierce was none too happy about having to hire a competing
P.I. as a lookout—especially when Bill Donelan seemed to watch more
than her back. But then Lauren's client turned up dead, and she became
the next target....

#300 GUILTY AS SIN by Cathy Gillen Thacker
Legal Thriller
All the evidence said that wealthy, powerful Jake Lockhart was guilty of
murder in the first degree. Only his attorney was convinced of his
innocence. Susan Kilpatrick was sure Jake had secret information
that could set him free. More than the trial was at stake if she was
wrong—so was her life.

AVAILABLE THIS MONTH:

#293 FAMILIAR REMEDY
Caroline Burnes

#294 THINGS REMEMBERED
Kelsey Roberts

#295 TIME AND TIDE
Eve Gladstone

**#296 SOMETHING BORROWED,
SOMETHING BLUE**
Adrianne Lee

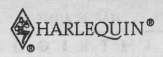

EDGE OF ETERNITY
Jasmine Cresswell

Two years after their divorce, David Powell
and Eve Graham met again in Eternity,
Massachusetts—and this time there was magic
between them. But David was tied up in a
murder that no amount of small-town gossip
could free him from. When Eve was pulled into
the frenzy, he knew he had to come up with
some answers—including how to convince her
they should marry again…this time for keeps.

EDGE OF ETERNITY, available in
November from Intrigue, is the sixth book in
Harlequin's exciting new cross-line series,
WEDDINGS, INC.

Be sure to look for the final book, **VOWS,** by
Margaret Moore (Harlequin Historical #248),
coming in December.

HARLEQUIN®

I N T R I G U E®

INNOCENT UNTIL PROVEN GUILTY...
IN A COURT OF LAW

Whether they're on the right side of the law or the wrong side—their emotions are on trial...and so is their love.

Harlequin Intrigue is proud to continue its ongoing "Legal Thriller" program. Stories of secret scandal and crimes of passion. Of legal eagles who battle the system and undeniable desire.

Next on the docket is

> #300 GUILTY AS SIN
> Cathy Gillen Thacker
> November 1994

Look for the "Legal Thriller" flash for the best in taut, romantic suspense—only from Harlequin Intrigue.

HARLEQUIN INTRIGUE—NOT THE SAME OLD STORY!

HARLEQUIN®

INTRIGUE®

WHO IS THIS

They say what makes a woman alluring is her air of mystery.
Next month, Harlequin Intrigue brings you another *very*
mysterious woman—Madeline St. Claire. We're proud to
introduce another writer to Harlequin Intrigue, as the Woman
of Mystery program continues.

And not only is the author a "Woman of Mystery"—
the heroine is, too!

Lauren Pierce is hiding—from the trained eyes of
a rival P.I. who's taken by her beauty but not by her
impersonation...and from the lethal eyes of a killer
about to step out of the shadows....

**Don't miss
#299 PRIVATE EYES
by Madeline St. Claire
November 1994**

Be on the lookout for more "Woman of Mystery" books in
the months ahead, as we search out the best new writers,
just for you—only from Harlequin Intrigue!

"HOORAY FOR HOLLYWOOD" SWEEPSTAKES

HERE'S HOW THE SWEEPSTAKES WORKS

OFFICIAL RULES — NO PURCHASE NECESSARY

To enter, complete an Official Entry Form or hand print on a 3" x 5" card the words "HOORAY FOR HOLLYWOOD", your name and address and mail your entry in the pre-addressed envelope (if provided) or to: "Hooray for Hollywood" Sweepstakes, P.O. Box 9076, Buffalo, NY 14269-9076 or "Hooray for Hollywood" Sweepstakes, P.O. Box 637, Fort Erie, Ontario L2A 5X3. Entries must be sent via First Class Mail and be received no later than 12/31/94. No liability is assumed for lost, late or misdirected mail.

Winners will be selected in random drawings to be conducted no later than January 31, 1995 from all eligible entries received.

Grand Prize: A 7-day/6-night trip for 2 to Los Angeles, CA including round trip air transportation from commercial airport nearest winner's residence, accommodations at the Regent Beverly Wilshire Hotel, free rental car, and $1,000 spending money. (Approximate prize value which will vary dependent upon winner's residence: $5,400.00 U.S.); 500 Second Prizes: A pair of "Hollywood Star" sunglasses (prize value: $9.95 U.S. each). Winner selection is under the supervision of D.L. Blair, Inc., an independent judging organization, whose decisions are final. Grand Prize travelers must sign and return a release of liability prior to traveling. Trip must be taken by 2/1/96 and is subject to airline schedules and accommodations availability.

Sweepstakes offer is open to residents of the U.S. (except Puerto Rico) and Canada who are 18 years of age or older, except employees and immediate family members of Harlequin Enterprises, Ltd., its affiliates, subsidiaries, and all agencies, entities or persons connected with the use, marketing or conduct of this sweepstakes. All federal, state, provincial, municipal and local laws apply. Offer void wherever prohibited by law. Taxes and/or duties are the sole responsibility of the winners. Any litigation within the province of Quebec respecting the conduct and awarding of prizes may be submitted to the Regie des loteries et courses du Quebec. All prizes will be awarded; winners will be notified by mail. No substitution of prizes are permitted. Odds of winning are dependent upon the number of eligible entries received.

Potential grand prize winner must sign and return an Affidavit of Eligibility within 30 days of notification. In the event of non-compliance within this time period, prize may be awarded to an alternate winner. Prize notification returned as undeliverable may result in the awarding of prize to an alternate winner. By acceptance of their prize, winners consent to use of their names, photographs, or likenesses for purpose of advertising, trade and promotion on behalf of Harlequin Enterprises, Ltd., without further compensation unless prohibited by law. A Canadian winner must correctly answer an arithmetical skill-testing question in order to be awarded the prize.

For a list of winners (available after 2/28/95), send a separate stamped, self-addressed envelope to: Hooray for Hollywood Sweepstakes 3252 Winners, P.O. Box 4200, Blair, NE 68009.

CBSRLS

OFFICIAL ENTRY COUPON

"Hooray for Hollywood"
SWEEPSTAKES!

Yes, I'd love to win the Grand Prize — a vacation in Hollywood —
or one of 500 pairs of "sunglasses of the stars"! Please enter me
in the sweepstakes!

This entry must be received by December 31, 1994.
Winners will be notified by January 31, 1995.

Name _____

Address _____ Apt. _____

City _____

State/Prov. _____ Zip/Postal Code _____

Daytime phone number _____
(area code)

Account # _____

Return entries with invoice in envelope provided. Each book
in this shipment has two entry coupons — and the more
coupons you enter, the better your chances of winning!

DIRCBS

OFFICIAL ENTRY COUPON

"Hooray for Hollywood"
SWEEPSTAKES!

Yes, I'd love to win the Grand Prize — a vacation in Hollywood —
or one of 500 pairs of "sunglasses of the stars"! Please enter me
in the sweepstakes!

This entry must be received by December 31, 1994.
Winners will be notified by January 31, 1995.

Name _____

Address _____ Apt. _____

City _____

State/Prov. _____ Zip/Postal Code _____

Daytime phone number _____
(area code)

Account # _____

Return entries with invoice in envelope provided. Each book
in this shipment has two entry coupons — and the more
coupons you enter, the better your chances of winning!

DIRCBS